Scott Hunter was born in Romford, Essex in 1956. He was educated at Douai School in Woolhampton, Berkshire. His writing career began after he won first prize in the Sunday Express short story competition in 1996. He currently combines writing with a parallel career as a semi-professional drummer. He lives in Berkshire with his wife and two youngest children.

SILENT AS THE DEAD

Scott Hunter

Acknowledgements

Thanks to Andrew and Rebecca Brown (Design For Writers) for the cover design, my insightful editor, Louise Maskill, and Tom Marcus (author of *Soldier Spy [Penguin, 2017]*), an inspiration for the character 'JC'.

To the memory of my late grandparents

I would always look for clues to her in books and poems,
I realised–
I would always search for the echoes of the lost person,
the scraps of words and breath,
The silken ties that say, Look: she existed
–Meghan O'Rourke

Prologue

'They found him – I take it you've been informed already?'

'Yes, Sir. I'm aware.'

I try to make myself comfortable. The chair's hard and I'm tired. Of course I've been informed. They found him all right – what was left of him. I lick my lips, look down at my new trainers. There's a scuff on the right toe. Probably did that against the bar foot rest.

'LK was one of our best,' the man behind the desk says.

They always refer to us by our initials. Never a name. Safer that way.

Anyway, I've no quarrel with what the guy just said. LK *was* one of the best. *Was* ...

The man fiddles with a pale, meerschaum pipe, taps the bowl. Takes out a pipe cleaner. 'Can't smoke the damn thing in here, sad to say. Best I can do is a spot of maintenance.'

No answer to that. Sometimes I have to put a smoke on, if I'm on ops, but I never inhale. Pipes, smoking – mug's game, if you ask me. So I just shrug. 'Yeah, of course.' Am I supposed to smile?

He carries on with the pipe. After a bit he looks up.

'You knew him pretty well, JC, is that right?'

1

He has one of them old BBC voices, like you used to hear on Radio Four. Still do sometimes. Toffs, the lot of 'em. But I know I have to be careful. He might be a toff, but he's not stupid.

'Couple of years, yeah.' I nod.

'Couple of years,' the man repeats. 'Long enough to know someone pretty well.'

'I suppose.' I scratch my head. Hopefully this won't take long. We've been through a full debrief already, but I guessed this was coming. LK blew it and, for someone who'd been around the block as many times as he had, that was worth a few questions from higher up the food chain. I've only met this guy once before, just after they recruited me. I was fresh out of the Army back then, cocky as hell. Maybe that's what they liked about me. Or it might have been my photographic memory. He's looking at me, waiting for an answer. 'We used to banter a bit, yeah,' I say. 'LK was solid.'

Truth is, I feel crap about it – about what I had to do. But I need the money. LK knew the risks. He could have got himself out. I thought he *would*, but Black's bodyguards, once they were sure, they were right on the money. They didn't give LK a chance. That Niall guy, he's a right psycho. The way the corner of the pub cleared and the tables emptied – the regulars knew who the visitors were, all right. Hope I don't need to drink with Niall again in a hurry. Probably have to, though. He's close to Black.

'What do you think happened, JC?' the man asks, all quiet like. As if he was asking me about the weather, or something.

I'm ready for this question. I look him in the eye. 'Simple. They sussed him. Maybe he got careless. It only takes the smallest thing to blow your cover. He was a painter

2

decorator, right? That was the scam. So he had the white van outside, the paint on his hands and hair, all that. But these guys are good, they know when there's something wrong, some detail. Maybe they felt his radio as they brushed past him. Maybe they didn't like the way he drank. Maybe he paid for his drinks with a twenty-pound note instead of change.' I shrugged. 'Could be anything. The smallest detail out of place. That's the game we play.'

He's quiet for a bit. Then he gets busy with the pipe again. 'Quite so,' he says after a while. 'The smallest detail.' He sighs, put the pipe down. 'They tortured him, you know, JC.'

Keep cool. Don't think about it. Maintain eye contact.

'But I'll spare you the details. Chap like you has enough on his plate. You mustn't dwell on it. I'm sure you did your best.'

Time to toe the line. Sounds like he's finished. Hope I've done enough to convince him. 'Yes, Sir.'

'You'll catch up with these people. Last night's setback is just that. They may have won a battle, but they haven't won the war yet, not by a long chalk. Whatever they're planning, I have every confidence you'll come up trumps.'

'We'll do our best, Sir.'

'I'm sure you will.'

'Will there be anything else?'

'Not for the time being, JC. Thank you.'

'Sir.' I'm on my feet and at the door. I'm knackered. It's been a long night. Suddenly, he calls me back. I stop, half-in half-out, look back. He's smiling.

'Thanks for everything you do, JC. Take care of yourself, won't you? I can't afford to lose any more of my best.'

'Sir.'

The corridor's empty. I lean on the wall, my shirt sticking

to my back. I feel sick to my stomach, but it looks like I got away with it.

For now.

Chapter 1

The salt-laden breeze hit him like a slap in the face. Nowhere else smelled like this, and for sure nowhere else *felt* like this. DCI Brendan Moran watched the land approach, only subconsciously aware of the noise of the ferry engines, the crashing of doors and bustle of passengers. He took a deep breath and went below.

Twenty minutes later the port was behind him and he was heading west on the N25. The plan was to arrive at his destination by tomorrow – mid-afternoon at the latest. At least that's what he'd told Donal. Moran didn't mind either way; if he was half a day out, so be it. This trip was off the record and by the time he got there, if what Donal had told him was to be believed the trail would have been cold for over a fortnight. And when it came to abduction, a cold trail was a poor starting point. If it *was* abduction. Moran hadn't said as much on the phone, but it could just as easily be murder.

Or suicide.

He pulled into a service station; the engine was sucking air after the long journey through Wales to Fishguard. He filled the tank till the pump clicked; he'd need all the fuel he could get, driving as he was to a tiny village on the Dingle Peninsula, about as far west as you could go. Moran grabbed a sandwich, paid, smiled to himself at the cashier's accent and got back on the road. After an uncomfortably early start he intended to find a B&B somewhere near Youghal and catch up on his sleep. He wasn't getting any younger and journeys like this took it out of him in a way he found annoying and slightly alarming. Funny how the small things that never used to matter seemed to get under your skin after you'd hit fifty. Or fifty-*something*, he grudgingly conceded.

But certain things had *always* annoyed him.

Like being followed.

Moran glanced in his rear view a second time, just to be sure. The Passat was still there, about the same distance behind him as before. Moran wasn't doing much over fifty-five; it could have overtaken anytime.

Time to put its commitment to the test.

Moran floored the accelerator. It took a heartbeat for the Passat to respond, but respond it did, closing the gap and maintaining the same distance as before. A lay-by appeared a few hundred metres ahead. Moran checked his mirror and slammed on the brakes. The Passat sailed past in the fast lane as Moran dragged his vehicle off the road, tyres screeching in protest. He had just a second to clock the Passat. Two guys, the passenger bearded, heavy-set, looking his way. Couldn't see the driver. Moran let the engine idle.

Paranoia?

He waited four, maybe five minutes before rejoining the dual carriageway in the wake of a passing Guinness lorry. Moran settled himself a few car-lengths behind and chewed on his sandwich. Not for the first time he questioned the wisdom of agreeing to Donal's request. It had felt risky from the start.

But that's probably why you agreed in the first place, Brendan …

The service station was twenty minutes behind him before he caught sight of the Passat again, easing itself into its customary position. Observation, Moran decided. That's what these guys were about. They'd had plenty of opportunity to run him off the road, sidle up to him at the service station, bundle him into the boot, or whatever else they might have intended. As it was, they seemed content just to keep him in view. Which was OK with Moran. They were going to have a boring twenty-four hours, what with him stopping over and all. Moran resolved to find an opportunity to make life more interesting for them – should such an opportunity present itself.

Casting an occasional glance at the rear-view to check the Passat's position, Moran turned his mind to more pressing concerns, the frontrunner being how he was going to cope with meeting his late fiancée's family for the first time in years. This was something that had been worrying him since Donal's phone call. Sure, dealing with the reality of Janice's murder was no longer as intolerable and ruinous as it had been in the early days. Nowadays it was more of a distant ache – but nevertheless an ache that didn't take much prompting to flare up. A date on the calendar, a whiff of perfume, a song on the radio – these were the minutiae waiting to derail him. Small things, big impact.

And there was the Hannigans' attitude towards *him* to take into consideration, too. Donal had always, albeit irrationally, blamed Moran for his sister's death. It went something like this: the bomb had been intended for Moran, therefore if he'd never existed, Janice wouldn't have gone anywhere near the car. Moran got that; Donal's thinking was an inevitable consequence of post-traumatic 'what if' syndrome, and Moran had engaged in plenty of that himself. What if they hadn't changed their plans that day? What if he'd sent Janice home, as he'd originally intended? What if he'd decided to drive himself to the meeting instead of walking? What if he'd never suggested she take his car to save herself a soaking? What if it hadn't rained that afternoon? And so on, and so on.

Moran took a deep breath. There was Janice's sister, Geileis, to consider as well; what did she think these days? As far as he knew, Geileis still lived in London, and he'd not seen her for years. Just Donal for the moment, then. He let his breath out in a long sigh. The first few hours would present the greatest challenge.

Just get through those, Brendan, and then the next hour, then the one after that ...

He tapped the radio button, checked for the Passat's by now almost reassuring presence, and fixed his speed at sixty. The music did its distraction thing and he settled into the rhythm of the road, humming the tunes he knew and tapping his fingers on the steering wheel to the ones he didn't. It passed the time and he found himself entering a trance-like state as the car sped westwards.

Moran toyed with the idea of pressing on towards Cork, but it was getting late and he didn't fancy kerb-crawling in the dark in search of a half-decent B&B. He turned off the N25, following signs to Ardmore. His buddies in the Passat were almost taken unawares but they made the turn in time and settled for a thirty-mile-an-hour, unhurried 'we're taking in the sights' sort of pursuit – which seemed to confirm Moran's earlier assessment of their intentions.

Thirty minutes later he had found a B&B with sea view, a pleasant if talkative landlady, an opportunity for high tea and a bedroom with a picture window. It was one of many boarding houses dotted along the coast road but Moran had selected this one not for its ambience, but for the fact that there was nowhere for the Passat to lurk while he was in residence.

It was a pleasant evening, if a little chilly, and after he'd excused himself he took a stroll down to the beach. As the sun sank he thought about Janice and the life they might have had. When the tide began to lick his boots he retraced his steps. Over to his left, towards the edge of the car park by the toilet block, the Passat was one of three remaining cars, an empty windscreen gazing sightlessly out to sea.

Chapter 2

Moran would never have claimed to be one of nature's early risers, but the following morning he felt an unexpected lightness of heart. Something to do perhaps, with his midnight visit to the beach car park where he had used a pair of steel clippers to sever the ignition coil wire on the Passat's distributor cap. He'd been right about his shadows: once they'd figured he was settled for the night they'd only had a couple of entertainment options: the car or the local bar. Moran put his money on the bar. After all, he'd gone out of his way to create the impression that he was in for the night.

Nevertheless, he'd been quick with his sabotage. To have been caught *in flagrante* wouldn't have been a great idea, not with him being a copper and all – the Gardai would have taken a dim view. But everything had gone to plan. His only real worry had been the landlady, whom he suspected would have taken an equally dim view of a guest creeping about during the night. However, Mrs Keene had proved herself a heavy sleeper and his clandestine exit and re-entry passed without incident.

It was in this happier frame of mind that Moran rejoined

the N25 and pointed the car towards Cork. He reckoned it would take most of the morning for the Passat guys to source a new ignition coil, and by that time he would be way west. They'd no doubt track him down eventually but by then he would have figured out who he was dealing with.

Know your enemy …

Who had said that? Moran racked his brain. Some Chinese warlord, maybe? Well, it was damn good advice. Know their strengths, know their weaknesses …

Traffic began to thin after Cork and the towns and villages he passed through were quiet and nondescript. A bar, a café, a church, the houses mostly grey-rendered and run down, but a few picked out in vibrant yellow, blue or red – an attempt, Moran suspected, to bring a little colour into routine, unremarkable lives. By the time he'd passed Killarney Moran was beginning to miss the Passat's companionship; it had given him something else to think about. Its absence meant that his mind inevitably found its way back to the late Seventies and once there the film began to roll without any further prompting.

A last-minute arrangement to meet Janice for lunch, the deferment of a meeting until later in the afternoon. They laugh, make plans. Chicken sandwiches and a glass of orange juice for him, for her, smoked salmon salad and a Babycham. She's wearing a cord jacket and a silk scarf picked out in autumnal colours. Her hair is loose, full of sun. They leave the pub and the bright morning has succumbed to grey, a light rain beginning to fall as they walk arm-in-arm to the car, parked just up the road near the local butchers. A sudden thought: why don't *you* take the car? Save you getting soaked. I've only to visit number thirty-six, just up the road.

Meet you at your ma's tonight? I'll get the bus, no problem.
A kiss. Watch her walk to the white Cortina, a cheap old
banger – all he could afford on a junior garda's salary – just
a few hundred yards away. She turns, smiles, waves. They'll
be married in three months. He watches her unlock the car,
get in. Smiling, he turns away. Then comes the blast of hot
air, driving him back, sending him sprawling. Shock,
confusion. What just happened? He rolls, dazed. Now he's
on all fours. He turns his head and the sight which greets his
eyes is impossible to process. Flames, smoke, drifting flakes of
upholstery settling on wet tarmac like fiery butterflies …

The car. The car. Oh God. Oh God, no, please God, no …

A lorry sounded its horn, jolting Moran back to the
present. He moved over, the lorry overtook. The driver
glared. He raised his hand apologetically. Coffee. That's
what he needed. Moran opened the window. Cool, diesel-
laced air circulated and he breathed it in deeply.

Get a grip, Moran. You're not even there yet …

He pulled over at the next café and bought a bitter, cheap
coffee. He sat in the window, watched the rain. Even now,
thirty-five years later, it was still too soon to come home.

'You're looking well, Brendan. The years have been kind,'
Donal Hannigan said, handing Moran a half-filled tumbler
of Irish. 'I mean it. England must suit you.'

Moran accepted the glass and raised it. 'You're not looking
so bad yourself, Donal. Good health.'

'And to you.' Donal raised his glass in response. He was a
thick-set, ruddy-faced man of around Moran's own age. A
life in hill farming had hardened him to the elements and he
carried little excess weight. His hair was grey, but thick and

abundant, as was his beard, which he wore longer than Thames Valley fashion would prescribe. 'My only trouble is the knee,' he told Moran. 'But I'll have a little op soon to put that right. When all this is blown over.'

'Tell me what happened,' Moran said. 'Everything you can remember from your last few conversations with Aine.'

The fire sparked in the grate as Donal began to speak, hesitantly at first and then, as he warmed to his theme, more confidently. He spoke about his relationship with his wife, the early years when strong opinions and optimistic idealism had prompted many an explosive argument – when political passion had all but wrecked their passion for each other. But things had mellowed with the passing of time and inevitably the demands of a young family had prompted a reprioritisation. Old contacts fell by the wayside. The farm prospered. Ireland moved on, and the Hannigans moved with it.

'The thing is, Brendan,' Donal said, placing his empty glass carefully on the polished occasional table next to his armchair, 'she's been so *happy* these last few years.' Donal shook his head. 'I can't see that she would have any reason to just up and … *leave*, as she's done.'

'From what I remember of Aine, she always knew her own mind,' Moran said. 'So if there were problems, issues, whatever, once she'd made a decision she'd more than likely–'

'–We're all right, Brendan,' Donal interrupted. 'Let's get that straight. The two of us. Now the kids are grown and doing their own thing – well, not Padraig, maybe – we get on just *fine*. The only stuff we argue about these days is whether to watch Gogglebox or Strictly.'

Moran laughed. 'I wouldn't know what either of those are, Donal. Look, I don't want to pry but you've asked me here for a specific reason. The Gardai have come up with zilch …' Moran spread his hands. 'So, I just need to know, well, how things are, that's all.'

Donal nodded. 'Sure. I'm a little over-sensitive just now, as you can imagine.'

'It's been over three weeks?'

'Twenty-four days.'

Moran nodded. Donal suddenly looked tired, worn out. He was a year younger than Moran but recent events had clearly taken their toll.

'Hello?' The lounge door swung open.

'Padraig – you're back.' Donal was on his feet. 'Here's the lad keeping the wolf from the door.' Donal smiled broadly. 'Padraig, this is my very old friend, Brendan Moran.'

Moran extended his hand.

Padraig's grip was dry and firm. 'The policeman. Da told me he called for you.'

'I'm here as a friend, Padraig,' Moran said.

'Sure you are. You're going to find out what happened to Ma when the Gardai have been over every inch of this county and found *nothin*'?'

'Padraig–' Donal began.

Moran raised his hand. 'It's all right. You've had a stressful time, I understand.'

'Oh, you *do*?'

'Padraig, please–'

'I hear you're doing a grand job on the farm,' Moran said as Donal placed a pacifying hand on his son's shoulder.

Padraig shrugged. 'Nothing that Da hasn't been doing for

a lifetime.'

'You're damn good at it, Padraig. You've a better feel for it than I ever had.' Donal clapped his son on the arm. Padraig was an inch or two taller than his father, with reddish brown hair as thick and abundant as Donal's. As Moran had feared there was more than a trace of his late aunt in the contours of the young man's face, something about the way his mouth turned up slightly at the corners, the almost delicate flare of his nostrils, the colour of his eyes, somewhere between grey and green …

Padraig moved towards the door. 'I'll away and put the quad to bed for the night. I'll not be wanting any tea, Da. I'll be at O'Neil's if you want me.'

The door closed and Padraig was gone. Moran heard the roar of the quad bike's engine receding into the distance.

'I'm sorry.' Donal stood by the fireplace, empty tumbler in hand. 'He's taken Aine's disappearance hard. He's looking for someone to blame. And that'll be me.' Donal covered his eyes and lowered his head. His mouth formed a thin line. After a moment he said, 'Hell. I'm sorry.'

Moran took Donal's shoulders and gripped them firmly. 'Listen to me, Donal. We'll get to the bottom of this, I promise. I'll have a wee wander about tomorrow; maybe I'll hear things you're not party to. Now come away into that fine kitchen of yours and I'll show you how to make a mixed grill you'll remember for years to come.'

Donal ran a hand through his hair, took a steadying breath and grinned. 'For all the right reasons, I'm hoping.'

Moran encouraged the laughter that followed, all the more so because he knew it was unlikely to last.

Chapter 3

Moran woke suddenly. For a brief moment he had no idea where he was, but the wooden beams above his bed provided the first clue and the gentle lowing of a cow outside the small window the second. He'd slept well, a pleasant surprise.

Moran lay on his back and wondered where to begin. *Locally* was the obvious answer. The outskirts; the outer strands of the spider's web. He knew from experience that it only required a small agitation of the appropriate thread to bring the bigger insect – or insects – scuttling. The trick was not to be stuck in place when they did.

He eased himself into an upright position with a short groan and performed the daily leg massage routine before committing his weight to the bare boards of the guest bedroom. He'd managed to wean himself off the stick a few months back, contrary to his physio's advice, but then Moran had never been much good at taking advice. Besides, it felt better not having to rely upon what DI Charlie Pepper laughingly referred to as his third leg. Nearly three years had passed since the explosion at Charnford Abbey which had almost claimed his life. It didn't seem possible. Where had the time gone?

*Into the dustbin of history, Brendan my lad. That's where it all goes
…*

Downstairs he found a note from Donal explaining how best to use various kitchen appliances and letting him know that he and Padraig would be out for most of the day. Moran also found a table laid for breakfast and a cosy atmosphere courtesy of the ancient range, the heart of the farmhouse. Moran remembered sitting in almost this exact spot when the farm had belonged to Donal's late parents. The ghosts of those earlier generations, of which he had been a part, moved quietly around him, their spirits as tangible as the farmhouse walls. There was Mrs Hannigan, apron-clad by the range, stirring a home-made stock and toasting muffins for the teenagers. Over there was young Donal, and next to him his sisters, Geileis and Janice, while over there by the back door Moran himself had lingered, the awkwardness of adolescence tripping his tongue.

'Are youse comin' in or stayin' out in the cold, young Brendan?' Mrs Hannigan teased.

'I'm comin' in, if that's all right, Mrs H,' Moran heard himself speak aloud.

'I'm thinkin' young Janice'll be pleased to hear that, so I am,' Mrs Hannigan's ghost replied.

Moran sat at the table and allowed the images to disperse in their own time. Pinching the bridge of his nose between thumb and forefinger he squeezed his eyes tightly shut.

Come on, Brendan, keep it together…

He helped himself to a slice of bread which he then set about toasting by means of the intriguingly designed range toaster. Pleased with the results, he fried an egg to go with it. A pot of fresh coffee had already been prepared and he helped himself to two mugs in quick succession. Pleasantly caffeinated, he sat at the broad breakfast table and considered his itinerary.

It was time to agitate the first thread.

The path down to the beach was a cross between a walk and a skate; loose stones beneath his feet and the restrictions of a damaged leg made Moran question the wisdom of his descent on several balance-challenging occasions. But he wanted to feel the wind on his face, to assess the land from the shore, order his thoughts – the beach seemed a good starting point. The path petered out and he found himself on even ground. The beach was deserted, the tide coming in. He walked past rocky outcrops onto an expanse of sand slicked with pools of sky-reflecting saltwater. The temperature was moderate, a mild autumn for the wild west coast.

It was a haunted landscape, and it was all too easy to believe the local legends and mysteries, of which there were many. The story of Jenny MacLennan came to mind. She had lived on this very stretch of coastline with her invalid husband, he a shell-shocked veteran of the First World War, she a front-line nurse traumatised by her experiences of the Western Front. Here, apparently, amid the beauty and tranquillity, she had cold-bloodedly murdered her friend, Orla Benjamin, the wife of a senior war cabinet official. MacLennan had protested her innocence right up to the end, however, citing the ghost of a long-dead landowner as the perpetrator of a crime which had fascinated and horrified the nation in equal measure. And then there had been the policeman – Keene? Keefe, was it? – who had disappeared under mysterious circumstances whilst continuing to pursue the murder investigation post-retirement. He had apparently never believed Jenny MacLennan capable of murder, and had spent the last years of his life in an obsessive quest to find the truth.

A haunted landscape, indeed…

Moran dug his hands deeper into his coat pockets and looked out to sea where the humps of the Blasket Islands rose from the water like a school of primeval monsters. Uninhabited since the late Fifties, the islands were raw and inhospitable. You could get a ferry over to have a look, if you fancied it. Maybe he'd do that later in the week. Beyond Great Blasket, one or two grey hulls broke the distant line of the horizon – passing trade from America no doubt, en route to who-knew-where. This coastline had seen them all; Viking warships, Spanish Armada remnants, wallowing oil tankers, distant convoys, U-boats, ships which just disappeared…

Like the policeman.

Like Aine Hannigan…

He walked along the line of the incoming tide, maintaining a short distance from the foaming water, and thought about Aine. Strong-minded, fiery, self-sufficient. Capable. Not the disappearing type. Abducted then? Or absconded with a lover? Both unlikely scenarios. Donal and Aine were, although an odd match in some ways, devoted to each other – as far as he knew. And, as Donal had told him last night, all was well between them. Apparently.

The church was visible from his wide vantage point on the beach, as he had known it would be. The old stone building had changed little, although closer inspection would no doubt reveal that its proximity to the shore and commanding view of the sea came at a price. Wind, rain and the passage of time would keep the masons at their never-ending task of restoration. But still it stood, defiant against the elements and the indifference of younger generations. Moran felt his feet reluctantly change direction towards the tiny path which led from the beach to the churchyard, hidden from view from where he stood, but never hidden from his thoughts.

By the time he reached the gate he was out of breath and his leg was aching. He paused for a moment to settle his thoughts as well as his heart. An elderly lady was attending to some horticultural task by the porch and he nodded a silent greeting as he passed. She looked up and met his gaze and for a moment they were two souls in empathy. She too had loved and lost, and it was plain to Moran that her task was one which she undertook not only as a willing member of the church community, but also because it allowed her to spend time in close proximity to the earthly remains of her loved one.

He walked slowly now, following the route he had taken the first time – on the day of her funeral. Janice's grave was tucked in the far right-hand corner, beneath the shadow of the high wall but facing west, out to the wind and the open sea. She would have liked the location. It was peaceful and quiet, yet at the same time encapsulated some sense of agelessness. Moran wouldn't have described himself as religious, but from time to time, given the right location, the possibility of something greater than himself, higher than his own thoughts and perceptions, seemed inescapable.

It had been years since he had stood on this spot, but he remembered how he had felt at the time.

And nothing had changed.

He bent and scratched the moss from one or two letters which were missing their inlay. Worn or stolen? Moran couldn't understand how anyone could pinch lead or gold plate from a gravestone. The plot was tidy nonetheless; Donal would be a frequent visitor, and no doubt Geileis paid her respects from time to time. Moran got down on his haunches, but soon sank forward until he was kneeling, palms pressed flat on the mound. The inscription blurred before him:

Janice Hannigan

B. 2nd January 1954
D. 11th April 1974

A loving daughter, a faithful sister

Here was Janice, *his* Janice. And who could say if they would ever be reunited in some future existence? He found himself speaking aloud. 'I'm here. I'm always here. Forever. You and me. Always, always, *always*.' He breathed in, then slowly out. How could this have happened? How could she be dead? How could the perpetrators of such a crime walk the earth? How could they live, laugh? How could they endure, when he had been consigned to this hopeless, grief-bound existence? He lowered his head until his forehead touched the grass.

It was only when the wind got up, carrying fresh rain with it, that he eventually roused himself and made his way back along the path between the stones.

He looked at his watch. Nearer to midday than not, which

meant that the local bars would be open for trade. He couldn't think of a better opening gambit than to start there, the hubs of the local community. Right now Moran was thirsty and there were questions to be asked. Subtly, of course, but asked nonetheless.

As he headed back the way he had come, he wondered how long it would take the Passat's occupants to catch up with him. He had intended to mention it to Donal last night, but something had held him back. Instinct, probably.

And instinct was something that rarely let him down.

Chapter 4

'A pint of black, is it?'

'That'll be right,' Moran nodded. 'And a round of chicken sandwiches, please.'

'No problem, sir. Be five minutes or so.' The barman drew the dark, treacly beer with care and presented it to Moran with a practised flourish. 'Good health to you.'

Moran raised his glass. 'And to you and yours.'

'You've a familiar look about you,' the barman said. 'Wait, don't tell me.' He stroked his chin. 'Come on now,' he said, countermanding his own directive seconds later, 'help me out, would you?'

Moran smiled. He'd already recognised a face from the distant past. Jerry O'Donaghue. Older, but recognisable, nonetheless.

'Oh my goodness!' Jerry's puzzled expression gave way to surprise. 'You know me too, I can see that!' He clicked his fingers. 'Merciful saints. If it isn't Brendan Moran himself, in the flesh.'

'Hello Jerry. It's been a long time.'

'It's been a *hell* of a long time.' Jerry reached over the bar and pumped his hand. 'Wait a second – I'll get the girl to do your sandwich.' He disappeared to the rear and Moran heard him issuing instructions. He was back in an instant, found himself a glass and banged it against one of the optics. '*Slainte*! Now tell me; what in the name of all that's good brings you back to this god-forsaken place?'

'I had a call from Donal.'

Jerry's face clouded. 'Ah yes. Of course.' He shook his head and a strand of thinning hair fell across his forehead. He brushed it back absently, a gesture he probably made a thousand times a day. 'Terrible thing. Strange, too. She's a fine woman, is Aine.'

'D'you keep in touch with Donal?' Moran sipped his stout.

'Brendan, you know as well as I do it's hard *not* to keep in touch with folk out here. There's not a lot going on I don't get to hear about.'

'That's what I thought.'

Jerry drained his glass and helped himself to another. The kitchen door opened and an attractive girl with shoulder-length auburn hair placed a plate of chicken sandwiches in front of Moran, smiled shyly, and scurried back to her duties. Moran heard low voices and a burst of female laughter.

'Pay no attention.' Jerry winked. 'A new face is always worth a comment or two.'

Moran nodded through a mouthful of chicken sandwich. It wasn't bad; a bit heavy on the mayonnaise, but tasty enough. Jerry rattled on between slugs of whiskey.

'Donal's a worry, right enough,' the barman said. 'He wants to sell up, but Padraig's not for it. The boy's good at the job, y'know. But between you and me Brendan, Donal had something better in mind for the lad. Somethin' better than bein' up to your neck in sheep shit all day long.'

24

Moran sipped his stout and the flavour hit his palate like a time bomb, the memories crowding his mind, jostling for attention. The five of them: himself, Donal, Aine, Geileis and Janice – five teenagers on the cusp of change. For Moran the months ahead would see his entry into the Gardai as a cadet. Geileis would head off to London and university. Janice would begin her studies in Cork. Donal and Aine would be married within two years. But for now, for these moments, they were carefree, young, full of life, enthusiasm and the future.

'You all right, Brendan? You look a wee bit pale, sure you do.'

Moran shook his head. 'I'm fine. Just being here brings it all back.'

Jerry nodded sagely. 'I'm sure it does. Where does the time go, eh?' He finished his whiskey with a flourish.

'So you know that Aine's missing.' Returning to the subject, Moran finished the last of his sandwich and wiped his mouth with a napkin.

Jerry found some glasses to polish and set to work with a grubby tea towel. 'Like I said, it's hard not to know what's going on locally.'

'Any ideas? Donal's all over the place. He just can't square it with how things have been these last years. They've been fine together, he tells me.'

Jerry avoided eye contact, focused on his polishing. 'Well, well. I can't say for sure when I last saw Aine, that's God's honest truth. She keeps – kept – herself to herself. Donal too. I mean, he's always busy up at the farm. Semi-retired, he says, but he's always up to something.'

'But she's not really the leaving type, Jerry, is she?' Moran was doing his own re-focusing, nudging Jerry back on track.

'Well you see, I just don't know the lady well enough anymore, Brendan.' Jerry paused for a second, glass in hand, tea towel poised.

'Come on, Jerry. You hear things all the time. You must have formed an opinion.'

Jerry leaned over the bar, voice lowered. 'I have a quiet life here, Brendan. I'd like to keep it that way. If you get my meaning.'

Moran took a deep pull of stout and set his glass down on the bar's scarred wooden surface with a firm *clunk* which made Jerry blink. He held the barman's gaze.

'I'm here to find out what happened, Jerry. I could use a friend or two. I need to know I can count on you. Feathers are going to be ruffled a little, but I can't help that. Now I'm asking – for old time's sake – can I count on you?'

Jerry pursed his thin lips and looked at the floor. The sound of clanking pans and female voices drifted into the bar from the kitchen. A local came in with a gust of rain and nodded briefly before taking a stool at the opposite end of the bar.

'Jerry.' Moran kept his voice low. 'I was followed from the moment I drove away from the ferry. Two guys, driving a black Passat. I left them east of Youghal but they'll get here eventually, if they're not here already. Any idea who they might be?'

The barman gave him a look and moved off to serve the other customer. When he came back his expression had changed from evasive bonhomie to one which Moran recognised at once. There was no mistaking the branding of fear stamped across the man's face.

'Not here, Brendan.' His voice was little more than a whisper. 'Not with the girls working out the back and my locals coming and going. Meet me tonight at Geileis' cottage and I'll tell you what I know.'

'Geileis is *here*?' Moran was stunned. 'I thought she lived in London?'

Jerry shook his head. 'Her husband died three years ago. She came home.'

'Donal never said… My god, I'm amazed. Geileis, of all people …'

'Back of the high street, up the hill near the church. You'll see it on the right. Blue gate. Seven o'clock.'

Jerry turned his back on Moran and went into the kitchen. Five minutes later he still hadn't reappeared, so Moran gave a brief nod to the bar's only other customer and left.

Set slightly back from the lane on the gentle slope leading away from the village, the cottage was easy enough to find. Moran unlatched the blue gate and ducked under low branches to the front door. He found himself hesitating on the threshold.

Geileis. It had been so long. Too long. Moran was seized by a sudden panic. The impulse to turn and walk back the way he had come was almost overwhelming. Before he could change his mind he took the tarnished brass knocker in his hand and gave two sharp raps.

And waited, heart bumping in his chest.

The sound of footsteps, but not from within. He turned in time to see a woman of around his age appear at the corner of the cottage, carrying a wicker gardening basket in the crook of her arm. Her hair was greying at the temples but the flame-red tresses he remembered had not vanished entirely; they were tied in a long plait which fell over one shoulder onto a lightly-patterned pinafore dress. The green eyes met his and for a moment all he could see was Janice. He opened his mouth but found no words.

It was Geileis who broke the silence.

'I heard you were in town. My god, Brendan, but you don't look too bad. Not bad at all.'

Geileis smiled and Moran's world rocked unsteadily. The similarities between Janice and her sister had always been marked, but time had closed the gap even further. It was Janice's smile which greeted him, *her* voice inviting him to *come away in*. They hugged and Moran caught a faintly familiar perfume.

At last he found his voice. 'Nice to see you,' he said, and realised how weak a greeting it sounded.

'Jerry's just arrived.' She tapped her basket. 'I thought I'd have half-an-hour or so to bed in the last of the spring-flowering bulbs before you joined us,' she said brightly. 'I'll put the kettle on.'

Geileis slid the front door open with a practised movement of her foot. 'The wood's a wee bit swollen after the rain. Mind your head.'

Moran followed her in, ducking under the lintel as instructed, and found himself in a cosy front room which smelled faintly of roses and woodsmoke – a homely, comforting, female kind of fragrance. There was a two-seater settee, a spindle-backed rocking chair and a more serviceable-looking armchair by the unlit fire. Jerry occupied the latter, but made no effort to rise. He was nursing a glass in one hand, and raised the other in half-hearted greeting.

'You came, then.'

'Of course.' Moran wrinkled his nose as he caught the unmistakable tang of liquor on the man's breath. 'Weren't you expecting me to keep this appointment, Jerry?' Moran held Jerry's gaze until the barman looked away, his fingers nervously stroking the rim of his glass.

Geileis bustled back into the room and handed Moran a steaming mug. 'Tea. Strong, a dash of milk. No sugar.'

Moran smiled as he accepted the drink, seating himself on the settee. 'You remembered. I'm impressed.'

'I remember a *lot* about you, Brendan Moran,' Geileis' eyes twinkled as she moved towards the rocking chair.

There was more than pleasure reflected in those eyes and Moran found himself responding with a nervous smile while a confusion of emotions raged inside him. He was saved from further embarrassment by Jerry's abrupt intervention.

'She's left of her own accord, Brendan. I'll tell you that much.'

'And why would she do that, Jerry?' Moran said quietly, and took a sip of tea as he waited for Jerry's response.

'Why indeed?' Geileis agreed. 'She has absolutely no reason to go off on her own to do *anything*. Her life is here. She was perfectly content when we met up last month. At least she *seemed* to be. What have you heard, Jerry? Is she in debt? Has she had some kind of breakdown?'

'No, no. Nothing like that.'

There was a sudden noise from outside, a scuffling, scraping sound followed by a metallic *clang*. Jerry jumped, and whiskey splashed from his glass onto his trousers. He sprang from the chair as if stung.

Moran was at the door, shooting Geileis a quizzical look

over his shoulder. He unlatched the front door and looked out. All was still.

'It's probably our local fox. Or cats.' Geileis was at his shoulder. 'Always trying to get into the bin.'

Moran waited for a few seconds, listening intently, as Geileis went down the side of the cottage, held up the bin lid with a grin and a shrug, and secured it in position, weighing it down with a brick for good measure.

Jerry was pacing the floor as they went back inside. Geileis shut and bolted them in, and then drew a pair of heavy velvet curtains across the front door – more for Jerry's benefit, Moran suspected, than for any security concerns of her own.

'It's all right, Jerry.' Geileis placed her hand on his arm. 'Just a fox.'

It took a few minutes and a large refill to calm Jerry down sufficiently that they were able to continue the earlier conversation.

'You were saying, Jerry?' Moran prompted. 'Aine *had* to leave? But why?'

Jerry raised a shaking finger. 'She left to protect them – Donal, Padraig and Caitlin, I reckon. I think she *had* to go, y'see.'

'Protect them from what, Jerry?' Moran posed the question but he already suspected what the answer might be. Aine's background had always been something of a blank page, which Moran had found easy to fill with questionable associations – but they'd all been aware of that, especially her husband-to-be. As promised, she'd cut all such ties a long time ago, slipped the leash of her past and made a new life for herself as a sheep farmer's wife.

But now Moran could see a bleak possibility in Jerry's terrified eyes.

Perhaps the leash had been reapplied.

Perhaps Aine had been recalled.

Chapter 5

The stillness of the cottage wrapped itself around the three of them as Moran and Geileis digested Jerry's words. Geileis made a low sound in her throat and rocked gently on the rocking chair, one pale hand over her mouth and an arm wrapped protectively around her midriff.

'*Who*, Jerry?' Moran placed his empty mug carefully on the side table by the settee. 'Who are we dealing with here?'

Jerry moistened his lips. 'I've said too much. I should never have come. Just leave it there, Brendan. You wanted to know why. Now you know. You'll understand why she had to go. Donal knows; he just won't admit it.'

'No choice,' Moran said quietly. 'She had no choice, is that it?'

Jerry looked into his glass. Geileis went quickly into the kitchen and reappeared with a half-bottle of whiskey. She poured a shot into Jerry's empty glass and returned to the rocking chair, shooting Moran a covert glance of encouragement as she passed by.

Jerry took another deep slug. His face was grey and drawn, thinning hair dishevelled. Moran remembered him as a youngster from way back – up for anything, two years younger than the rest of their group and always eager to impress. His pranks had passed into their – and local – folklore, but now here was this skinny, frightened middle-aged man who looked ten years older than he was, trembling over his whiskey like a drunken informer from some gumshoe TV series.

Jerry allowed his gaze to fall somewhere between Moran and Geileis. Into the air he said, 'No choice. You're right, of course. Like you always were, Brendan. On the button, as they say nowadays.'

Moran leaned forward. 'I need a name, Jerry.'

Jerry's tongue flicked nervously over his bottom lip. 'I know you do. But I can't give you one. God's truth.'

'Think hard, Jerry. At least give me something to go on. The last thing I want is to compromise your safety.'

'Oh, is that right?' Jerry snorted. 'These folk don't mess around, Brendan. They'll kill me, I'm tellin' you.'

'Knowledge is empowering, Jerry. The more you tell me, the more chance I have of getting to the bottom of this and making an end of it. If that's what you want.'

'It's never over, is it? No one can make an end of it. It doesn't matter what bloody agreements the politicians put in place.' Jerry stared miserably into his tumbler. 'There's always a few who'll not accept it.'

Geileis broke her silence. 'You said it, Jerry. A few. That's the point. The majority have moved on. It's just the remnant that's left. And that's the cancer that's got to be cut out.' Her voice trembled a little and she lifted her cup, took a sip of tea.

'Easy to say.' Jerry's voice quavered.

'I thought things had changed for the better when I

decided to come home,' Geileis went on. 'And they have. But we have to keep it that way. We have a responsibility.'

'Responsibility?' Jerry's voice rose. 'To get ourselves killed?'

'To make sure the peace is kept. To make sure we have a stable country for our kids' generation, Jerry.' Geileis' voice carried a slight tremor.

'I *have* no kids.'

'But Donal does, Jerry. Caitlin's a fine young woman. And like me she'll want to come home one day, I know. So let's make sure she, and others like her, have the option.'

'Caitlin's living away?' Moran asked. 'Donal never mentioned that.'

'There's a lot Donal doesn't mention.' Geileis' mouth was a thin line. 'And that's the problem.'

'Where is she?'

'London, I believe. But Donal tells me she's buying in Reading. Nice flat, apparently. Boyfriend too. She's doing well.'

'My patch,' Moran said, half to himself.

'You should look her up,' Geileis said. 'She'd be pleased to see you.'

'I wouldn't recognise her,' Moran said. 'Last time I saw her she was running around the bay with a sunhat and little else.'

'She'll just *love* being reminded of that.' Geileis smiled broadly for the first time and Moran's heart lurched. Not just the smile; Janice was in the eyes too. He hid behind a cough and took a sip of tea.

Jerry had fallen silent during this exchange. However, he had apparently reached some decision, because he got up rather unsteadily and addressed them both.

'You'd be best talking to the islander, Brendan. He's out of it now, but he'll have the information you need.'

'The islander?'

'That's what they call him.' Geileis looked slightly alarmed. 'He lives on Great Blasket. On his own. His name is O'Shea. Joseph O'Shea.'

'On *Blasket*?' Moran frowned. 'No one lives on Blasket.'

'Well, O'Shea does,' Jerry waved his tumbler. 'Nowhere else would have him.' He laughed, a cracked, strained sound.

'Ex para?'

'What do you think?'

'ONH?'

Jerry shook his head. 'Even they rejected him. Unmanageable, they said.'

'OK, now we're getting to it.' Moran paused as Geileis recharged Jerry's tumbler. Once the operation had been completed the barman sank back into the armchair. Moran pressed home his advantage.

'So this guy, O'Shea, can point me to the organisation responsible for Aine's recall?'

'Depends how he is when you find him.' Jerry shrugged. 'Like I said, he's not an easy one to manage.'

'It's a question of approach, Jerry. I've done this sort of thing before.' Moran sounded more confident than he felt. He became aware of Geileis' eyes on him.

'Just keep me out of it, OK?' Jerry's hand shook as he raised his tumbler to pale lips.

'We're already past that stage, Jerry,' Moran said evenly. 'We're in it already, so we pull together and we finish it together. Just like the old days.'

*

After they'd seen Jerry off, a little unsteadily, down the lane, Geileis turned to Moran with an unspoken invitation, and moments later he found himself in the lounge with a stronger drink in hand.

'He's terrified,' Geileis said, arranging her plait to fall over her right breast. She sipped from a glass of red wine, her long fingers curled around the stem.

'He knows more than he's letting on.' Moran settled into the sofa and sipped the Irish, enjoying the smoothness as it slipped down his throat. It was easy to drink. Far too easy.

'Are you really going to visit this O'Shea?' Geileis' eyebrows drew together in concern. 'He sounds wild – dangerous. You don't know what he might do – or who he might tell,' she added, nipping her bottom lip in consternation. 'Why not leave it to the Gardai, Brendan? They'll know how to handle it.'

'They've made a grand job of it so far, right?'

'But you're just one man,' Geileis pointed out. 'I mean, you don't know what you're up against. If it's something to do with, you know, the paramilitary, then … oh, I don't know. It's far too risky, Brendan.'

Moran nodded slowly. 'So what do you suggest I tell Donal? Sorry, brother, it's out of my league? You'll just have to wait and see what happens?'

'No! I mean, obviously not. Oh, I don't know *what* you should do – what *we* should do.' Geileis drank deeply from her glass. When she looked up her eyes reflected the firelight. 'Will you stay for something to eat? I've made a casserole – it's too much for one person. I could freeze the rest, I suppose, but…'

'Thanks. I'd like that.'

There was a brief lull in conversation as Moran digested the implications of the offer and the alacrity of his positive response.

Is this wise, Brendan?

Geileis broke the silence. 'We both know there's an elephant in the room, Brendan. We can talk about it, if you like.'

Moran took a deep breath and slowly exhaled. 'It's hard, Geileis. I nearly didn't come. I wasn't sure how I would handle all … all this.' He waved his hand vaguely. 'I mean, seeing you all again. Being back here. Coming home.' He trailed off.

Geileis rose from her chair and joined him on the sofa. She placed a hand on his knee and he tensed.

'It's all right, Brendan. I know it's hard. God knows, it's hard for us all.'

Moran felt a mixture of emotions at the physical contact. He cleared his throat. 'It's good to see you, Geileis. I didn't know you'd come back.'

Her hand remained. 'You could have called me. I wasn't that far away.'

'I know. It's just–'

'–Just that you're a man. And men handle things their own way.' Geileis smiled. 'And we know what men do, don't we? Bottle it up and hope it'll go away.'

Moran shook his head. 'You're wrong. I know it'll never go away. Every night I see her, Geileis. Every night I remember. I see it all. The rain. The car. The smoke.'

'I don't blame you. You know that, don't you? I never blamed you.'

He nodded, not trusting himself to speak. He got up and

moved to the fire, stood with his back to the flames. A spark spat in the grate as the wood settled. Geileis said nothing, just watched him, one long leg crossed over the other.

'I know you don't,' he said eventually. 'But I'm not sure about Donal.'

'It wasn't your fault, Brendan. It wasn't *any* of our fault. Donal knows that.'

'Maybe logically. But emotionally?' He shook his head. 'Different story.'

Geileis rose gracefully from the sofa and held out her hand. 'Let me get you a refill.'

He nodded and handed her the empty tumbler. He watched her walk to the kitchen, hips swaying as she moved, head held confidently. She had lost none of her poise. The quieter of the two sisters, Moran had always been conscious of Geileis' warmth towards him – even after he and Janice had got together. If his relationship with Janice had caused her pain then she had masked her disappointment well. She treated him as the close friend he was – as a brother. And in a way, that's exactly what he was – or had been – to the Hannigans.

Moran settled into the sofa, remembering the day his parents had broken the news of their impending move north. Before he could open his mouth to object his father had held up his hand. 'It's all right, son. You're staying put. The Hannigans will take you in, as long as you behave yourself and bring credit to the Moran clan. Think you can do that?' His father's eyes twinkled. 'I've no choice, son. The firm want me moved and so that's how it'll be. But your mother and I know that your life is here. Your friends, your school. Everything. Am I right?'

'Right, Da.' Moran muttered to himself.

'What's that, Brendan?' Geileis reappeared with two recharged glasses.

He shook his head. 'Nothing. Just daydreaming.'

'That'll be right. Sure, it'll do you a power of good to relax a little.' She smiled and handed him his drink.

'Thanks, but I'm hardly here to relax.' Moran managed a stiff smile. 'Let's just call this evening a minor diversion.'

'Agreed.' She raised her glass. 'Well, then. Here's to us.'

'To us,' Moran reciprocated, 'and to Aine's safe homecoming.'

They drank and set their glasses down in unison. It felt orchestrated and they both laughed. The tension lifted a little.

Geileis' expression became thoughtful. 'I was thinking, Brendan. Maybe Jerry's got it wrong. Maybe Aine *has* just taken off, on her own, like.'

'It's possible,' Moran agreed. 'But unlikely, for two reasons.'

Geileis cocked her head to one side. 'Namely?'

'Number one, the state Jerry's in. Would he be as jumpy as he is for no other reason than some sort of paranoia concerning the past? I don't think so. But number two is the clincher for me.'

'Go on.'

'I was followed here. Two guys.'

'Are you sure?'

'As eggs is eggs.'

'What happened to them? I mean, are they still watching you?'

Moran sipped the Irish. His head was remarkably clear

and he was enjoying the excellent quality of the whiskey; Geileis' taste was impeccable. 'I last saw them east of Youghal. They'll catch up – soon, I imagine.'

'God. You *will* take care, Brendan, won't you? This doesn't sound good at all.'

'I'm used to this kind of stuff, Geileis. It's what I do. My DCS would rather I spend my time behind a desk, but somehow that never seems to happen.'

'Because you don't *let* it happen, I'm guessing. There's plenty of youngsters able to do the dangerous work, Brendan. You should let them. You've done your bit.'

'It's not about doing my bit. It's just … I don't know, how I am, I suppose. The thought of being trapped in an office all day fills me with horror.'

Geileis shook her head and laughed softly. 'I'll bet. You were always an outdoor lad, as I remember. Hiking, climbing, whatever – you'd be the first in line.'

Moran smiled ruefully. 'Those days are gone. Time just seems to go faster. I always seem to be working.' He shrugged. 'That's how it is.'

'Maybe you need to slow down, Brendan. We're not getting any younger. Why not give yourself some space, a little time to think and reflect?'

'God, that's the last thing I want to do.'

'I know – I didn't mean–' Geileis' face fell.

Moran gave a dismissive wave. 'I know you didn't. It's all right.'

There was a moment of silence – not awkward, just pensive.

'*Anyway*,' Geileis said eventually, 'we should eat before the casserole morphs into a burnt offering.'

Moran laughed. 'Sure. I'll give you a hand.'

'Gosh, a domestic policeman. I *am* impressed.'

'Ask Donal about my mixed grill next time you see him,' Moran countered. 'Once eaten, never forgotten.'

Chapter 6

He couldn't remember the last time he'd enjoyed a meal so much. Geileis was sparkling company, the wine was on a par with the whiskey and the casserole one of the best he had tasted. Afterwards, Geileis served coffee, two perfect double espressos. Moran sat back in his chair and gave a sigh of contentment, the purpose of his visit temporarily forgotten. Somewhere in the recesses of the cottage a clock chimed eleven, each stroke a short but insistent reminder.

'Good grief. Is it that late?' He glanced at his watch for confirmation.

'What's the hurry? You don't have to get up for work.'

'No, but I want to make an early start. I have a boat to catch.'

'I can't dissuade you?'

'I'm only going to talk to the guy, that's all. What's the worst that can happen?'

Geileis shivered. 'I don't want to think about it.' She reached over the table and took his hand. 'I care about you Brendan. I always have done. You know that, don't you?'

'I know. We're family. That's why I'm here – to help.'

Geileis' hand applied a light pressure. 'You never married.'

'No.' The amber light which had begun to glow dully in Moran's head now switched to a vibrant red. 'I was sorry to hear about your husband,' he added.

'Yes, thank you.' Geileis looked down at her shoes – gathering her strength, Moran thought, so that she could comment appropriately. 'He was a good guy. Solid, dependable, you know. Bit dull, I suppose.'

Moran, slightly taken aback, gave an awkward laugh.

'Well, he was.' Geileis smiled. 'But I do miss him. What happened wasn't fair. He went through a lot of discomfort. But then,' she sighed, 'we're all headed that way, aren't we, at our age? Something ghastly comes along and *whoosh*, that's it, we're done.'

'Well now,' Moran said, 'you are the cheery one, aren't you?'

'But it's true, isn't it?'

'We have to make the most of what we have, I suppose. You know, enjoy life as much as it–'

'–As it allows us to.' Geileis sighed, withdrew her hand and gave him an ambiguous look which Moran interpreted as rather more than family-friendly. He felt himself wilting under Geileis' scrutiny and made a play of finishing the non-existent contents of his coffee cup.

Time to go before things get out of hand, Brendan, old son…

He scraped his chair back. 'Let me give you a hand with the clearing up.'

'Don't worry.' Geileis gathered up the coffee cups and went to the far corner of the kitchen. 'I'll just pop the lot in the dishwasher. It's no bother.'

'If you're sure, then.' Moran stood irresolutely by the kitchen table.

'Maybe just collect the glasses from the living room? Then you can be on your way. Your early start and all, remember?'

Geileis' tone had become more formal, as if he had somehow mishandled the intimacy of their conversation and was now being penalised for his ineptitude.

'Sure. I'll bring them in.' He went into the lounge and found the empties, was about to return to the kitchen when the half-open drawer of a small bureau caught his eye. Some ingrained sense of tidiness impelled him to cross the room to close it, but as he reached down he caught a glimpse of something metallic. A moment's guilt gave way to a policeman's curiosity and he slid the drawer fully open.

A small automatic pistol lay half-covered in a soft muslin cloth; three loose bullets lay beside it. He stepped away quickly and returned to the kitchen.

'Here you go.'

Geileis looked up from the dishwasher. 'Just put them over by the sink. I'll hand-wash those.'

'Well.' Moran spread his hands. 'It's been a lovely evening. Thank you.'

Geileis wiped her damp hands on a dishcloth and held her arms out. They hugged.

'I can't tell you how nice it's been to see you, Brendan.'

'You too.' The image of the gun was forefront in Moran's mind as she leaned forward and kissed him lightly on the cheek.

'You can't keep your heart locked away like this, Brendan. You're not giving yourself a chance. Nor anyone else,' she added quietly.

Moran cleared his throat, found no words.

'You know the boat times?' she asked quickly, covering his

embarrassment. She smiled as she read his expression. 'Of course you do. Well then. Take care. See you later in the week?'

'You will. Goodnight, and thanks again.'

As he made his way along the lane towards Donal's farmhouse he asked himself a thousand questions. Was it her gun? Why would she have a gun in her cottage? Maybe it belonged to someone else. If so, who? He passed the local bar and thought of Jerry. Had Jerry lent it to Geileis? Was he *that* scared?

The churchyard was a field of irregular shapes to his left, the lights of Donal's farmhouse just visible in the near distance. Down the slight incline of the lane to the unmade road and he was home and dry. He felt slightly lightheaded and regretted the last glass of wine. No matter; tomorrow he would begin to get to grips with Aine's disappearance – with O'Shea's cooperation. Moran was confident in his ability to obtain information; it was just a matter of approach. And what did O'Shea have to lose anyway? The guy had not only opted out of whatever para involvement he might have had in the past, he'd also apparently opted out of society altogether. It would be no skin off O'Shea's nose to share a little information. Moran just had to get alongside him, get him talking. He made a mental note to bring a bottle – a little lubrication might help loosen O'Shea's tongue if it came to that.

He was so engrossed in working through his strategy that he failed to notice a shadow detach itself from the hedgerow a few metres ahead. The first blow came out of nowhere and Moran reeled to his right, for an instant imagining that he had collided with some unseen object in the dark. Then someone caught his arms from behind, yanked them back and held them. Reflexively he tried to tear himself away, but whoever had pinioned his arms was strong and very determined. He could feel breath on his neck, a sour smell of garlic, or something stronger. Moran tensed, guessing what was coming next, but instead of a fist a masked face appeared an inch from his nose.

'You're not welcome here, see? So you get in that wee car of yours and head back to the ferry, understand? First thing tomorrow, if you've any sense.'

Moran tried to place the accent but it was obvious he was deliberately masking it, speaking in a low and clipped tone. The guy behind pulled Moran's arms further back than they were anatomically intended to go and Moran winced. 'Get this.' The first spoke again. 'If you're still here in twenty-four hours you won't be driving anywhere again. Ever. Understood?'

Moran was checking the eyes out, the only visible part of the face in front of him. They were deep socketed, maybe brown or dark grey. Hard to tell.

'I said, *understood*?'

The punch came fast and hard, doubling him up as the breath was driven from his lungs. He managed a croaked response and the pressure on his arms eased. He heard their retreat, a pattering of rubber soles on the road's unmade surface. After a few minutes he felt able to straighten up and walk the three hundred metres to the farmhouse.

He fumbled for the key Donal had given him and let himself in. The house was in darkness, Donal no doubt fast asleep in preparation for his customary early rise. Moran took the stairs slowly and found his bedroom door ajar. He edged it open cautiously.

The bedside light was on and a note was sitting on his pillow. He closed the door behind him and checked the ensuite. Empty. He went to the bed and picked up the note.

Blasket ferry might be cancelled tomorrow – incident at Dunquin Pier. Jerry mentioned you had a mind to go over to Blasket. I thought you'd like to know. D.

The grapevine had lost none of its efficiency, then. Perhaps Jerry had called in on his way home, or perhaps Donal had been out and about, had helped Jerry on his way. In any case, the news about the ferry was a potential spanner in the works of his planned trip.

Moran cursed silently and returned to the bathroom. The mirror revealed an impressively swollen area just under his left eye, the skin unbroken but already turning an interesting shade of blue which was only going to get worse before it got better. He soaked a face flannel in cold water and applied it gingerly to his damaged flesh. His head was pounding, a combination of the whiskey and the blow he had received.

After a few minutes he removed the cold compress, went back into the bedroom and sat heavily on the bed. His stomach ached where he'd been punched and he felt a hundred years old. His watch told him it was a quarter to midnight.

Sure, you've made a fine start, Brendan.

Chapter 7

Dunquin jetty was clearly not designed for motor vehicles. It was accessed via a high-sided, narrow walkway which twisted down to the small harbour. No one in their right mind would attempt it in a car, let alone a four-by-four.

Moran stood by the road and looked down at the Land Rover wedged securely between the two walls. There were always exceptions, of course. While human beings walked the earth there would *always* be exceptions. Moran shook his head ruefully and wondered how long it would take to unwedge the vehicle so that he, and a handful of other hiking hopefuls could make their intended journey across to Great Blasket.

Two gardai vehicles and a small fire engine were attending to the task in hand but it looked to be touch and go as to whether the walkway could be cleared for the scheduled morning crossing. It then occurred to Moran that there might be more to the four-by-four driver's ineptitude than first met the eye: what if news of his intentions had reached the wrong ears? What if this was a deliberate attempt to delay his crossing? Moran elected to loiter for a while and observe.

He felt the wind on his face and grimaced. Pretty much all of him hurt, his cheek and the area around his eye-socket being the worst. He'd skipped breakfast, despite Donal's comprehensive and hospitable preparations; his stomach just wasn't up to it. He'd also drawn a few curious glances on his way through the village. And no wonder – he looked as though he'd been the loser in some dodgy bare-knuckle sweepstake. Maybe O'Shea would be impressed. Maybe he wouldn't care. Maybe he'd think Moran was just plain stupid to get involved.

He wrapped his coat more tightly around him. It was getting colder, the sea choppier. He watched the firemen hooking up the four-by-four's chassis. A guy in a duffle coat and cap was gesticulating urgently at the firemen. The driver, no doubt. He looked *pukka*; hard to imagine he was anything to do with last night's reception committee. Raised voices drifted over, floating on the sea breeze. Duffle Man was clearly concerned about damage to his vehicle. *Should have thought of that before, pal.*

Moran jammed his hands deeper in his pockets and sat on a nearby wall. He glanced at his watch. At this rate it was going to be a wasted day. No boat, no Blasket, no O'Shea. Even when he reached the island he still had to find the guy, and that could take a while. Four square kilometres didn't sound too bad, but on foot it was a lot of island to cover.

Still, he was well prepared; Moran had found a bag on the farmhouse doorstep earlier containing some basic provisions: water, a bottle of whiskey, an apple, a flask of coffee and three rounds of chicken sandwiches. There'd been a note – *'Thought you might need these today. Keep warm. Gx'.* He glanced at the other hikers, stereotypically bearded, bespectacled, earnest-looking bog-trampers, all waiting patiently, like himself, for news. They all sported rucksacks of gargantuan proportions, as if they were expecting to spend the rest of their lives on Blasket Island.

It was hard to imagine, Moran mused, that as recently as the Fifties an entire community had done just that – eked out a basic, ascetic existence, cut off by the sea and solely dependent on each other for survival. The ruined village, with its decaying shells and grass-covered pathways, was the only reminder of that long-vanished community. Perhaps O'Shea had commandeered one of the old buildings and made a rudimentary home for himself. Or maybe he'd elected to move further into the island and built a shelter of his own in a more remote location. A few houses at the top of the old village had apparently been restored, and Moran reckoned that the hikers had probably reserved rooms in these. He hadn't had time to organise a room himself, but felt confident that he could beg a little floor space from whoever might be officially renting; if there was any strong objection he could always produce his warrant card. Not that it carried any weight in Ireland, but the sight of it might swing things in his favour if it came to that. His preference, however, would be to spend as little time on the island as possible – find O'Shea, see if he had anything useful to impart, and board the evening boat back to the mainland.

If it runs to schedule…

Moran got up and walked towards the gaggle of firemen and *gardai*. Duffle Man was still talking animatedly to one of the officers, but as Moran approached he jumped smartly into the police car's passenger seat. There was a further brief exchange between Duffle and the driver before the vehicle reversed smartly and took off up the lane. Moran frowned. Had the driver been arrested? Had the gardai found something in the Land Rover?

'Half an hour or so, sir.' One of the gardai, interpreting Moran's quizzical expression as the unspoken question on everyone's mind, delivered his estimate with good-natured bonhomie. It sounded optimistic to Moran, but at least there was some expectation that things might get moving before midday. He raised a hand in acknowledgement. That was better news, the first of the day. Moran hoped to add to that tally once he got to Blasket.

As it turned out, it wasn't difficult to find O'Shea. The man was waiting for him.

Moran knew it was him just by the way he was standing; there was something unhurried, laconic, almost idle about the way he was watching the passengers disembark. A tourist would be more animated, while anyone affiliated to the island's nascent tourism industry would be acting more purposefully – and would probably sport a more welcoming demeanour. Not that O'Shea looked hostile; Moran reckoned he just looked indifferent.

The islander was lean and tall, dressed in jeans and black jumper, bearded with grey-streaked hair caught into a long ponytail. Moran stepped gratefully onto dry land – boats weren't on his hobbies list, especially dinghies – and approached O'Shea with his hand outstretched.

'I'm Moran. How did you know I was coming?'

'Does it matter?' O'Shea's voice was soft and low, his eyes guarded. 'I don't have many visitors.'

'Well, I appreciate the welcome anyway.'

'What happened to your face?'

O'Shea's expression was difficult to read. He probably knew exactly what had happened. Moran dissembled. 'Difference of opinion in a bar.'

'Yeah, right.' O'Shea seemed amused. 'And you a policeman an' all.'

'Not here I'm not. Anyway, thanks for taking the trouble to meet me.'

'You'd never have found me in a million years. Thought I'd save you a wasted visit.'

'Very kind. Is there somewhere we can talk?'

O'Shea looked Moran up and down. 'We're talkin' now.'

'I meant somewhere more comfortable. Somewhere I can offer you a drink.'

'Ah. Now that's my kind of talk. No bars on the island, more's the pity.'

O'Shea turned and began to lope up the slipway, surefooted on the seaweed-strewn rock. He was wearing knee-length boots which glistened with some water-resistant coating. Moran followed, taking extra care on the uneven ground. His stick would've been handy right enough and for a moment Moran regretted his hasty decision to abandon it. *Stubborn as ever, Brendan …*

But O'Shea was lengthening his stride, leaving Moran and his dinghy companions behind. Moran'd be damned if he'd ask O'Shea to slow down. He scrambled up the slipway and eventually found more solid ground beneath his feet.

It was an uphill climb but Moran found himself shivering in spite of his exertion as he passed the village's crumbling remains; he could sense the ghosts of the long-gone islanders in the shadows and maudlin, decaying piles of stonework. 'Is it far?' he called out to O'Shea's back.

The tall figure stopped and turned, silhouetted for a moment against the horizon. He shouted: 'The Englishmen not keeping you fit, Brendan?' Then he presented his back once again and Moran concentrated on placing one foot after the other.

To the east, the smaller island of Beiginis, home of the local grey seal population, lay like a flat, green disc in the blue waters of the sound while far away on the mainland the fin-like elevations of the Three Sisters stretched heavenwards towards a sky filled with bloated, grey-white clouds. It was a warm afternoon for late September, and soon Moran was sweating profusely. After twenty minutes he detected a slight slowing of O'Shea's pace and took the opportunity to rummage in his bag for a drink. He found the plastic bottle of mineral water and drank deeply, wiping sweat from his brow with his free hand.

Shortly the route began to slip into a gentle decline. O'Shea made a slight course alteration and gestured. Moran shielded his eyes against the sun and found himself looking at a long, low building on raised decking, set into the lee of the hill. It looked like one of those eco-houses Moran had seen on some prime-time TV show a while back. O'Shea was evidently taking his long-term survival seriously – you'd have to, really, Moran thought, living in this kind of isolation. As he got closer Moran noticed the solar panels, the large plastic containers beneath the building, the charcoal burner and a smaller outhouse, the purpose of which was self-evident.

As he approached O'Shea's head appeared from one of the windows of the main building. 'Are you comin' in or what?'

Chapter 8

Moran climbed the wooden steps onto the decking, ducked his head and entered. The house was more spacious than it appeared from the outside. It was split into three areas: a main living room, a bedroom, and the last presumably a kitchen or food preparation area of some sort. In the centre of the room, an open grate beneath a conical central chimney was packed with wood ready for a fire to be lit.

'Sit down.' O'Shea pointed to a threadbare armchair. 'And tell me what it is you want.' He perched on the edge of a plain table, its surface covered with ephemera relating to, as far as Moran could tell, the outdoor life: fishing lines, saws, a hunting knife, a few blocks of shaped wood. There was also, he noted, a shotgun propped up against the far wall.

The islander rapped the table with his knuckles. 'See this? Good solid stuff. Spanish. From an Armada wreck. Made it myself. Like most things here.'

Moran set his bag on the floor, which was dry, clean and bare apart from a thin oriental rug which extended beneath the table and was speckled with loose wood chippings.

'Take a look at this,' O'Shea offered, the gleam in his eyes showing that despite his gruff exterior he was enjoying the rare opportunity to show off his creation. 'When I built the place I didn't just opt for natural resources – I wanted to recycle what I could. Whatever was practical to get over here from the mainland.'

Moran joined him at the rear of the cabin, a translucent arrangement of small windows forming an interlocking wall of glass. 'Surplus stock – aircraft windows,' O'Shea explained. 'Got them from Shannon. Cheap as chips – there's an English expression for you, Brendan. Make you feel at home. Come and take a look out here.' O'Shea held the back door open, and Moran stepped cautiously onto a shorter area of decking upon which a peculiar contraption was sited – a kind of cross between a fork-lift truck and a fence trellis.

'Observation platform,' O'Shea explained. 'Finished it last month. Watch this.' O'Shea stepped onto a squared-off sheet of metal, closed a gate behind him and pressed a button.

Moran stepped back in amazement as the islander was hoisted rapidly into the air.

'Old scissor-lift. Fairground junk,' O'Shea called down. 'No mains power – I've built a wood and dung furnace to fire up the generator.'

Moran waited for the platform to make its descent and watched O'Shea disembark, closing the gate behind him with an affectionate pat. 'See for miles up there. Like it?'

'Remarkable,' Moran agreed.

'Anyway, you're not here to be impressed by my DIY, are you, Brendan? So.' O'Shea motioned for Moran to walk ahead of him into the house. 'What is it you want?'

'Simple. I'm looking for Aine Hannigan. Wife of a friend of mine.'

'Sure. Donal's wife.'

Moran wasn't surprised. There were connections going back here, maybe a long way. 'I was told you might be able to shed some light.'

O'Shea picked up a hunting knife and began to whittle at a piece of wood. 'Light? I haven't shed light for a long, long time, Inspector Moran. There's not much light in a human heart, as far as I can tell – but you'll know that anyway, being around the same age as myself.' O'Shea's eyes glinted with what might have been amusement even if the short, deft stokes he was making with the knife seemed to contradict that interpretation.

'I'm not here to discuss philosophy,' Moran said, 'and I'm not here to delve into what you might or might not have done in the past – let's get that straight to begin with. This isn't about you.'

A gull shrieked somewhere above the house and in the short silence which followed Moran could hear waves breaking against the shore below in a slow, rhythmic wash.

'No?' O'Shea rested the point of the knife on the table and rotated it slowly back and forth. 'Well that makes a change, right enough.'

'So, can you help me?' Moran found the whiskey bottle in his bag and held it up in an unspoken question.

O'Shea clattered the knife onto the tabletop with a thump, disappeared into the kitchen area and returned with two glasses. Moran went to the table, poured two shots and held up his glass.

'Your health.'

'And yours.' O'Shea resumed his half-standing, half-reclining position at the table.

Moran studied his new acquaintance. Here was a man used to being on the alert – never able to relax, always ready for action. Moran had little doubt regarding the nature of his past actions. Everything about O'Shea proclaimed his trade: *Warrior. Freedom fighter. Survivor.*

'Aine heard that someone was looking for her,' O'Shea said finally. 'Figured she'd get out of the way while she could.'

'Where?'

O'Shea shrugged. 'She's gone off the radar. For a time. But he'll find her.'

'Who?'

'Ah, now, I can only go so far, Inspector.'

'Someone from your old organisation, I presume.' Moran sipped his drink, watched for O'Shea's reaction.

'Now what would *you* know about *my* old organisation? A fella who took off to work for the English.'

'I had my reasons for leaving,' Moran replied evenly. 'No political agenda.'

'True enough,' O'Shea agreed. 'A broken heart, was it, Brendan?'

Moran stiffened. 'We're talking about you, O'Shea. And Aine Hannigan.'

'You don't mind me calling you Brendan?' O'Shea drained his glass. 'This is a friendly visit, right?'

'I don't care what you call me. I just need to know where I can find my friend's wife.'

O'Shea scratched his beard. 'You'll need to get to her before *he* does. He doesn't like to be crossed.'

'Don't play games, O'Shea. I want a name.'

O'Shea clunked his glass on the table. One stride and the

shotgun was in his hand, barrels pointing at Moran's stomach. 'The last time a fella came over here making demands, Brendan, I sent him off with something else to think about. He's not been back since.'

Moran was unfazed. Even O'Shea wouldn't be rash enough to shoot a serving Detective Chief Inspector, English or otherwise.

'Let me guess,' Moran said. 'They don't like you cluttering up their nice shiny heritage site.'

'Spot on,' O'Shea nodded. 'But it's a free country, right? I don't give a toss if they've bought Great Blasket or the whole of the USA. There's no one going to tell me where I can or can't choose to live.'

'I'm sure your point of view will be carefully considered.'

O'Shea frowned and his face darkened. The shotgun moved a fraction, shifted in the islander's grip; his lips twitched. A gust of wind made the rafters creak. The distant sound of an engine suggested a passing motorboat – an end-of-season outing, perhaps. Moran felt sweat trickle down his neck.

O'Shea gave a snort of laughter, lowered the shotgun, broke it and propped it against the table. 'You've picked up the English humour, I see, Brendan. Only thing I like about the English.'

Moran relaxed a fraction. Not for the first time he wondered at the wisdom of tackling O'Shea alone. Jerry's terrified face swam through his mind – the face of a man in fear of his life, in fear of people like O'Shea. He dismissed the image, got to his feet and refilled both their glasses.

O'Shea nodded his thanks. 'It's about family, Brendan, isn't it?'

'Isn't it always?'

'But they're not your own, are they? Not really.'

This time Moran was taken aback. O'Shea knew a *lot* about him, which was a little unsettling but, in a stranger way, also curiously reassuring. Moran felt as though he were on the verge of discovering something deeper than a missing woman's whereabouts. He hid his discomfort by raising his glass to his lips, aware of O'Shea's analytical gaze resting upon him. The whiskey seared his throat and warmed his stomach.

After a moment he said, 'They're family to me, and that's all that matters.'

O'Shea gave him a long look. 'I don't know why I'm even *entertaining* this. First you'll be giving me your word you'll not do anything … rash.'

'I just want to get Aine back safely. That's all.'

O'Shea gave a bitter sigh. 'All right. Well, the guy I'm talkin' about, we've not seen eye to eye for many years. And it's got worse since I found out what he's planning.'

Moran nodded. A close friend, then. He studied O'Shea's body language. No, not a friend. More than that …

O'Shea shot Moran a knowing look. 'You're not a DCI for nothin', eh Brendan? You've sussed it. Sean's long since lost the surname, but he's still my brother. It's Sean Black you're dealing with, no less. Heard of him?'

'Indeed I have.' Moran tried not to show any emotion, but it was a struggle.

Sean Black.

Sean Black, who had worked closely with Rory Dalton, back in the day.

Rory Dalton, who had come close to ending Moran's life

at Charnford, the same way he'd ended Janice's.

'See, Brendan,' O'Shea went on, 'the trouble is, the authorities have a habit of puttin' everything in nice neat boxes. So if Sean's in one, they'll put me in it too. Nice and tidy, like.'

Moran nodded.

'Only it's not.' O'Shea studied his glass, and looked up again after a long moment of contemplation. 'It's not tidy at all. I'm done with it, Brendan. Finished. I like it here, and I want to keep things the way they are.'

'I can understand that.'

'I think you can.' O'Shea nodded. 'But Sean, you see, he's different.'

'He can't let go.'

'That's exactly right. He can't let go.' O'Shea emphasised the last two words, the imperative his brother had ignored.

'He's planning something. And he needs Aine?'

O'Shea banged his glass on the table and began to pace the room. 'I must be out of my mind – spillin' to the likes of you.' He went to the door and raised his arms to the top of the frame, leaned forward into the gap and stretched long and hard, as if trying to exorcise the realisation that he needed help.

From a policeman…

Moran sensed the inner conflict. He had to clinch a deal before the moment was gone. 'We'll work it out together,' he said. 'For our mutual benefit.'

'Oh God, *mutual benefit*. Will you listen to him.' O'Shea disengaged from the doorframe and stood over Moran. 'You'll not harm him, understood? That's the deal. He's my brother, whatever he's doing.'

'I understand. I had a brother. Our relationship was…' Moran searched for the right words, '… strained, to put it mildly, but in a different way.'

'You worked it out, though?'

Moran shook his head. 'Not really. He died – unexpectedly.'

'I'm sorry to hear that.'

'Thanks. It was a while ago.' No point bringing that up, going into the detail. Patrick Moran had been murdered – along with Kay Kempster, an ex-girlfriend of Moran's – during the Charnford case, at the hands of Rory Dalton. Moran had dealt with it, shelved it after Dalton had gone down, excised the fresh atrocity from his mind. It was hard, though, not to be softened by O'Shea's curiosity. He opted for a kind of forced levity, worked up a tight smile. 'Life carries on.'

O'Shea gave him a strange look. 'It does that, Brendan. But the ghosts are always there, right?'

'Yes.' He nodded. He hadn't expected to feel quite so vulnerable – this guy seemed to have the knack of getting under his skin, almost as though he'd cast himself in the role of confessor specifically to figure out what made Moran tick.

'So, we have an understanding. But do we have a *deal*?'

'Deal.' Moran got to his feet.

O'Shea nodded, helped himself to another drink. 'It'll not be easy,' he said quietly. 'I'll tell you now I don't rate your chances.' He shook his head.

Moran extended his hand. '*Our* chances.'

O'Shea's grip was firm. 'I'll be in touch. Now get the hell out of here before I change my mind.'

*

Sean Black. Moran let the name ring in his head. The spray kicked up as the boat tacked its last few metres towards the jetty and Moran tasted salt on his upper lip.

His leg was killing him and he was hungry. It'd been a long trek back from O'Shea's and he was impatient to get to his car. O'Shea had hinted that he had been in Aine's company recently; she was scared, compromised somehow. And, whatever the reason, she had been compelled to go into hiding. Had she gone directly to O'Shea for help, knowing that he was the only one close enough to understanding his brother's psyche – the only person qualified to offer advice? Did O'Shea *know* where she was, and had simply declined to share the information?

And what of Sean Black? Once described by the British press as a 'loose cannon' during the lengthy and protracted peace process, he was known to have masterminded a notorious shooting at a border town and claimed responsibility for a number of bombings. Despite his unstable reputation he had evaded capture primarily, it was said, by having friends in influential places. Moran wondered if these 'friends' would describe themselves as such. Unlikely; he was pretty sure they'd be too scared to reveal anything much.

The thing was, if Aine had been summoned by Black but had cut and run instead, there was plenty of emotional leverage at Black's disposal: Donal and Padraig were vulnerable, so why hadn't Black made a move in that direction? Moran fingered his bruised face. Sure, he had people keeping an eye, but nothing Donal had said gave Moran the impression that his friend considered himself to be in any danger.

Moran raised a hand to the skipper as he disembarked. It was just himself and an older couple making the return journey; the others, as predicted, had stayed on Blasket. He wondered if they'd have been so keen if they'd known who was living on the far side of the island – and what he had stashed in his eco. Moran hadn't missed the long, wooden boxes stacked almost out of sight in the kitchen: explosives, and maybe guns and ammunition.

But O'Shea wasn't active; of that, Moran was pretty certain. Sure, the islander might have squirrelled away a stash for a rainy day, but it would have to be some thunderstorm for O'Shea ever to use it in anger.

Moran was so absorbed that he only looked up when he reached the top of the walkway and began his customary pocket-patting in search of car keys. That was when he noticed the two gardai vehicles boxing his own into the verge. As he approached he could see the yawning boot and the expression on the approaching officer's face.

'This your car, sir?'

'It is.' Moran's stomach contracted. This was going to be bad, no question.

'In which case, sir, I'd like you to accompany me back to the station.'

'Why? What's the problem?'

'That's the problem.' The officer pointed to the open boot.

Curled up in a foetal position, Jerry's body looked even smaller and more vulnerable than ever. But vulnerability wasn't something Jerry was likely to be worrying about any more.

Jerry was dead.

Chapter 9

Moran's mind was racing faster than the garda driver. Donal would vouch for him, of course. And Geileis. And there was no proof. Moran hadn't laid a hand on Jerry.

Or had he? Had he touched any of his old friend's belongings, personal effects? Even if he had, so what? They couldn't pin this on him – no evidence.

Except that the body was in his boot.

The car braked to a halt. The door opened, hands reached for him.

They led him down the side of a grey-rendered building and ducked his head under a weatherbeaten wooden door.

Moran resisted. 'Wait. Aren't you going to book me in officially?'

'Shut up. We do things *our* way here.'

A narrow corridor, a row of cells. What the hell *was* this?

'You can't just–'

'Get *in*.' The push sent him staggering forward. The door slammed.

The cell was tiny, as Moran had anticipated. This was a small village. The occasional drunk on a Saturday night or maybe the odd punch-up outside O'Reilly's would pretty much sum up the extent of the lawlessness the local garda would have to deal with on a routine basis. The harsh smell of disinfectant and the engrained stench of urine appeared to confirm his analysis.

Moran sat on the bench and put his head in his hands. What could he remember from the assault on the road? The first thing the garda would want to know is why he hadn't reported it – and also what he'd been doing on Blasket. O'Shea would be known to them. The boat skipper had been close enough to observe their meeting. Two and two make five.

The cell door clanked and swung open. An officer he hadn't seen before beckoned with an impatient gesture.

Moran knew the drill. He followed the uniform into a small room. One table, two chairs, a recording machine. Another officer came in. He was shorter, dark. No smiles.

'Interview with Detective Chief Inspector Brendan Moran begins–' The first officer looked at the wall clock. '8.32pm. Sergeant James O'Mahoney. Garda Liam Buchanan also present.' O'Mahoney fixed Moran with a level gaze. 'Visiting a friend, Inspector Moran?'

'Yes. Donal Hannigan.'

'Old friend?'

'Yes. I lived with the Hannigans in the Seventies.'

O'Mahoney nodded.

'You knew Jerry O'Donaghue well?'

Moran cleared his throat. 'He was in my social group at the time. Yes, I knew him well.'

'What happened to your face?' The dark guy, Buchanan, asked.

'I was set upon. Last night. Late.'

'And you didn't report it? Looks painful.' O'Mahoney tapped a pencil on the table, rubber side down.

'No. I didn't want to make a fuss.'

'They take anything?' Buchanan again.

'No. I don't believe so.'

'Then why did they attack you?' O'Mahoney tucked the pencil behind his ear and steepled his hands.

'I have no idea.'

'Yes, you do,' Buchanan said. 'You're just not letting on.'

'Listen.' Moran spread his hands. 'I've been on Blasket all afternoon. The car's been parked up since late morning.'

'Did you shove auld Jerry in the boot last night, maybe?' Buchanan picked his teeth with his pinky nail. 'I used to enjoy a dram in his bar, y'know. I kind of warmed to the man.'

Moran took a deep breath. Rain spattered on the small window. 'I did not.'

'When did you last see Mr O'Donaghue?' O'Mahoney again.

'Yesterday evening. At a friend's house.'

Nods.

'He was fine.' Moran went on. 'He'd had a few drinks, but no more than usual, I wouldn't say.'

'Oh, you wouldn't?' Buchanan said.

'The guys who went for me. You'd be better off questioning *them*.'

Buchanan leaned forward. He had a shaving cut on his chin, a tiny piece of tissue clinging to the small wound. 'See, here's our problem. We haven't a description of these people. You didn't report the attack. No one has seen any strangers about. Apart from yourself, that is. What were you doing in Jerry's bar yesterday?'

'Having a drink.'

'Asking questions is what I heard. You have an old score to settle? Against Jerry? That why you're back here?'

'No.'

'Really?'

'Look.' Moran leaned back in his chair, which creaked ominously. He quickly redressed the balance by leaning forward again. 'You're aware, I'm sure, that Mr Hannigan's wife is missing. I felt that I might be able to support Mr Hannigan in the meantime. He's an old friend and very upset. I'm sure you can understand that.'

'Bollocks,' Buchanan said. 'You thought you'd have a crack at finding her yourself.'

'The investigation into Mrs Hannigan's whereabouts is continuing,' O'Mahoney broke in smoothly. 'And we don't encourage members of the public to get involved. I'm sure you'd take the same line on your own patch, Inspector.'

'Are you charging me or just warning me off?' Moran felt his face reddening. 'You know damn well that I didn't kill Jerry O'Donaghue. OK, the body was in my car. I can't explain that, except to say that whoever attacked me more than likely dumped him in there last night – I didn't open the boot this morning. You haven't a scrap of evidence to link me to Mr O'Donaghue's death. Forensics will confirm that.' He paused, read their expressions. 'You *have* handed the car over to forensics, haven't you?'

O'Mahoney and Buchanan exchanged glances.

'Who's the SIO on this?' Moran posed the question in a calmer tone. No point in getting them agitated.

'It's still a local affair,' Buchanan said.

'You're kidding. You've a murderer in town and you're treating it like a minor burglary? Come on, *really*?'

'That'll be all for now, Moran.' Both men got up. 'Interview suspended 08.45pm. Officers O'Mahoney and Buchanan are leaving the room.' O'Mahoney stabbed the tape machine button.

'Now wait a minute–' Moran was on his feet.

'After you.' O'Mahoney indicated the door.

Moran went out, walked the few paces to the cell.

Buchanan opened up.

Moran stepped reluctantly in and turned to face them. 'How long d'you intend–'

But the cell door heaved to. Bolts clunked into place and footsteps receded.

Silence.

Moran stood by the cell door awhile, cursing silently. He knew they couldn't hang onto him for long without evidence, but the one thing which had struck him about the two gardai gave him little confidence in the prospect of his release: O'Mahoney and Buchanan were acting as if they had all the time in the world. Patience was their watchword, it seemed. They'd been patient all the way from the ferry; more so now with a suspect in custody.

Suspect or target? Moran favoured the latter. It was Buchanan who'd given the game away. He knew Moran had got a look at him on the N25, so he'd done the obvious: he'd shaved his beard off.

Chapter 10

Someone was trying to insert a screwdriver between his ribs. The pain was tolerable at first, but worsened in a matter of seconds. Moran twisted, tried to pull the steel out of his body but it was no good – he couldn't reach it. The point of the screwdriver probed his body, searching for the most sensitive areas. It gave a final twist and Moran sat up with a cry. Sweat was pouring down his torso.

He felt behind him and found the culprit; a screw head had come through the surface of the bunk. Moran cursed. The place was falling apart.

He looked at his watch. It was just after four. Then he heard a scraping sound. Rats? More than likely.

A bolt was drawn. The cell door creaked on its hinges.

'Moran.'

It wasn't a question. The shape in the doorframe knew he was there.

'Well? Are you comin', or stayin' with your wee whiskered buddies?' O'Shea shone a thin torchbeam into the small space.

'A moment.' Moran slipped into his shoes and joined O'Shea at the door. The building was silent, wrapped in darkness. 'I won't ask how.'

'Best not.' O'Shea said, *sotto voce*. 'You'll have guessed by now that this building isn't part of the official Gardai Station.'

Moran followed O'Shea out the way he had come in. The fluorescent light flickered dimly as they passed, like a failed attempt to capture photographic evidence. Moran hesitated, imagining for a moment that he heard a muffled voice behind a door marked *Toilets*, but O'Shea was already outside, holding the door open.

Moran hesitated at the threshold. Technically, he *was* under arrest, and his departure would not only be considered unlawful, but perhaps also an admission of guilt – at least in the minds of O'Mahoney and Buchanan. However, the fact that he'd been kept in some dodgy lockup was confirmation enough that the two were acting independently of the official gardai, so Moran reasoned that a choice between the cell and O'Shea's alternative was no choice at all.

They walked quickly across the road and into a narrow alley. O'Shea turned left at the end and clicked a key fob. A four-by-four's twin headlamps lit up like cats' eyes. Moran stole a glance behind but the alley was still and lifeless.

He sank gratefully into the passenger seat as O'Shea gunned the engine. He didn't ask where they were going. He'd find out soon enough.

O'Shea drove fast but accurately. They hit the coast road for a bit and then turned inland again. Moran checked the dashboard clock; it was 4.25. Felt like it, too. He rubbed his eyes with the heels of his hands.

'Coffee's what you'll be needin'. Plenty available presently.'

'The gardai. They followed me from Rosslare. Why would

they do that?'

'Sleepers.' O'Shea indicated right and they turned off the roundabout into a row of nondescript terraced houses. He deftly parallel-parked the four-by-four and killed the engine, turned to Moran with a raised eyebrow. 'On Sean's payroll. He'll have heard you were coming. Sent them to keep an eye – to begin with, at least.' O'Shea withdrew the ignition key and mimed a locking motion. 'Looks like they decided you needed to be kept out of the way.'

'They'd have just *left* me there?'

O'Shea nodded. 'Until it was safe to let you out.'

Moran raised an eyebrow. 'And that would be when, exactly?'

The islander gave him an odd look, half-pitying, half-amused. 'There you go with your questions again.' He opened the driver door. 'Wait for my signal, then follow.'

O'Shea cast a practised eye up and down the street. Satisfied, he motioned Moran to join him. Not the first, second or third house, but the fourth. O'Shea waited, performed his checks again then quickly mounted the steps to the front door.

The hallway was dark and narrow. Moran peered into the gloom. The house smelled musty, slightly damp. O'Shea went right and flicked a light switch. The room lit up slowly as the power-saving bulb illuminated. Sparsely furnished; peeling wallpaper, a coffee table, two used mugs, a pack of cigarettes. Standard safe house vibe. Moran shook his head ruefully as he recognised a turn of phrase he'd clearly picked up from his DI, Charlie Pepper. Pepper was Moran's right-hand officer – capable, ambitious, and making slow but steady progress following a recent attempt on her life. Moran had initially been hesitant to leave the team in her hands during his absence but the medical reports – and Charlie herself – had eventually convinced him. She was back, and hopefully for good.

Moran could hear O'Shea rattling around in the small galley kitchen. He reappeared presently with two mugs of coffee. 'No sugar.'

'Thanks.' Moran gratefully sipped the hot liquid.

O'Shea sat himself down on the threadbare sofa. 'So. What happened?'

Moran shrugged. 'They made the hit on Jerry O'Donaghue, planted the body in my boot. Laurel and Hardy turned up to make the *arrest*.' He made imaginary speech marks in the air to emphasis the word. 'That's it.'

O'Shea nodded. 'And now Sean will guess I'm involved.' He took a sip of coffee. 'Not good.'

A footstep on the staircase brought Moran's heart into his mouth. He half-rose from the armchair until O'Shea brushed his alarm aside with a wave of his tattooed arm. A figure appeared in the living room doorway. Slight, tousle-haired.

'What the hell kind of time d'youse call this, Joseph O'Shea?'

Moran did a double-take as he tried to reconcile the person in the doorframe with the Aine Hannigan he remembered from yesteryear. Her features swam in and out of focus, like a familiar photograph which has been retouched, or an old painting which has been restored; the familiar blended with the unfamiliar in one discombobulating moment of confusion.

'Who's your pal?' Aine cocked her head at Moran. 'What

happened to *no one else'll know*?'

'Aine,' Moran managed at last. 'It's Brendan.'

Her hand went to her mouth. 'Oh my *God*. It is too. What on *earth*?'

Moran held out his hand but Aine brushed it away and hugged him, pressed her cheek to his. She stepped back, studied his face. 'It's been too long, Brendan. But I can't say I'm as pleased to see you as I might have been. Not the way things are.'

'I'm here to help.'

She shook her head vehemently. 'You can't. Not with this. Not with *him*.'

Arms folded, she looked him up and down. 'Just go, Brendan. I don't know what Joseph's told you,' this with a glare in O'Shea's direction, 'but whatever, he didn't tell you enough. Or you'd never be here at all.'

'Donal and Padraig. What about them?'

Aine looked away, bit her lip. 'How are they?'

'As you'd expect.'

'When did Donal call you?'

'Last week. I came as soon as I could.'

Aine nodded.

O'Shea, who had been listening to this exchange in silence, interjected. 'And a right bloody cock-up he's made of it so far.'

Aine ignored the interruption. Still addressing Moran, she said, 'Does Donal know anything?'

Moran shook his head. 'No. You should send word. It's not right to leave him like this, just hanging.'

Aine put her face close to his. 'If I so much as *breathe*, Sean Black'll be onto me. Do you know what that means? Have

74

you any *idea?*'

'He wants you back on duty?'

She sighed, folded her arms. 'I could hardly believe it. It's been so long, I'd all but forgotten.' She squared up to Moran. 'It's like another life, Brendan. A long time ago.'

'Sure,' Moran said. 'For you, maybe. Not for him.'

'Anyways,' O'Shea said. 'You'll both sit it out here until I say so. No phone calls. No goin' out, no curtain-twitchin', nothin'. Got it?'

'I've just about had enough of *here*, Joseph O'Shea.' Aine's cheeks had coloured. 'With no change of clothes, no flamin' hot water, no *nothing*.'

O'Shea had raised both hands. 'All right, all right, I hear you. It's not the Hilton, but it's *safe*. I can't—'

'Being safe isn't going to get me very far,' Moran broke in. 'We do this together, or not at all.'

O'Shea shook his head. 'Don't start, Brendan. You're not in Berkshire now.'

Moran was looking at Aine. 'If Black can't find you, he'll try something different. Another way, another approach.'

'Like what exactly?' Aine's arms were still folded. She was wearing an open-necked blouse which emphasised her cleavage, the more so by the supporting action of her posture. Moran noticed O'Shea's eyes straying.

The islander took a packet of gum from his jeans pocket and offered it to each in turn. Both declined; he carefully unwrapped a stick for himself. 'Our policeman's right, Aine. He'll want to flush you out.'

'Oh God. Padraig?'

Moran shook his head. 'He'll start with the weakest. The target that'll be sure of success. Padraig's a big lad. Might be problematic. Donal's on his guard. Who are you closest to?'

'Well, Caitlin, but she's—'

'He'll not touch her,' O'Shea broke in. 'No way.'

Moran was taken aback by the islander's reaction. O'Shea's hands were balled into fists and his mouth was twisted into a grimace of – what? Anger? Fear?

Aine plonked herself on a faded armchair. A faint cloud of dust rose with the small impact of her behind on the cushions. Her fingers worked busily, twisting her wedding ring around her finger. Her face was drained of colour. 'He wouldn't. He can't. Not Caitlin. I mean, she's in England …'

O'Shea, chewing vigorously on his gum, went to the window and checked the street. Moran noted that he did this without disturbing the curtain. Satisfied, the islander turned and faced the room again. He'd composed himself, but Moran could see that some weighty conclusion had been arrived at in the preceding few moments.

'Aye, he might. You'd better believe it.'

Moran frowned. 'You're saying he'll send someone that far afield? The UK's well out of his jurisdiction these days, surely?'

O'Shea shook his head, swept a hand through his hair. 'Not at all, Brendan. The UK's bang in the centre of his thinking. Always was. He'll have people there already.'

Chapter 11

'Best get word to your daughter.' Moran spoke to Aine gently. 'Just in case.'

'She's in the process of moving. To Reading,' Aine said, half to herself, her voice quavering. 'London's too expensive, and there's Crossrail coming, you see. She'll commute … let me think…she's moving this weekend, or was it last weekend? Oh *God*, now I'm losing track of time…'

'Well, Reading is my jurisdiction,' Moran said. 'I'll get my DI to contact her. What's her address? Mobile phone number, email. Whatever you've got.'

'It's a new apartment,' Aine said. 'She's doing so well.' A brief smile. 'I've got the address somewhere. Hang on. It's in my handbag.' She made for the stairs.

There was an uneasy silence as they listened to Aine bumping around in a bedroom. Eventually O'Shea shook his head. 'You'd better get this right, Brendan.'

'That sounds like a threat. We're on the same side, remember? My DI can handle it. Trust me.' Moran finished his coffee and grimaced. Cold dregs.

O'Shea grunted. 'I have a laptop, registered to a dummy name and address.'

'Fine. So we could use social media.'

'Traceable.'

'But not easily. IP addresses take time. Wifi?'

'Hacked into the local bar's wifi. It's down the street a wee bit. Signal's pretty dodgy. Won't give you long if he susses you, but maybe long enough.'

'OK. We'll have to risk it.'

'Here.' Aine came back into the room, her face flushed. She'd applied a little makeup and had a cardigan thrown over her blouse. She handed Moran a scrap of paper.

'I'll fetch the machine – and other stuff, while I'm about it.' O'Shea went out. They heard the front door close, a key turn in the lock. Aine shot Moran a look.

'Precaution,' Moran said. 'He's not taking any chances.'

'Joseph's all right,' Aine said. 'I don't know what I'd have done without him.'

'Right. An angel compared to some of his friends.'

'What's *that* supposed to mean?'

'Forget it,' Moran said. 'Let's focus on Caitlin, get her into protective custody. We'll worry about us later.'

'Where *is* he?' Aine paced the front room. She lit another cigarette, took a long drag and exhaled. Blue smoke filled the air and Moran coughed. He wanted to open the window, but O'Shea had been insistent that they opened neither windows nor curtains.

'Hell, sorry. Bad habit, I know.' She flicked the filter with her thumb, an automatic gesture Moran had grown used to in the preceding hours.

Moran waved a dismissive hand. 'Not a problem.'

'What's the time?'

He glanced at his watch. 'Just after eleven.'

'Where *is* he, then?'

Moran studied Aine. She was a few years his junior, five-two or three, still slim, quite attractive. They'd never hit it off, right from the word go. Nothing unpleasant had occurred between them; it was simply that they were different. The times they'd spent together had been as members of their social group with little one-to-one interaction. Donal quickly discovered he'd landed a girl with strong political views, which Aine hadn't shied away from airing whenever the opportunity presented. The occasions when she and Moran had chatted, argued maybe – about life the world and everything – had been few and far between. Moran had been as good a listener then as he was now, and so he'd listened, maybe proposed the odd counter-argument, perhaps begged to differ on occasion, backed off when things got a little too heated.

Aine's background had been implied rather than fully known. Now, it seemed, there was more to her politics than anyone in the old group could have guessed at the time. Moran wanted to know more. He cleared his throat. 'Probably nothing to worry about. He doesn't strike me as the sort of guy who'd say one thing and do another.'

'What if he's run into trouble?' Aine dragged on the cigarette. 'What if they know where we are?'

'Like I said, he's probably just being cautious. That's how he operates. At least that's the way it seems to me.'

'I *have* to call Caitlin. What if they've got to her already? … Oh *hell*.' She stubbed the cigarette out in the already overflowing ashtray.

'Ten minutes. Then I'll go to the bar and make a call.'

'All right. All right. Yes.' She sat on the sofa, face pinched. 'Thank you, Brendan.' She felt in her pocket, took something out – a small photo booklet. 'Here, look. This is Caitlin.' Aine flicked through the clear plastic leaves, selected one, held it up.

Moran examined the print. A pretty girl sitting in a restaurant, smiling. The red hair, the warmth in the eyes – the inherited Hannigan good looks, all in place. Moran smiled appreciatively. 'She's a beauty. You must be proud.'

'I am. Very.' Aine gave the photo a long look before closing the booklet and returning it to her pocket.

'Tell me about Sean Black. You knew him pretty well, I'm guessing.'

Aine compressed her lips. 'Well enough, I suppose.'

'You were involved in frontline stuff, back in the day?'

'Hardly frontline.' Aine smoothed her jeans with both hands. 'I – I knew people who were, of course. I suppose I moved in those circles, a little. Then I met Sean. He was young then, just a boy really.'

'As were we all,' Moran murmured.

'He … he had a compelling kind of personality. He was–'

'Charismatic?'

'Yes, that's exactly right. Charismatic. People would listen to him. Even as a young man, he had something about him. A passion. Or a vision, maybe.' Aine examined her nails, first one hand then the other.

'You were an item?'

She looked up. 'No. Maybe I'd have liked that. I don't know. It's a long time ago.'

'But he hasn't forgotten you. Why's that, d'you think?'

Aine's brow furrowed. 'Are you interrogating me,

Brendan? Or telling me how unmemorable I am?'

'No, no. I didn't mean that. Listen, the more I know, the more I can help. You have to be one hundred percent honest with me, Aine. If you're not, you're putting more lives at risk.'

'What do you mean, *more*? Who—?'

'Jerry O'Donaghue was murdered.'

'Jerry? Oh my *God*.' Aine's shoulder's slumped. 'What happened?'

'Not sure, yet. Someone killed him, put him in my car. Wanted me to take the rap for it.'

Aine's head lowered. When she looked up, she said 'It's ten minutes now. Nearly.'

Moran nodded. 'OK. Stay put. Do *not* leave the house.'

The bar was pretty typical. No frills, Formica top on the counter. Fluorescent lighting, Mary Black easing her silken voice through the speakers:

Last night I dreamed you were back again. Larger than life again, holding me tight again...

Placing those same kisses on my brow — sweeter than ever now, Lord I remember how...

Black. No relation, Moran supposed; it was a common enough name ...

The song played on.

...I wonder if I'm past the point of rescue.... Is no word from you at all the best that you can do ?...

No word. He thought of Donal, waiting. Not knowing. Maybe he should call, tell him Aine was all right. No, he couldn't risk it.

'What'll you be havin'?'

'Half of Guinness, please.'

The barmaid nodded. Her hair was scraped back into a tight bun. 'Essex facelift, guv,' one of his sergeants had once described the style. A deft flourish with the knife took the head off the Guinness, and he paid. 'Thanks. D'you have a payphone on the premises?'

'In the corner, by the fruit machine.'

'Thanks.'

He walked across the lino to the old-fashioned, Perspex-hooded booth. It had seen a bit of life, right enough. Four, maybe five taped repairs across the nicotine-stained plastic barely held the canopy in place. Moran picked up the handset – in a similar state of disrepair – and dialled the operator. Two minutes later he was speaking to DI Charlie Pepper.

'Why is it I always get a bad feeling when you're away and you call in?'

Moran sighed. 'I can't imagine.'

'Everything's OK, guv. Honest. And I'm fine.'

'It's not you, Charlie. I know you're fine. Listen up…'

Moran outlined the situation, leaving out much of the detail regarding himself, the gardai and Jerry Donaghue's murder; those events didn't concern Charlie and the team. Instead he majored on Caitlin Hannigan, the potential threat to her life, and the possibility of a UK incident in the making.

'I'll get onto the chief, guv. He'll have to sanction any action, of course.'

'He will. And that's fine. The Met will be on high alert as it is after Westminster, but whatever Black's planning may wrong-foot them – it may not be London. And his MO is likely to be quite different.'

'Got it.'

'I'll get back to you when I can. But don't wait. Just get after that girl and keep a close eye.'

'Will do, guv.'

'Thanks, Charlie.'

'Guv?'

'Yep?'

'Take care, won't you?'

'You know me.'

'That's why I said it.'

'Right. Bye, Charlie.'

'Bye.'

Moran hung up. The smell of cooking was drifting into the bar from the kitchen, and he realised how hungry he was. He hadn't eaten since the night before – a scrappy plate of fish and chips, courtesy of the two gardai. He ordered sandwiches, two rounds, one for himself and one for Aine, and kept an eye on the street through the narrow window. No sign of the four-by-four. For the first time, Moran considered the possibility that something had happened to O'Shea.

The sandwiches came. He paid, left the bar, crossed the road and took the steps two at a time to the front door. Which was ajar.

Moran stepped immediately to one side and the sandwiches hit the ground. With his left arm he eased the door open to the point where he could slip through the gap. A cigarette packet lay on the hall floor, just outside the living room door. Smoke still hung in the air. Moran shuffled along the internal wall and stole a careful glance into the living room. Empty. He went upstairs, came down, less cautious now. Downstairs toilet, kitchen. Nothing.

An empty house.

Chapter 12

'George? You busy?'

DC George McConnell looked up from his screen. 'Always.'

Charlie plonked herself on the end of George's desk. 'This is probably more urgent.'

McConnell frowned. It was Friday. He'd told Charlie once that he hated Fridays – something to do with his Catholic upbringing when his convent junior school had forced the fish thing. His refusal to comply had drawn the attention of a particularly sadistic nun whose *modus* of encouragement had apparently been to beat the young George with a steel ruler. Charlie supposed that McConnell hated fish as well.

George was a short, wiry Scot with a close-cropped ginger beard which no one was allowed to refer to as 'ginger'. It was a banned word in McConnell's vocabulary and countless new joiners and visitors had fallen foul of his acerbic wit through ignorance of this simple rule. George was a good copper, though. Forensically thorough in his investigations, he was one of Charlie's 'go to' officers when an unscrambling of potentially conflicting facts, alibis or conundrums of one sort or another was needed, even despite his sometimes irritating tendency to over-summarise the current status of an investigation or finer point of detail. Her only real concern was George's liking for a drink. But he was a Scot after all, so maybe that was just hard-wired, and maybe she shouldn't worry about it too much.

Maybe.

She became aware that George was looking at her expectantly. 'So,' she said, before George had time to interrupt, 'we have a young woman potentially under threat. I'll fill you in with the details later, but can you pay a quick visit and go over McConnell's patent security brief, chapter and verse?'

'Righto. Where?'

'Town centre, new apartment block. She's in the process of moving in.'

'Posh?'

'Irish.'

'Can't be both, I suppose.'

'Hey – my grandmother was Irish.'

'Oops. Sorry.' George McConnell grinned. 'And our source?'

'The guv.'

'What? Really?'

'I know, I know. He dishes out more work when he's away than when he's sitting in his office. But this sounds serious. Could be a potential terrorist threat in tandem.'

'What? Not those IS bastards *again*.'

'The clue's in the nationality, George.'

'Ah. Got it.' George tapped the side of his nose. 'But not the IRA surely?'

'I don't know any more than you right now.' Charlie ran a

hand through her spiky blonde cut. 'But the guv'll be back in touch soon, so he tells me.'

'Can I take Brit?'

'Tess might be better. Female empathy and all that?' Charlie handed George the address Moran had provided. 'And keep me posted.'

'OK. Modern apartment'll have good security, I'd've thought.' George was on his feet, but Charlie still had a height advantage of two or more inches. 'Video entry system and so on. All helps. They might have installed one of the new–'

'All right, all right, George. Spare me the *Gadget Show* highlights. Just make sure this young woman is extra vigilant, OK?'

'D'you want Tess to stay with her?'

'Let see how the land lies.'

George nodded, an action that never failed to put Charlie in mind of a small terrier. 'Righto,' he said brightly. 'You're the boss.'

'There you go.' DC Tess Martin's finger jabbed at a large building swathed in two enormous banners which read, '*Luxury apartments for sale. One and two bed. Available now.*'

'All right for some, eh?' George McConnell steered the car into the service road alongside the block and eased into a parking space.

'The girl's doing good if she can afford this, that's for sure.'

Several calls to Caitlin Hannigan's mobile number had gone straight to voicemail. Her old apartment was empty. Her employers had apparently given her the week off. *Ergo*, George, reasoned, she must have moved – or be in the process of moving – into her new place.

A motorbike exploded into life a few metres away and Tess flinched.

'You OK?' George shot her an anxious glance.

'Yes. Stop taking my temperature, George, will you?'

'Sorry.' George raised both hands apologetically and killed the engine. It had been just over a year since Tess had been maliciously wounded in a revenge attack linked to the Ranandan drug cleanup op. The woman responsible, a young Chinese by the name of Sheu-fuh, was behind bars and likely to remain so for a good many years. The assassin's MO, a custom motorbike, garrotte and knife, still made George shiver. They'd lost one colleague, strangled in his bed, and almost a second when Tess' maisonette had been targeted. Tess' attitude had been commendable from the start, but her determination to bounce back after her encounter with Sheu-fuh had transformed George's admiration into something else altogether. He knew he was being overprotective, but what could he do? She was his partner in a potentially dangerous job. Which meant that he was obliged to lead her into dangerous situations. It went right against George McConnell's grain. He bit his tongue and nodded.

'My bad. Let's go.'

The foyer of the new apartment block was plush. And locked. George shaded his eyes and spied a desk strategically placed dead-centre just above the short stairway leading from the foyer. Behind the desk a suited individual was shuffling papers and speaking into a mobile phone. Sales rep. New apartments, so rep on site. That figured.

He rapped on the glass door. The man looked up, finished

what he was doing and came down the stairs at a brisk trot. Tess showed her ID.

'Ah, right. Nothing amiss is there, officers?' The guy was what George would have termed a typical new homes estate agent. Smart, a little obsequious – not unpleasantly so – but way too heavy on the aftershave.

'I'm John. I work for the agents. How can I help?'

Tess explained: 'We're trying to trace a young woman. We understand she's bought an apartment here recently.'

'I see. Well, quite a few people have. They're very nice apartments.'

'I'm sure,' George said.

'You have a name?'

'Caitlin Hannigan,' Tess told him. 'Twenty-six years old. Fair, reddish hair, just above shoulder length.'

'Irish.' John nodded. 'Yep. I know her. Very pleasant. In fact, she was the first to complete.'

'Right,' Tess said, 'so she's not moved in yet?'

'Not yet, no. She has keys, though. I expect she'll be moving in anytime.' He scratched his bald pate with his biro. 'I can't recall if she said this evening or tomorrow. This weekend, at any rate.'

'You have security cameras.' George glanced around the foyer. 'On all floors, or just down here?'

'All floors,' John told them with a hint of pride colouring his voice. 'State of the art. IP camera system. You can monitor all floors – and the car park – in real time online. From your phone if you want.'

'Security guards?'

'Sadly not.' John allowed himself a regretful smile. 'Too much of an overhead. But the cameras obviate the need for human intervention.'

'I see. Well, thanks for your time. You're here until?'

'Six o'clock.'

Tess gave the agent a card. 'If you see – or hear from – Miss Hannigan, can you ask her to call me as a matter of urgency?'

'Nothing serious I hope?'

'We hope not.' Tess smiled her professional smile.

The smile stayed with George as he led the way back to the car. He guffawed as he unlocked it. '*Obviate the need for human intervention.* He's in the wrong job, that fella. He should be on *Countdown* with Carol Vorderman.'

Tess giggled. 'Carol Vorderman? She left the show *years* ago, George.'

'Aye, well, whatever.'

'So, now what? Wait until Caitlin turns up?' Tess turned the sunshade down and checked herself in the mirror.

Don't bother, George thought, *you look just fine to me.*

'Better idea.' George unclipped his seat belt. 'Technology is our friend, remember?'

George returned a couple of minutes later. 'Simples. Courtesy of Countdown John, I have the app name, login and password for the security system. We can monitor on my iPhone. Soon as she turns up, back we come.'

'Impressed.' Tess raised her eyebrows. 'So you *are* entering the UK Mr Multi-Tasker awards, 2017 after all. I'd heard a rumour, but I wasn't sure if it was your thing.'

'Funny.' George started the engine. 'Let's away – I'm in the middle of a car reg trace.' He glowered. 'As it happens.'

But deep inside he felt a pleasant warmth. He'd impressed Tess. That was one cool way to close off the week.

They queued to get onto the main road. Traffic was bad and getting worse by the minute. Something was going on.

'It's Friday evening,' Tess reminded him. 'It's always bad.'

'No.' George shook his head. 'This is definitely a lot worse than usual. Can you get hold of Traffic?'

A swift call confirmed George's assessment. Two lanes of the M4 westbound were shut, one lane eastbound too. RTA, multiple vehicles.

'Damn.' George drummed his fingers. The inner distribution road was clogged as far as the eye could see. He'd wanted to knock off by half six, maybe squeeze in a pint or two on the way home. Think about his next move with Tess. The car in front had turned his engine off; the driver was standing on the door sill, peering ahead to see what could be causing such an irritating obstruction. George turned his own engine off and sat back in exasperation.

Fridays. He hated Fridays.

'OK, George,' Charlie said. 'Thanks for that. Keep a close eye, please. I'm not a hundred percent on the IP camera thing. We need closer obs until we've found Miss Hannigan and briefed her.'

'It'll be all right,' George said, a little tersely. 'I've checked the tech – I can see all floors, and the lift interior too. Reading's gridlocked; we'd never get a car over there now in any case. Soon as she shows you can call her up.'

'*If* she has her phone on.' Charlie knew that George was like a dog with a bone once he'd made his mind up. Best to reinforce the details and let him get on with it.

'She will, won't she? It's probably out of charge just now.

Or something.'

Or something. Charlie held her tongue and left George to his vehicle checks. She wanted to calm the nagging feeling that Caitlin Hannigan had already been found, but by other interested parties. What had happened to the guv's promised update? This was too like the Cernham case – guv goes away, finds a problem, phones in, goes offline.

Not good.

Chapter 13

When in doubt, keep moving. It was an imperative Moran had always stuck by. Yes, he was wanted by the gardai – or at least some unofficial version thereof; yes, it was probably unsafe to move around freely and yes, he was now beginning to have second thoughts about O'Shea. He'd therefore concluded that to stay in the safe house would be anything but.

So, keep moving was the first imperative, but the second was to find Aine. She couldn't have gone far, not without transport. But, he supposed, it was possible that O'Shea had returned while he was speaking with Charlie and that, for whatever reason, Aine had simply gone with him. In which case they could be anywhere. But then, why didn't they wait for him?

Moran reached the end of the street and turned into another, wider and longer, dotted with shop frontages in a variety of contrasting primary colours. The first, a butcher's, told him what he'd already suspected; he was in Dingle town itself. He'd been here before, of course, a long time ago, and before it had become the tourist hub it was today. A gentle breeze ruffled the shop awnings and Moran tasted salt on his lips.

Memories, poignant and insistent, flooded back. He lifted his face to the weak sun and felt the warmth of a time long gone by. Donal, Geileis, Janice, Jerry. The *auld* group. And someone else. But who? The face swam in and out of focus, defying recognition. Probably unimportant. Nevertheless, as Moran continued up the street, peering into each shop in turn, he couldn't shake the nagging feeling that the missing memory was significant in a way he couldn't quite put his finger on.

He let it go, consigned it to his subconscious while he concentrated on searching for Aine. She was a mother, and a worried mother at that. Contact with Caitlin would now be an all-consuming need. No phone. So what would he do? Did they still run internet café's here? Maybe – with 4G not yet fully rolled out. He passed a coffee bar. Cheeky, but worth a punt. The proprietor was friendly and gave him directions. Next street, turn right, third on the left. He couldn't miss it. Moran thanked the guy and bought a packet of biscuits to salve his conscience.

The internet café was painted a lurid green and Moran didn't miss it. Sitting at the rear, face glued to a screen, Aine was concentrating hard and didn't look up as he approached.

'Any joy?'

Aine started as if stung. Her shoulders slumped. 'How did you find me?'

'It's not rocket science. If O'Shea didn't abduct you, this was an obvious alternative. Have you got hold of her?'

Aine shook her head. 'Not responding.'

'She's moving house. Busy girl.' Moran opened the biscuits and offered one.

'No thanks. Look, Brendan. This is not your problem. I don't want you involved.'

'Bit late for that.'

She sighed, pushed her hair back from her forehead. The café was half-empty. A backpacking couple were busy at a neighbouring PC, no doubt looking up B&Bs or cheaper alternatives. The remaining computer stations were empty and the waitress looked bored. Season's end was closing in.

'I can look after myself. I have friends.'

'Like O'Shea?'

'He's all right, I told you.'

'Then you should get back to the house. He obviously has a plan.'

'Drink?' The waitress had appeared at his shoulder. 'Sandwich?'

'Coffee. Black. Thanks.'

The waitress hovered, more interested in the raised voices than a sale. Moran waited until she had sidled away. He lowered his voice a little. 'O'Shea warned you about Caitlin. So he *is* thinking about her.'

She nodded. 'Of course he is. But it's my welfare which concerns him too.'

Moran pulled up a stool. 'Ah. Now it makes sense.'

'We're not an item, Brendan. There was something, once, but this is about friendship. Loyalty.'

'That's not how it looks from where I'm standing. Ah – thanks.' Moran nodded to the waitress and placed a few coins on her tray. 'I'll not be staying long.'

'Whatever.' Aine fumbled in her handbag. 'I'm going outside for a smoke.'

'Keep out of sight.' Moran tasted the coffee. Luke warm.

He called after Aine. 'And don't go wandering off.'

'Fat chance with you on my case the whole time.'

Moran drank his coffee, all the time keeping Aine's slight figure in view. She was standing half-in, half-out of the café taking short, nervous puffs on her cigarette. If it wasn't for the small matter of his being wanted for murder he'd have no difficulty in reaching a decision about the way forward: he'd frog-march Aine back to the farmhouse, leave her with Donal to sort things out and be on his way.

Or would you, Brendan?

He finished his coffee, leaving a centimetre of sediment at the bottom of the cup – at least it was real coffee. Moran hated instant coffee almost as much as he hated loose ends. Especially loose ends like a potential terrorist threat in the UK *and* a possible abduction on his patch. So no, he wouldn't walk away now. He'd see this through, whatever the consequences.

Moran returned his empty cup to the counter. The waitress gave him a smile which could have been coquettish, or it could have been his imagination. 'Your girl's taken off.' She gestured with her chin. 'Best get after her.'

'What–?' Moran spun on his heel and strode to the door.

He looked right, then left. Aine's sprinting figure was just visible, threading through the crowds.

Muttering expletives under his breath Moran followed, breaking into a run when he realised he'd never catch up at a fast walk. A few seconds later he knew he'd *never* catch her.

A diesel engine roared behind him. Moran turned, imagining a vehicle mounting the kerb, intent on mowing him down. It was the four-by-four. O'Shea's head appeared through the window. 'Get in.'

Moran got in, and O'Shea floored the accelerator.

'Your idea or hers?' he asked, tersely.

'Watch out!' Moran tensed as O'Shea spun the four-by-four past a family group. He looked back – the father with raised fist, shouting, the mother clutching a toddler.

'Take it steady.' Moran took out a handkerchief and mopped his brow. 'Her idea, since you asked.'

O'Shea's mouth was set in a determined line as he urged the vehicle down the street. Aine's blouse came into view. She'd slowed down, thinking she'd lost him.

O'Shea pulled over. In a second he was on the pavement and had grabbed Aine by the arm, dragging her into the Land Rover. Aine turned the air blue as O'Shea took off with a screech of tyres, scattering tourists and shoppers.

'Welcome back,' Moran said.

'I got you a phone,' O'Shea said over his shoulder. 'You can call from the house.'

Defeated, Aine lapsed into fuming silence.

'Sorry to keep you hanging around, darlin',' O'Shea said. 'Had a few things to sort out. Oh, I bought you some clothes too – on the back seat there, look now, in the bag. Jeans, a couple of tops. Underwear. Hope you like them. Shampoo as well – if you want it.'

'Thanks,' Aine said grudgingly. 'Can I use the phone now?' Her voice was laced with irritation.

O'Shea fumbled under the dash. 'Help yourself.' He threw the device over his shoulder. Aine caught it deftly in one hand. 'Burner. Chuck it when you're done.'

They turned into the safe house road and O'Shea performed his customary circle around the block. Satisfied, he found a space and parked up.

'Hello? Hello? Oh, thank *God*. Where have you *been*?'
Aine's tone veered unsteadily between relief and anger.

A pause as Aine listened. O'Shea was making irritated gestures for them to follow him into the house. They did so, Aine still glued to the mobile.

'Right. That's good. Now listen to me, Caitlin. There's no need to be alarmed. I have an old friend here, a policeman. He's going to have a word. I want you to do exactly as he says.'

Another pause.

'No, I can't explain everything. It'll be all right. You just need to listen carefully and do as he says, please?' Aine held out the handset and Moran took it.

'Caitlin? My name is Brendan Moran. I work for the Thames Valley Police. Where are you now? In your apartment? Good. Now listen.'

As briefly and gently as he could, Moran explained their concerns. Caitlin understood. She sounded frightened, but in control. A chip off the maternal block. She'd moved the remainder of her furniture into the new apartment – or rather, she'd overseen the move. The furniture guys had gone. No, she wasn't intending to go out again that evening. Traffic was apparently bad – some issue on the M4. Yes, she had everything she needed for a night in. Her first. She was excited. Her own apartment, first sleep. No, she didn't think anyone else was in the new block yet. She was the first. The sales reps had gone for the day. So yes, she supposed she was alone in the complex. No, that wouldn't normally have worried her. It did now. Moran understood. The apartment had a security entry system. Could she check it? Sure.

Thirty seconds elapsed, Aine riveted to Moran's every

word and gesture.

Caitlin came back on the line. Yep, all good. Video entry working. No one outside. Door double-locked. Sit tight? Of course. Yes, she was happy for Moran to send someone to check on her later. Would she like the number, just in case? Absolutely. Moran gave it.

'Ask for DI Charlie Pepper. If she's not available, DC Tess Martin, OK? Now, I don't want you to worry unduly, Caitlin. You're safe where you are.' He listened to the response and nodded.

'I can't tell you any more just now. I'm sorry. Your mother is fine, and I saw your father a couple of days back. No need to worry on their account. Just be vigilant and stay put. We'll give you chapter and verse soon. I'll hand you back now.'

O'Shea came down the stairs two at a time. Checks complete. But he looked worried about something.

Aine signed off, handed the phone to Moran. 'Call your people. Please.'

'Seems like a level-headed girl.' Moran took the phone and began to punch in Charlie's number. 'Took it well, considering it's the last thing she'll have been expecting.'

'She's always been strong,' Aine said, lighting another cigarette. 'Ever since she was a wee thing.' She inhaled deeply. 'Once, on the farm, she fell and cut her leg badly. There was blood everywhere, but Padraig had scratched his arm on a bramble patch while they were out together and all she could think of was her brother.'

'I'm away out for a while,' O'Shea broke in. 'I strongly advise you both to stay put.'

'If there's something I need to know, O'Shea–' Moran began, but O'Shea was in the hall and out the front door.

They heard the four-by-four start up.

Moran was holding the phone to his ear. No loudspeaker. Just in case there was something Aine shouldn't be party to. It rang. And rang.

Come on, Charlie.

'DI Charlie Pepper.'

Moran clocked the tension in her voice immediately.

'What's up, Charlie?'

'Guv – George has the apartment block security cams on his iPhone. Someone's outside. Hoodie, something under his arm.'

'Could be legit. Workman?'

'I think not, guv. He's looking through the glass … oh *what?* – He's buzzed the lock open, guv. He's *in* …'

'Get someone over there, Charlie.'

'It'll have to be on foot. Reading's gridlocked.'

'What's happening? What *is* it?' Aine was at his side, grabbing at the phone.

Moran held up his hand, flicked over to loudspeaker.

'Charlie, you're on speakerphone. I have Caitlin's mother here.'

'Right. Understood. Stay calm please, Mrs Hannigan. Your daughter is safe in her apartment. She's double-locked in. *Oh–*'

'Talk to me, Charlie.'

'Hang on – sorry, guv. It's just that – George has the security cam app open. He's switched to the atrium view.'

'And?'

'Guy's taken the left-hand door from the atrium. Let's see – apartments three to fifteen. Odd numbers.'

'Caitlin's in five.' Aine's voice was barely a whisper.

'He knows,' Moran said under his breath. 'He knows exactly where she is.'

'Well, do something for God's sake.' Aine's hand was shaking as she reached for another cigarette.

'Guv? Bola and Tess are on their way.'

'OK, thanks. Listen, can you get Caitlin on her phone? I want to keep this line open.'

'Will do.'

They heard Charlie punch the number into a landline desktop. Then her voice again, slightly fainter.

'Hello? Caitlin? This is DI Charlie Pepper from Thames Valley. Pardon me–? No, *wait. Do not* answer it. Caitlin? *Caitlin?*'

Chapter 14

Charlie gripped the handset.

Seconds passed.

George's lips moved in a series of silent curses as he navigated the app. His iPhone screen stubbornly refused to refresh. All he could see was the entrance lobby.

Caitlin's voice back in Charlie's ear, tremulous now: 'There's someone outside. He's wearing a *mask*.'

'Caitlin. Listen up. You're on the ground floor. Your window opens onto the internal quad, right?'

'Yes. He's *banging* something on the door. Can you hear–?' Caitlin's voice was a tense whisper.

Charlie and George exchanged glances. They could both hear the sound of a determined assault on the door.

'Yes I can hear it, Caitlin. You're double-locked and the door is solid. You have time. Please be calm and listen.' She turned aside and muttered to George. 'Where are Bola and Tess?'

George held up his hand, spreading the fingers.

'Five minutes is *too long*. Yes – yes, I'm here Caitlin. Go to the window in the living room. It'll probably have a security catch.'

'Boss?' George held up the iPhone for Charlie's inspection. The image showed an internal corridor. Odd numbers, three to fifteen. Someone was battering at one of the apartment doors with a fire extinguisher. The hoodie was pulled back; the head was enclosed in an eye-socketed balaclava. They watched as the intruder stepped forward and slammed the metal container against the wood. They felt the silent impact.

The door held.

Charlie was still speaking to Caitlin. 'You found the catch? Good. Now there'll be a way to open it fully.'

'He'll be through the door any minute, It won't *hold*. Oh *God…*'

'It'll hold. Concentrate, Caitlin. My officers will be in the building very soon.'

'All right. The window's open. I'm climbing out—'

Charlie heard banging and scraping. The apartment door shaking under a fresh assault. She held the phone to her chest, muffling the mic.

'George, can you get me a visual on the quadrangle?'

'Trying.' George stabbed at the iPhone, scrolled up and down. 'Hang on. Ah, got it.'

They examined the screen. Caitlin was visible in the central space, running from door to door, trying each, looking for a way out.

George stabbed the screen with his forefinger. 'There. Service door. Looks ajar.'

Charlie spoke into the handset. 'Caitlin? You see the narrow door to your right? By the corner? It has a short ramp. Yes. There. It looks open.'

They watched as Caitlin lunged for the service door. She

glanced back and her face froze in shock. 'He's at my window. Climbing out.'

She wrenched the service door open and disappeared from view. Seconds later the intruder appeared, something long and metallic in his right hand – a rifle, or a shotgun, maybe. He traversed the quad and went through the service door.

'Hello – he's carrying.' George was back on the app. 'ARU job.'

'Where does it lead George? Come *on*.'

George's radio sprang into life. 'George? We're here. Status update please.' Tess sounded breathless.

George spoke quickly. 'Caitlin Hannigan is on her way down to the car park. There's a garage door by the canal. I'm calling up ARU. There's a guy in there and he's armed. Do not engage. Repeat do not engage.'

'ARU won't get here, George. I've got to get that girl out.' Tess spoke matter-of-factly.

'No – wait. Is Bola there?'

'Yes, he's here.'

Charlie glanced up. George's face was pained. 'Look, just stand by, Tess.' She held the phone up to her ear again. 'Caitlin? Caitlin are you there?'

'Yes. I'm here.' A whisper.

'*Where* Caitlin? What can you see?'

Barely a whisper now. Then, 'I'm in the car park. In the bins area. He's *coming*.'

'Sit tight. We're going to get you out of there.'

DC Bola Odunsi was a good cop and he knew it. He'd had a few wobbles, sure, particularly after Detective Sergeant Steve Banner's murder and the ensuing DCI Wilder debacle, but he'd got over that. He was on the good guys' side now, and proud of it. He and Tess worked great together, and Bola had a lot of time for his tenacious but talkative partner. Thing was, there was an armed guy in the building and his sense of … well, *rightness* wouldn't allow him to rank Tess lower than himself in the safety and due diligence stakes. That meant she stayed outside while he went in for the girl — *if* there was a way in. But it wouldn't be easy. Tess wasn't one to hang fire and he'd have to insist.

They were at the rear of the apartment block, by the concrete ramp which led down to the electronic car park door. Which was shut.

Their heads were close together. Bola said, 'You can open these from inside. Button to open, button to close.'

Tess looked the metallic slats up and down. 'Helpful.'

Bola made a frustrated face. 'What I mean is, if she can get to the door, hit the button, she's out.'

Tess shook her head. 'He's in there, close. He has a gun. He'll pick her off as soon as she breaks cover.'

'Maybe he won't shoot her. Maybe he just wants to put the frighteners on her.'

'We don't know enough about what's going on here, Bola.'

'Do we ever?'

'Point taken. But we can't risk it.'

'So what, then?'

'I'll talk to him.'

Bola shook his head. 'Uh uh. No way.'

'Then we'll check with the boss.' Tess thumbed her radio.

Charlie's voice: 'Go ahead, Tess.'

'George, there must be another way in,' Charlie said. 'Let

me take a look.'

'Just what's on the screen, boss. That's it.' George proffered the iPhone.

Charlie peered at the small screen. Garage door, closed. Refuse service door to the right. Locked – combination. Electrics – door to the left. No good. She was about to go back to Tess when she gave a cry of alarm.

'What?' George grabbed the phone. For a second he couldn't see any change, then he saw what Charlie had also clocked: a face had appeared behind the mesh of the bins area, pale hands gripping the fencing. Looking for a way through.

Tess: 'Boss? She's here. Hang on.'

Tess, and then Bola, came into view. Tess was up close, talking to the girl. Bola was trying the door, getting frustrated, pulling at it. No go.

A voice, harsh and metallic. Moran now, on the other phone, patience exhausted. 'Charlie? Update, please.'

At that moment there was a flat, backfiring sound through Charlie's phone speaker and Tess screamed, staggered back. They all recognised the sound – a shotgun discharge.

Chapter 15

'He's got her, guv.' Charlie's voice was flat, but Moran knew that to be a poor indicator of his number two's emotional condition. When Charlie reached her point of highest tension, she switched into ice-woman mode.

Except when she rammed her car into a shopfront, seriously wounding a suspect, a small voice reminded him. But that was a while back, and Charlie had had an extended convalescence. She was over that. The shrinks had given her the all-clear.

'Anyone hurt?' Moran's patted Aine's shoulder, as reassuring a gesture as he could make. He felt her flinch and withdrew his hand. She moved to the far side of the room, chewing her finger.

'Negative, guv. It was a warning shot. Made a mess of the wire fencing but Caitlin's OK. For the moment.'

'Tess and Bola?'

'Shaken, stirred, but intact.'

'Good. What's ARU's ETA?'

'That's the problem, guv. Reading's a mess this evening. Gridlocked. Last ETA was ten minutes; that was three minutes ago.'

'Has George still got a visual?'

Moran heard Charlie ask the question and George's gruff response.

'Negative. iPhone's not playing ball.'

'So much for hi-tech,' Moran said. 'The roof, then.'

'Guv?'

'There'll be some kind of service ladder. Bound to be. You might find a rooftop service door open.'

'They *have* to do something. Tell them they *have* to–' Aine was at his side, pale and trembling.

Moran's hand went up. 'A *moment*, Aine. Charlie?'

'Here, guv. We checked. No ladder.'

'OK. ARU'll cover front and back. *When* they get there. Keep Tess at the rear and Bola covering the front for now. Any uniforms in the area?'

'Called them up. Any time now.'

'Right.' A siren wailed somewhere outside. Moran went to the curtain, drew it back. All clear. Someone else's problem. For now. He sat on the armrest of the faded sofa and tried to picture an empty building, a desperate gunman and a frightened girl. Outside, two unarmed detectives. It could end badly. He said to Aine, 'It'll be fine. Try to relax.'

Aine blew smoke, forced a smile.

'Guv?'

'Yep.'

'Caitlin's mobile phone is still on. She must have put it in her pocket.'

'Can you get a fix?'

A pause. Then, 'Not yet. Sounds like they're back in the main building. On the move. No echo. I can hear Caitlin. She's talking.'

'Bola in position?'

'Affirmative, guv.'

'Brendan?' Aine was at the window. 'Gardai.'

'Hang on, Charlie. I have a problem.'

A quick glance through the curtain confirmed Aine's warning. *Hell*. Where was O'Shea?

The gardai vehicle came to a halt at the top of the street and two uniforms got out. Not Buchanan or his buddy. Moran watched them approach the first terrace. Door-to-door. Old school.

'Guv? Everything all right?' Charlie still sounded calm.

Moran returned his thoughts to the drama unfolding in Reading. 'I think so. For a while,' he told her. 'But I may have to relocate in a hurry; if I drop out, I'll come back to you when I can.'

'Got it. ARU have arrived. They're deploying down the side street and–'

The line went dead. 'Charlie? Hello? *Hello?*'

Moran glared at the mobile. Damn. 'Dropped signal,' he muttered.

Two hefty clatters on the door. Moran froze.

Aine motioned him upstairs. 'I'll answer it.'

'You're in no state – *and* you're a missing person. If you want to stay missing, probably not a good idea.'

'They're not looking for *me* right now, Brendan, are they?' Aine cocked her head as she replied.

Moran nodded. She had a point. 'They might search the house,' he said, 'if they smell a rat.'

'Just get up there, Brendan. Leave it to me.'

Through the letter box: 'Hello? Gardai. Open up, please. Open up *now*.'

Chapter 16

'Donal. Come in.' Geileis moved to one side and caught a waft of stale alcohol as her brother ducked his head under the beam. 'Whatever's the matter?'

'It's Jerry.'

Donal had never been one for preamble, and as he collapsed into an armchair Geileis felt a zigzag of shock as she caught a first glimpse of his pale, drawn face and heard the agitation in his voice. This was going to be bad. She took a deep breath. 'What about Jerry?'

'He's dead, Geileis.'

'*What?*'

'He's dead. They found him in Brendan's boot.'

Geileis' hand went to her mouth. 'Oh *God* ... but where's Brendan?'

Donal passed a brawny hand over his eyes. 'That's the thing. The gardai took him, but he's disappeared.'

'I need a drink.' Geileis went into the kitchen and returned with two glasses, each a quarter full. She offered one and Donal took it gratefully.

The spirit did a little to dispel Geileis' shock. She composed herself and sat on the settee. 'Jerry's dead? I can't believe it. Why? I mean, who?'

'Not Brendan, that's the only certainty in my mind.'

Geileis looked down at her glass. Her stomach was unsettled again today and she had been about to make herself a hot chocolate to calm it. She sipped the unplanned whiskey and grimaced as it found its way to the root of her discomfort. She cleared her throat, coughed.

'Brendan went to the Blasket. To find O'Shea.'

'He did *what?*' Donal shook his head angrily. 'Sleeping dogs should be left well alone. What the hell is he trying to stir up?'

'It was already stirred, Donal. This isn't Brendan's doing.'

'I thought he'd gone inland. Then maybe to Dingle.'

Geileis shook her head. 'Jerry told him about O'Shea. I didn't want him to. But … well you know what Jerry's like – *was* like – after a drink, and Brendan was very insistent. Jerry said O'Shea would know what was going on. With himself, I mean, and his … wider family.'

Donal frowned. 'What's O'Shea got to do with Aine?' A pause. 'Is there something I should know?'

Geileis looked away. A fine drizzle was spotting the leaded windows of the cottage. A blackbird perched on the ledge for a moment, fluttered its wings and was gone.

'You know something, don't you?' Donal's voice was low, but his disappointment was loud and clear.

'I didn't want to say anything.' Geileis spread her hands. 'In case … you know, in case it was nothing.'

'One of my oldest friends is dead. Another's missing. Aine's still missing. Hardly qualifies as *nothing.*'

'Don't be angry, Donal. I've been so worried.'

Donal's eyes narrowed. 'Do you know where Aine is,

Geileis?'

'No! Absolutely not.'

Donal was on his feet now. 'I'll talk to this fella O'Shea myself, if he's the man with the answers.'

'*No*. Donal, please, leave this to Brendan.'

Donal leaned in close, his nose an inch from hers. 'Brendan's my *guest*, Geileis. I *invited* him here. If he's in trouble, I've got to help.'

Geileis put her arm on his. 'Be careful, Donal. Keep an eye on Padraig.'

'Padraig? What's the boy got to do with this?'

'Nothing, it's … nothing. Just take care of yourselves, that's all.'

Donal gave her a long, penetrating look, slammed his tumbler on the table and in two strides was at the front door. He turned as if to speak, changed his mind and clacked the latch open.

'I'll ring you if I hear anything,' she called after him. 'I promise.'

The door shuddered on its hinges.

Geileis downed her whiskey in one and set the heavy tumbler onto the mantelpiece. She covered her eyes, fighting back tears. 'Pull yourself together, woman. Do something useful, why don't you?' she said aloud. Her voice sounded weak and frightened in the sudden silence of the cottage; the thick walls and low ceiling absorbed her words, flattening their bravado.

She went into the kitchen, took her coat from behind the door, wrapped a scarf around her neck and selected a hat from the dresser drawer. She checked herself in the mirror. Not bad. A little puffy around the eyes, maybe, but he probably wouldn't notice. A moment's hesitation. Could she do this? And the answer came back.

Yes. You have a part to play in this.

Geileis carefully locked the front door, took a deep breath, and began to walk towards the village.

Jerry's was closed, shutters down. No sign of life. It would be the other bar, she knew, at the far end of the village. It was a bar frequented by a certain type, predominantly male, with an air of exclusivity about it. It wasn't the sort of place a woman on her own would be drawn to. But he'd said that's where he'd be found, if ever she was looking. At the time she'd thought. 'Right, and that'll be never.' But she'd kept her counsel, because she knew things about him already. His name was Liam Buchanan and they'd got talking at a local dance a while back, just after she'd moved into the cottage. He was ten or maybe fifteen years younger, but that hadn't stopped him making advances. She'd been having a good time up to that point; she'd been introduced to a few of the locals she'd not yet met, had enjoyed the music and atmosphere. And the dancing. They were a friendly bunch, by and large. But she'd always known that would be the case – it was very much part of the reason she'd come home. Anyway, Liam had chatted, given her a dance or two, made his loyalties clear. He wasn't bad looking, but he wasn't her type, not that she was in the market. He was way too fond of himself to be in with a chance that she would find him attractive in *that* sense. They got on all right though, had a bit of a *craic* together, plenty of banter. It'd been fun. She'd run into him on a couple of other occasions including one lunchtime session which had turned – inevitably, given the backgrounds of those in the bar at the time – to politics. She'd mentioned the old days, her youth. Maybe a reference to a few people she'd known who'd been involved in various … initiatives. Drink talking, probably. But then he'd opened up as well, started bragging about who he knew, some big stuff that was still going on.

And it had frightened her, so she'd made her excuses and left.

And then Aine had disappeared.

Geileis nodded a greeting to one or two folk she recognised as she made her way through the narrow streets. The community had seemed a safe place to her, a refuge from the madness of London. Now it felt secretive, oppressive.

She turned a corner and there it was. It looked as unfriendly as she'd remembered it.

You're here now …

She went in. It was half-empty. But there he was, on a stool by the bar's end, reading a newspaper, as he usually did, often commenting aloud if there was an audience to hand.

He looked up as she approached. 'Well, look what the fair wind has blown in. Have a seat.' He patted the empty stool next to him and Geileis shuddered inwardly. 'Hello yourself,' she said casually. 'I was on my way past and just fancied a livener.'

Buchanan folded his newspaper and called the barman over.

Geileis settled on the stool, edged it a few inches further away. 'I thought you'd be on duty?' When you ask a question, make it sound like it isn't a question. Who'd told her that? Brendan, probably.

'I will be shortly,' he said, looking wistfully at his watch and empty half-pint. 'You should've said you were coming.'

'Just popped in on spec, like I said. I really thought you'd be busy, what with the murder and all?'

'Who told you about that?' Buchanan said sharply.

'Jerry was a friend of mine, Liam. And this is a small village, in case you hadn't noticed.'

Buchanan paid the barman. 'It wouldn't have been Brendan Moran who told you, by any chance?'

'No. It was Donal, actually.'

'Was it, indeed? And have you seen Brendan Moran today?'

'Why all the interest in Brendan?' Geileis asked innocently, 'He's just visiting Donal—'

'Because we think he might have something to do with what happened to Jerry.'

'What? That's ridiculous.'

Buchanan seized her wrist. 'Don't you be goin' tellin' me what is or what isn't ridiculous, now. If you see Brendan Moran, you tell me right away, got that?'

'You're hurting me, Liam.'

He released her with a muttered apology, withdrew his hand. 'Sorry, it's been a long day.'

'I have to go now,' she said. Time for a tactical withdrawal. She wouldn't get anything more out of Buchanan today, that much was clear. The garda was rattled, under pressure.

Buchanan protested: 'No. Listen, I'm sorry I snapped ...'

'Another time, maybe.' Geileis smiled sweetly and left.

Geileis' heart was pounding as she retraced her steps. So, Brendan had successfully escaped the gardai's attentions. Which meant her appeal for help had been heeded. That boded well. Her concerns that her old friend had been heading for trouble had been proved right. Now he had an ally, was less vulnerable. Geileis glanced behind her as a sudden commotion made her jump. A small terrier had spotted a cat and had collided with a metal bin in its haste to catch it. The bin rolled and clanked, came to rest against the little picket fence delimiting the post office garden. Geileis placed her hand on her chest, tried to calm herself. Sure, Brendan had someone watching his back, which was a relief.

But for now, she was on her own.

Chapter 17

Moran heard voices at the door, followed by Aine's careful response. 'No. I haven't seen anyone of that description. Yes, I'm on my own here just now.'

Another low voice. Not one he recognised.

Aine: 'I will, of course.'

The door closed. Moran breathed again. He made his way downstairs to rejoin Aine in the lounge. Given the current situation in Reading, he admired her coolness.

As Aine's mouth formed a question Moran cut her off: 'I'm doing it.' He tapped out Charlie Pepper's number. Two rings.

'Charlie Pepper.'

'Update, Charlie?'

'ARU just showed up – hang on, they're forcing the door ... *now*. George, can you get that view any bigger? Sorry guv, we've got the app on a desktop. Easier to see what's happening.'

Moran heard familiar Scottish muttering in the background. 'OK,' he told her. 'That's good. All exits covered?'

'About to be, guv – ah, that's better. Thanks, George.

Guv?'

'I'm here. Any update on the girl?'

'No further shots. That's all I can say at the mo–'

Silence.

Aine's face paled. 'What? What is it?'

'Hang on–' Moran held up his hand. 'Charlie?'

Low conversation at the other end, but Moran couldn't make out what was being said. George McConnell's voice, Charlie's, and then–

'Guv?'

'Yes, Charlie.'

'He's out. With the girl.'

'How the *hell* did that happen? What's ARU doing?'

'Just on the scene, guv. He came out the back. Crossed the canal. Wait–'

Silence.

Charlie's voice came back, cold, stiff. 'We've got an officer down.'

'Who? Who is it?

'Tess Martin. It's *Tess*. Guv, I've got to go.'

The line went dead.

Bola Odunsi was relieved to see the commotion at Jackson's Corner which signalled the arrival of the ARU. It only took a few seconds before the traffic, just starting to move again, ground to a fresh standstill as drivers slowed to get a look at the action. Six guys, one woman, heavily tooled up, which was fine because that was what they did. Bola approached the lead officer, a thick-set, hefty bloke around the thirty to thirty-five mark and introduced himself. 'The rear entrance is being covered by DC Tess Martin. Your mark's inside, armed. One hostage. Single shot fired in the underground car park at the rear of the building. Suspect and hostage believed to have returned to level one.'

'Thank you, DC Odunsi. We'll take it from here. If you and–'

The second shot seemed louder than the first, the sound of a twin barrel discharge echoing up the service road, bouncing off the polished glass of the apartment complex. Bola froze. '*Tess!*'

Before the ARU sergeant could intervene Bola was haring down the service road. The hooded man was out of the car park, running, ducking low, pulling Caitlin Hannigan close to his body, the shotgun bumping against his thigh as he ran. He reached the canal bridge steps, didn't look back. Caitlin Hannigan was pulling, fighting him, trying to get free. Her abductor cuffed her on the head and Bola flinched, but he had a higher priority; he left the gunman to the ARU, rounded the corner, and froze in his tracks before taking off again at a sprint. As he ran, he yelled behind him.

'Officer down! Ambulance now!'

Tess Martin was lying face-down by the car park entrance, groaning softly. Bola could see the blood seeping from her midriff onto the concrete ramp as he skidded to his knees beside her prone body. He bent to tend to her, only dimly aware of the clanking of multiple boots as the ARU pursued the gunman over the steel canal bridge.

'Sorry, Bola,' Tess tried to sit up. 'I let him go.'

He pressed her gently down. 'No, no. You did great. Stay put. You're going to be OK.'

Sirens in the distance, ululating.

'It hurts.' Tess' face was white.

Bola cradled her head. 'Shhh. You're all right. The medics'll be here in a minute.'

'I'm making a mess of your jacket.' Bola felt Tess reach for his hand. 'It's not your fault,' she whispered.

He stripped off his jacket and pressed it to her side. 'Might as well use it now, eh?'

Sirens, very close now, and the thrum of an engine almost on top of them.

Paramedics, and a voice which seemed to come from a long way off.

'All right officer, we've got this. Just stand back, if you would, that's it, thank you…'

Some time later, Charlie appeared at Bola's side. Her hand rested on his arm. 'What happened?'

Bola's mind was in stasis. He couldn't think. 'I – I don't know. I thought the rear was secure. He just came out, took a shot, I–'

'OK, Bola. I'm staying with the ARU. Our man's headed up the side roads near the RBH, still got Caitlin with him. Get yourself a hot drink and get back to the station. I'll need someone there.'

'You can't go alone,' Bola protested.

'I've got George. And an ARU team. This bastard is not getting away.'

'I'm going with Tess.'

Charlie nodded. 'All right. Yes, do that. Keep me posted. I'll see you later.'

Bola clambered into the ambulance and took a bucket seat by the door. He watch the paramedics bend over Tess' body, juggling tubes and saline as the driver took off and swerved between the kerb-clinging traffic. Five minutes to the Royal Berkshire Hospital. Bola bit his lip and held on.

Eldon Square, a satellite residential area of the Royal Berkshire Hospital, recalled the ambience and grandeur of a bygone era. In its centre, the small but tranquil King George V Gardens provided a peaceful lunchtime sanctuary for both office and medical staff. Many of the honey-coloured, stone-clad houses had been converted into flats, convenient and popular with hospital *locums* and registrars. Charlie's mental health specialist owned one of the larger, more secluded houses. As she arrived, breathless from sprinting the quarter-mile or so from the town centre she could see immediately what had happened. The ARU had horseshoed a building three or four houses in on the left-hand side. A *For Sale* notice explained the gunman's choice. A basement flat, potentially unoccupied. One entrance. Maybe another round the back, but inaccessible from the road. Charlie showed her ID to the two uniforms standing guard by their vehicles, parked across the entrance to the square with lights flashing. She was a few paces inside the cordoned-off area when her mobile rang. Charlie hesitated, but decided it might be important.

'DI Charlie Pepper.'

'Ah, I was told you had a good phone manner.'

The voice was soft, almost soothing, but Charlie's antennae were immediately on red alert. 'Who is this?'

'Does it matter?'

It was a male voice, but it wasn't the gender that bothered Charlie, it was the confidence. And the accent.

An Irish accent.

'Who gave you this number?'

'Oh, come now. Let's not propagate the blame culture. Not getting what I want isn't one of my problems, DI Pepper.'

'So what *do* you want?' Charlie watched the ARU sergeant discussing the approach with his squad. It wasn't going to be an easy one. Judging from the raised voices, there were a few options being bandied about. She began to move towards them.

'I want your friend Brendan to come out of the woodwork. And I want him to bring *his* friend with him.'

'You're not making any sense,' Charlie said. 'Don't call this number again.' Her finger was poised to kill the call.

'She'll die,' the voice said. 'Your wee girly hostage. And it'll be down to you to tell her ma why you wouldn't listen.'

Charlie's stomach lurched. Whoever this guy was, he was no crank. 'All right. I'm listening.' She'd reached the ARU team, flapping her free hand to get the sergeant's attention.

The voice went on, the tone reasonable, conversational. 'DCI Brendan Moran has been poking about in my business. I believe he's solved a wee problem for me, but I can't be sure.'

'The problem being?'

'Someone I need to find.'

'So what do you want me to do?'

'Put me through to Brendan. Don't tell me you don't have his number.'

'If I refuse?'

'Then I tell my man to cut the wee girl's throat. He's done this kind of stuff before. A lot. No skin off his nose, if you get my meaning.' A soft laugh. 'All in a day's work, you might say.'

'All right. Wait a moment. I'll speak to the ARU sergeant.'

'You do that,' the voice purred. 'Stand them down. No cowboys and indians today.' He finished with a low chuckle that set Charlie's skin crawling. She broke into the gaggle of armed police. 'Please. All of you. Listen up.'

The sergeant listened, nodded. 'All right. How long do you need?'

'Not sure. I'll liaise with DCI Moran. Bear with me.'

She took a deep breath and went back to her call. 'All right. ARU are stood down. This is DCI Moran's mobile number.'

'Much obliged. Keep your line free and those guns in their holsters. Be back to you as soon as I've had a chat with Brendan.'

'Right.' Charlie squeezed the phone until her knuckles whitened.

The caller rang off.

Chapter 18

Moran's phone buzzed and Aine started, fumbled for a cigarette.

'Moran.'

'Brendan. It's been *too* long.'

'Who is this?'

'I believe you're keepin' company with a friend of mine.'

Moran knew who it was. 'Black.'

'As the night.' Sean Black laughed softly. 'Now, listen. I have a wee situation here, Brendan. I reckon you can help me out.'

'What do you want?' Moran was thinking about mobile phone traceability, triangulation. But his handset was a burner. Should be OK for a bit.

'You know what I want.'

'Aine's not keen. Why's she so important to you?'

'That's between me and her. Important thing is, I have a gun to her baby's head.'

Moran glanced at Aine, chain-smoking on the sofa, watching his every expression. She seemed to have aged ten years in the last two hours.

'Did you get that, Brendan?'

'Yep. I got it.'

'So, I have the royal flush, agreed?'

'For now, maybe.'

'Listen to me, Brendan. I won't hesitate, you'd better believe it. My man doesn't give a toss about pulling the trigger.'

'OK, so he pulls the trigger. You still don't have what you want. What's your next move?' He turned instinctively away from Aine, drew the curtain back. The street was deserted.

Sean Black laughed heartily. 'I don't think you'd let that happen, Brendan. You're tellin' me you'd look Aine in the eye and tell her her daughter's brains are all over a wall in Reading? No, no, no. That's not *you*, Brendan.'

'So you want me to do what, exactly?'

'You'll bring Aine to me. I'll tell you where. When I have her, you say goodbye and the girl walks free.'

'And what about your man?'

'Between me and him, Brendan. He's a robust kind of character.'

'He'll need to be.'

'Oh, no threats please, Brendan. Not even empty ones.'

'All right. When and where?'

'That's the spirit. Send the lady to find a pen and paper, why don't you? She *is* there, isn't she?'

Moran made a writing gesture and Aine scrabbled around, found an old envelope, a biro.

Black gave an address. It meant nothing. Some obscure coastal village. 'Got that?' the voice purred.

'Yes.'

'So, you're somewhere near Dingle. It won't take you more than forty minutes. Just you and her. Is that clear?'

'Clear.'

The line went dead.

Aine's upturned face was chalk-white, enquiring, almost beseeching.

'We have to go.'

She nodded.

'Get them to back off, will you? At *least* ten metres,' Charlie called to the uniforms at the cordon. The press hadn't wasted any time. Cameras, tripods, intense-looking young reporters with tablets and smartphones had gathered like ants at a honey-spillage. 'The roads are bad enough already,' she barked. 'Get onto traffic – we need a couple of motorbikes on the London Road, by the RBH. Keep it moving.'

'Ma'am.' One of the uniforms stabbed buttons on his radio.

Charlie went back to the ARU team. Two had their guns trained on the narrow passage which led to the flat entrance. Another was covering the window.

'What about the rear?' she asked the sergeant.

'Two covering Eldon Terrace. High wall protecting the gardens. He can't get out that way without being spotted.'

'OK.' Charlie chewed her lip. Doing nothing didn't sit right. Not with Tess injured, maybe even–

No, she wouldn't think about that possibility. Not yet.

'How long do we wait?' the sergeant asked.

She shrugged. 'I don't know, Sergeant. I just don't know.' She mussed her hair, chewed her lip, aware how unsatisfactory it sounded. She added, 'as long as it takes, all right?'

'Ma'am.'

Chapter 19

The first problem was wheels.

The second was Aine. She was half-walking, half-running to keep up with him. 'Let me talk to her. *Please*. For god's sake, Brendan, she's a *hostage* …'

'Not yet.' He waved her objections away. 'I need to think.' Moran's leg was giving him hell after his earlier exertions, but this was not the time for hanging about. Not with the garda out searching, and not with O'Shea missing. Whatever that might mean.

'For the love of *God*, Brendan – *anything* might be happening…'

Moran found a car he thought he could work with. 'Wait. Keep an eye out.'

'What are you–?'

The side window caved in under Moran's elbow thrust. He was in the front seat, feeling under the dash. An older car, so in theory it should have … *there*. The engine started with a burst of black exhaust while Aine dithered on the pavement.

He leaned out. 'Get in.'

Moran knew his way out of Dingle; it was more a question of avoiding the garda.

'I can't do this, Brendan. I can't be near Black.'

'Hopefully you won't need to be.' Moran threw her a sideways glance. 'But you'd better fill me in, Aine – truthfully this time. Your daughter's life might depend on it.'

He gave Aine a moment to ponder this as he guided the car through the network of back streets and came to a halt at a set of traffic lights. A garda vehicle was waiting at the lights on the other side of the junction, engine idling. The lights changed. The garda passed by. Moran breathed again.

Aine broke the silence. 'Look, Brendan, I have *no* idea why Black wants me. We knew each other, sure, back in the day. But not well. And that's the truth. I just know that whatever's going down is not something I want to be involved in. Now give me the bloody *phone…*'

Moran's reply changed to a curse as a speeding car failed to stop at a mini-roundabout. It caught their vehicle behind the passenger door on Moran's side, slewing them to the right. Moran fought with the steering wheel, but it wasn't playing. A low brick wall ended their unscheduled diversion and the engine died on impact. Moran's head hit the steering wheel with enough force to trigger an airbag, had airbags been standard in the mid-Eighties when their car was manufactured, but it was just hard plastic. He saw stars, felt a stabbing pain in his shoulder. He was dimly aware of other voices – urgent, demanding voices, followed by Aine's scream, then nothing.

Steam rose from the punctured radiator in a series of aggravated puffs. A diesel engine somewhere nearby burst into life, rousing Moran into semi-consciousness. A screech of tyres, a hint of burned rubber and it was gone. Moran tried to figure out the direction but his brain wouldn't comply. The lights went out.

'He never intended us to get to the rendezvous,' Moran told Charlie. He was sitting in a bar two streets away from the scene of the crash. His head hurt like hell and he was holding a damp handkerchief to his forehead. The garda, fortunately, had dragged their feet getting to the scene, and after he'd come to Moran had been able make himself scarce, waving aside objections and offers of help from a small group of bystanders. He hoped the garda would file the crash under *joyriders*, but suspected that one or two upstanding citizens among the witnesses might offer a description. In which case, it wouldn't be a great idea to loiter.

'He wanted to catch me off guard,' he told Charlie, 'make sure I didn't pull anything funny. He must have *really* wanted Aine where he could see her.'

'But why?' Charlie said. 'I just don't get it.'

'Nor me. Not yet. But Black should be letting his man know that we've kept our side of the bargain. In a manner of speaking.'

'Will he call you, d'you think?' Charlie asked.

'He may well,' Moran winced as he shifted the handkerchief. The barman was regarding him with a mixture of sympathy and suspicion. Moran gave him a wan smile and raised his glass to his lips, took a sip.

Charlie said, 'I'll clear the line, guv.'

'Yes, you'd better, and–' Moran started as the sound of two muffled reports echoed through the handset. 'What the hell was *that?*

'*Gunshots*, guv. Inside the flat. Gotta go–'

The line dropped. Moran paled, dropped the burner in his pocket, sipped his whiskey. It did little to dispel the cold knot in his stomach.

Chapter 20

Bola had almost worn a hole through the squeaky-clean floor of the hospital corridor with his relentless pacing. Tess had been in surgery a long time. He looked at his watch.

An hour and a half…

That could mean anything. Something, or nothing. It was the not knowing that was killing him. And the guilt. The if-onlys had started the moment they had raced away in the ambulance. *If only he had stayed at the rear of the building. If only he had sent Tess to meet the ARU. If only, if only…*

The rubber doors flapped and a white-coated doctor appeared.

'DC Odunsi?'

Bola found that he couldn't respond. His mouth opened and closed silently. In the end he just nodded.

'I'm Dr Keogh, Mr Harriman's surgical registrar.'

Bola nodded again.

'DC Tessa Martin isn't in any danger,' Keogh went on, 'but she'll be weak and groggy after the anaesthetic. I suggest you come back tomorrow morning. She'll be more *compos mentis* by then, all being well. Hopefully we won't have to keep her in too long.'

'She's all right?' Bola felt relief sweep through him like a shot of amphetamine. 'She's really OK?'

'She was lucky,' Keogh said. 'The shot missed her vital organs. Most of the damage was superficial, you'll be pleased to hear. We had a good look around to make sure we didn't miss anything. She'll heal physically, but I suspect that the mental support will be more important,' he added. 'From colleagues, and friends.'

Bola pumped the man's hand. 'Of course, of course. Thank you, thank you.'

On his way out Bola met George McConnell on his way in. He grinned at the little Scot, an enormous good-to-be-alive grin. 'She's all right, George. She's going to be fine. Can't see her tonight, though, doctor's orders.'

'What the hell were you playing at?' George's tone was icy. 'Leaving her to man the fort on her own?'

Bola's face fell. 'Now wait a–'

George jabbed a stubby finger in Bola's chest. '*You* were supposed to be looking out for her.'

Bola took a step back. 'George, have you been drinking?'

'Are you my minder now?'

'Come on, George, not here. We can talk outside.' Bola touched George's arm. This wasn't good, not good at all. George had been off the booze for a while, as far as he knew, but–

'Get your hands off me.' George brushed him aside. 'Now, are you going to tell me where she is or do I have to find out myself?'

'George, this isn't a good idea. You can't see her right now. Look, she's just out of surgery. And she's going to be fine.'

George opened his mouth to reply but his mobile phone

got there first. 'McConnell.' He instantly modified his tone on hearing the caller: 'Oh, it's you, boss.'

Bola watched George with mixed feelings. Would Charlie be able to figure out the state George was in?

'Right. Got it.' George signed off. He looked Bola up and down. 'I'm wanted elsewhere, lucky for you. Standoff's over.'

'Over?' Bola's eyes widened. 'So what happened?'

'The girl's all right,' George said tersely. 'She's safe.'

A group of nurses passed them in the corridor and Bola stepped to one side to let them pass. George was already walking away. He hurried after the bristling figure.

'George, wait. They've got the guy responsible? The gunman?'

George picked up the pace, striding ahead. He threw the answer over his shoulder. 'Yes and no.'

'What's that supposed to mean?'

George burst through the exit into the overcrowded car park where an ambulance was unloading its fresh cargo of misery.

'It means,' the Scot said in a louder voice, 'that they have his body.'

'They *shot* him? ARU *never* take a shot, unless there's–'

George spun on his heels. 'He blew his own head off, all right?'

Bola watched George stride away, unsteady and angry. 'Go home, George,' he called after the retreating figure, only to receive a rude gesture in return.

At least George wasn't driving. And at least he wasn't in uniform. Bola glanced at his watch. Eldon Square was a couple of minutes away.

He started walking.

*

Eldon Square was doing a good impression of a war zone: blue light overload, uniform on the perimeter, press pressing against the cordon, and the ARU packing up, relieved maybe not to have been called upon to fire. Not that that was going to happen anyway – a last resort, and only in very rare circumstances. Just one shot fired, and that from inside the flat. He caught sight of Charlie, talking to the ARU sergeant. He waited for her to finish before catching her attention. 'Boss?'

'Bola.' Charlie scanned her DC's expression and liked what she saw. 'Tess is OK, right?'

'Yep,' Bola confirmed. 'She's going to be fine. Visitors tomorrow, the doc said.'

Charlie let her breath out in a long sigh. 'Thank God for that. Have you seen George? He's supposed to be on his way.'

'Actually, he's not well. Asked me to let you know. Gone home with a migraine.'

Charlie frowned. 'Migraine?' She studied Bola's expression. 'You're a rubbish liar, Bola.'

Bola shuffled his feet. *Damn. Now what could he say?*

Charlie sighed again, this time in frustration. 'OK, never mind. I'll sort George out later. You heard what happened?'

'Just the main points. The girl's unhurt?'

'Yep. She's over there – back of the second ambulance.' Charlie gestured to the main road where two ambulances had drawn up by the cordon. 'Seems unfazed by it all. Quite a self-possessed young lady.'

'So why did the gunman top himself?'

'We're trying to establish exactly what went on in the

basement flat. I'm second in the queue after the medics. Want to join me?'

'Sure,' Bola said. 'If you want me to.'

Charlie gave Bola a hard look. 'Bola, I don't blame you for what happened to Tess, OK? We'll talk later, but don't let it get in the way right now.'

'Thanks, boss. Appreciate it.' Bola tried a smile, which didn't come as naturally as he'd have liked. But the boss was on his side; that was a tick in the right box. George's reaction, however, was more worrying. It nagged at him like a sore tooth.

'Let's get to work.' Charlie spun on her heel and set off towards the ambulances, but then her mobile phone rang. 'Guv? Yep, sorry. Here's what happened…'

Charlie spoke quickly, gave Moran the salient facts. She finished with a question. 'Should we tell Caitlin the latest? That her mother's been abducted?'

Charlie listened to Moran's reply and nodded. 'OK. Straight bat. Agreed.'

Chapter 21

'Miss Hannigan? Can we have a quick word?' Charlie asked the question as much of the paramedic as the girl. Both nodded, the paramedic dismounting from the ambulance with a brisk 'All yours. Heart rate and blood pressure normal. But–' he raised a warning finger, 'a few minutes only, OK? – I'm obliged to take Miss Hannigan to the RBH for further checks. Just to be safe.'

'That's fine, thanks.'

Caitlin was sitting on the central trolley bed, back straight, legs neatly folded, hands clasped together. She looked calm and focused. Charlie gestured to Bola.

'Miss Hannigan, this is Detective Constable Bola Odunsi, and my name is Detective Inspector Charlie Pepper. I'd like to ask you one or two questions, if you feel up to it? I understand you're upset; that's only natural, but this'll only take a couple of minutes.'

'Go ahead.'

Charlie perched on a low stool opposite the trolley. Caitlin Hannigan held her gaze and maintained eye contact. She was a strikingly attractive redhead, hair fashionably styled in a face-framing cut just above chin length which shaped and accentuated her well-defined, but feminine, jawline. A light dusting of freckles around her nose and cheeks added a gamine quality which, judging from Bola's expression, wasn't doing her any harm in the male-attraction stakes. Charlie shot Bola a cautionary look before addressing Caitlin.

'First of all, we need to know as much as possible about your assailant.'

'Of course.'

Bola asked, 'What happened in the basement flat, Caitlin? Did he say anything to you? Take – or make – any phone calls?'

'No.' She shook her head. 'He only gave orders, like *sit down*. Or *keep quiet*, you know. He didn't make or receive any phone calls.'

Caitlin's Irish roots were only just discernible, her accent more southern counties than Southern Ireland. 'Did he hurt you?' Charlie asked.

'No. He had a firm hold of my arm on the way from my flat, but that's all.'

'Or threaten you in any way?'

A head shake.

Charlie glanced at Bola. 'In which case, I'll tell you what we know.'

'Thank you.'

'Have you been in touch with your father recently?'

'I spoke to him a few weeks ago, why?'

'You didn't get the impression anything was amiss?'

'No. What is it? What's happened?'

Charlie explained. Caitlin Hannigan nodded at intervals, ran a well-manicured hand through her hair. If she was upset, she hid it well. Shock, perhaps. Charlie had seen it before when breaking bad news, the recipient too numb to react.

'I'm sorry to be the bearer of bad news, Caitlin. Let me assure you that DCI Moran is doing everything in his power to find your mother.'

'Why can't the garda find out what's happened?'

'It's complicated, Caitlin. DCI Moran is doing all he can.'

'And this guy, today, I mean, he's – he was – something to do with my mother's decision to run away? What did he want? I don't understand? Why would he want to threaten me?'

Bola frowned. 'You said earlier he didn't threaten you.'

'Yes, sorry. Bad choice of words. I meant, what would he *want* with me?'

'Are you sure he said nothing at all, Miss Hannigan?' Bola was leaning forward, his voice low and encouraging. Charlie suppressed an approving smile. Bola was good at proactive prompting.

Bola continued, 'He didn't ask you *about* anything, ask you to *do* anything?'

'No. As I said before, he just told me to sit down, keep quiet.'

'And when he shot himself.' Bola raised his eyebrows a fraction. 'No warning? No reason? He just…' Bola made a barrel with his fingers and pointed them at his temple. 'Just *bang*, and that was it? He didn't say anything before he pulled the trigger?'

Caitlin swallowed and looked down at her hands, toyed with a ring on her little finger, twisted it round and round. 'No.' At last, a slight tremor in her voice. 'He just–' Now the hand went to her mouth. 'It was just like you said.'

'All right, Miss Hannigan. Thank you.' Charlie signalled to Bola – enough.

Caitlin brought herself under control with an effort. The hands were re-clasped. 'I should call my father.'

'Of course. But I'd wait till the hospital has given you the once-over.'

'I'm all right, really.' Her voice broke a little and she took out a handkerchief from her sleeve, blew her nose. 'Sorry.' The handkerchief flapped.

'You've been through a traumatic experience,' Charlie said. 'I've been through something similar. I can empathise with how you're feeling. You might feel fine now, but you may not later on.'

Caitlin nodded, and returned a weak smile. 'I'm sure you're right.'

'Would you like someone to stay with you tonight? I can arrange a WPC. She won't get in your way, just–'

'I'll be fine.' Caitlin nodded again, this time more decisively. 'I'm rather a private person. And there's my boyfriend.'

'He lives with you?' Bola was onto that one, smartish.

'No. He lives in Earley. He was coming over tonight, to help me sort things out – with the move, you know. What I mean is, he'll make sure I'm all right.'

'Very well. If you're sure.' Charlie got up and ducked instinctively as she remembered where she was. 'I'll arrange a car to take you from the hospital to your apartment. We have a specialist team onsite now – they'll make sure everything's fixed up for you – door, locks and so on, check everything over, make sure nothing's been taken.'

'I see. Is that absolutely necessary?'

Charlie caught the frostiness in the question. *Rather a private person.* Fair enough. It was no fun having a bunch of strangers poking around your apartment. A vivid flashback of the break-in which had almost cost her her own life caught Charlie unawares; the shattering of the front door glass, the desperate struggle with the knifeman, the sliver of window piercing his gut.

She shook the images away with a flick of her head, cleared her throat. 'Well – for your security, yes, of course. They won't touch anything they don't have to, don't worry on that account.'

A nod.

Charlie took out her wallet. 'Here's my number. Call me anytime if you're worried.'

'Thanks. I appreciate that. But …' Caitlin's composure faltered '… it won't happen again, will it? I mean, someone trying to break in, or–'

'You'll be perfectly safe,' Bola told her. 'We'll keep an eye on the flats, don't worry.'

'Thanks. That's very kind.' She shot Bola a wider, more relaxed smile and Charlie sensed the electricity crackling between them, a thousand hormones lining up for duty. The boyfriend thing wasn't something that would worry Bola. She might need to have a quiet word…

'We may need to ask some more questions in a day or so,' Charlie said in her best business-like tone. She indicated to the hovering paramedic that they had finished. 'Thank you, Miss Hannigan. We'll be in touch.'

They clambered down the ambulance steps and Charlie assessed the scene. The incident was being closed down. Police cars were departing with lights doused and sirens silenced. The ARU had left the Square; apart from the forensics team, only a brace of uniforms remained at the cordon. The gunman's remains were being stretchered up the basement steps, a body-bagged, anonymous shape. It would be interesting to see what pathology came up with – her first job tomorrow, Charlie decided. But this evening the first priority was to keep an eye on Caitlin Hannigan – a task to which, she suspected, Bola had already assigned himself. A call to the guv was in order, too. He'd sounded pretty shaken up. But experience had taught her that it was a dangerous thing to shake up the guv; it only made him raise his game.

'Want me to stick around, boss? Or–'

'–Maybe pop up to the hospital?' Charlie stuck her tongue in her cheek.

'Yeah, er–'

'Yeah, er… what?' Charlie cocked her head, enjoying Bola's discomfiture. She'd never seen a black man blush, but Bola was getting pretty close. 'Keep an eye on her, DC Odunsi. From a *distance*, OK?'

'Yeah, sure. Got it, boss.'

'And the boyfriend, if he shows.'

'Right.'

'Professional at all times, DC Odunsi. Everything PACE-compliant, remember?'

'Sure, no problem.'

Charlie watched him go and allowed herself a small grin. She turned, then, to the basement flat, and the besuited comings and goings of the forensics team.

She took a breath, went down the steps, lost the grin.

Chapter 22

George McConnell had no intention of following Bola's advice. What was the point? What would he do at home? Tess had been hospitalised by an Irish scumbag, and the guy was dead. That was good, but not good enough. It was too easy a way out. Someone had to answer for what he'd done, and George knew exactly where to get the answer he was after. They all met in the same place, these ex-pat Republicans, which was obliging of them: the Castle, off the Oxford Road.

George was one step beyond questioning the wisdom of what he was about to do. On the contrary – he felt empowered, full of righteous anger. He knew he'd had a few, but far from feeling lightheaded his mind was focused, his intentions beyond reproach.

The Castle was tucked around the back of Reading's Oxford Road, in a quiet cul-de-sac of neglected, sad-faced terraced houses, homes to a wide cross-section of Reading's lowlifes: prostitutes, dealers, pimps and – George felt it in his water, a generous sprinkling of Irish terrorists. As he turned the corner the first thing he noticed was a trio of dodgy teens on bikes hanging around on the other side of the road, doing nothing but watching everything. Lookouts, George told himself. Paid in fags and dodgy crack. Which not only meant he was on the right track, but also indicated that there might be a big shot or two in residence. That was good; the more the merrier. George stuck his chin out and kept walking. The pub's exterior was crowded with smokers standing around in groups, or lolling on damp bench seats under the cheap yellow exterior lighting. George ignored the stares, whispered asides and hostile mutterings, pushed hard on the heavy reinforced door and went in.

JC took the bottle of Bud, paid the barman and pushed his way through to the back of the pub. Multiple widescreens blared live football commentary, competing with the testosterone-fuelled banter and backchat. A shaven-headed guy he knew from last time, one of their minders, stopped him, patted his pockets, checked around his waist, inside his ears and waved him through. The end table had been cleared, a chair reserved for him, facing the bench seat opposite.

Which was occupied by three guys. Two he'd met before, one he hadn't. Stony – no *angry* faces. Something had gone down, something bad, but what? He felt a knot of fear in his stomach. If this went bad on him, it was game over. Permanently. These guys didn't mess about.

Think of the money. Keep your cool... You have something they want, something they need...

The guy in the middle looked up as he approached, nodded, pointed to the chair. JC took it, returned the greeting, sipped his Bud.

'We have a small problem,' the guy in the middle said.

'Looks like Niall's out of the game. You'll remember he was after talkin' to our expert, seein' as how the individual concerned's been a wee bit difficult of late. Well, we don't know why yet, or exactly what happened, but while discussing the problem with said expert, he seems to have taken a bullet. This'd be an hour or so ago. Thought you might be able to help, bein' in the know as you are.'

JC felt a trickle of sweat run down his neck. Niall Briggs, shot? Well, the guy had had it coming. There'd been some disturbance near the hospital; was that related? He'd seen the blue lights, the commotion, but he'd been on another – unrelated – stakeout this afternoon, an ISIS connection near Slough. Inconsequential, as it had turned out. He'd only got back a half-hour ago. Traffic was murder on the M4 after some pileup somewhere near Newbury.

'I've heard nothing,' he said. 'I expect I will, later on, if it impacts the team.'

'Better get your ear to the ground, then,' the man said. His voice was soft, but the menace of the slow, precise delivery lifted his words above the background noise loud and clear. 'And sooner rather than later. Niall finished his main job, so all's well there, but we might be needin' a slight change to the execution plan, dependin' on our expert's availability. I'll be wantin' to know you're still happily signed up. If things are as bad as they look, we might need you to take a more … central role.'

'Of course.'

'A copper was hurt,' the guy on the left said. 'She's been admitted to the RBH. You might start with her.'

JC took another swig of his Bud. 'Where did you get this information?'

145

Now the man on the right spoke up. He was small, but muscular. A long scar ran from his right eye to his chin. 'Young Brian's been keepin' an eye, but you're better connected. You can get to the bottom of it faster.'

'It might take a little time—'

'I don't think it'll take too long.' The small man ran his finger down his face, tracing the outline of the scar. 'Better get busy.'

'Sure. I'll be in touch.' He took a final swig from his bottle in what he hoped was a reassuring manner.

But as he pushed his chair back to stand up, he became aware of a subtle change in the atmosphere. Something was wrong. He turned to look. Someone had come in, someone who shouldn't have… JC craned his neck to see. There, by the bar. A copper. Stood out like a bandaged thumb. What a *dick*.

'The law. Get rid,' Scarface said. 'If you don't, we will. Know him?'

JC took another look, shook his head. The copper was at the bar, oblivious – or seemingly so – to the effect his presence was having. He was short and angry-looking but his whole persona telegraphed 'police'. Trouble was, his type had been at it so long they didn't twig that they stood out like snow in the Sahara. Obviously, this one hadn't done much, if any, undercover. And unless he got out quick he wouldn't likely survive long enough to get any practice in. Last thing these guys wanted was the rozzers sniffing around. Not now they were so close. He made a calming gesture, palm flat down. 'Leave it with me.'

He felt the triad's eyes boring into his back as he moved towards the bar. The TV crowd parted to let him through.

They didn't care much for him; they knew his game. But they didn't give him any hassle; they'd seen who he was with.

The copper looked up as he approached, all bristling and spoiling for a fight. JC could read the body language. What had possessed him to come in here? Ah, the eyes; slightly glazed, unfocused. The guy was half-cut. That explained a lot. Should make the job a bit easier.

JC grabbed him by the shoulder, hissed in his ear. 'Outside, now – if you want to get out in one piece.'

The guy pulled away, shook him off, reached in his pocket. The background banter quietened; all JC could hear was the TV, the ring of the cash register. He still had the bottle of Bud in his hand. He didn't want to do what he was about to do, but this copper was going to die if he didn't. He could feel the minders' eyes on him. The butterfly knives would be ready. *If you don't sort him, pal, we will…*

JC took aim, swung the bottle. He had to hit the forehead dead-centre for the glass to break. If he was out even by a fraction, the guy was going to be brain damaged. JC didn't want that. He had no argument with the police. As he brought the bottle down he yelled: '*Pig*! This is for my mates you banged up last month!'.

The guy saw it coming and his eyes widened. He'd come looking for trouble but hadn't expected to find it quite so soon. The bottle was half-way through its downward arc when he moved to his right, just slightly, but enough for the bottle to glance off the side of his head and onto his shoulder.

JC cursed, followed through with a push which sent the policeman stumbling backwards towards the door. A pair of tattooed punters helped him along with a further shove, and

JC was right behind. He and the policeman spilled out of the door like a couple of stuntmen in a spaghetti Western brawl.

Smokers scattered left and right as they demolished a trestle table. Wood splintered and an external heater went over with a loud crash. JC was on top. No one could see what he was doing. He stuffed his SECTU ID into the cop's face.

The guy stopped struggling. His eyes blazed but he'd seen it. He understood. JC made exit signs with his eyes, rolled off, stood up, brushed himself down. A crowd had gathered at the door, joining the smoking semicircle for a ringside seat. They all watched, jeering, as the pig got up, pulled his jacket straight, turned on his heels. Someone pitched a beer can after him. It glanced off the rozzer's back. More jeers and catcalls. JC, breathing hard, accepted the accolades, one or two pats on the back. 'Nice one, mate.'

He waited outside until he was sure the guy wasn't coming back. What an idiot. Hadn't done his own reputation with the clientele any harm, though. Which might prove useful over the next twenty-four hours. JC went back in, the crowd parting before him like he was Moses at the Red Sea. It didn't feel half-bad. He accepted his on-the-house Bud, downed most of it in one, looked at his watch, caught sight of one of the minders. The guy tapped his watch, made a 'vamoose' sign.

JC drained the bottle. Time to get going. He had another rozzer to deal with; at least this one would be a little less lively.

Chapter 23

Moran was sitting in the darkest corner of the bar to the left of the toilets. Not the most salubrious position but he had a clear view of the street. He'd checked for an alternative exit and found one in the fire escape door by the Gents.

He needed time to think; Charlie's call had added further unanswered questions to his already long list. He took a sip of coffee and began to arrange them in a rough order of priority. First, why did Black want Aine? Second, where had he taken her? No point visiting the address Black had given; it would be either non-existent or unrelated. Third, O'Shea. The islander was becoming conspicuous by his absence. Fourth, why had the Reading gunman shot himself?

He made a mental note to follow up both forensics and the autopsy with Charlie. He drained his coffee cup. Maybe the gunman would leave *some* clue as to Black's whereabouts. The suicide was puzzling; it made no sense.

Moran emptied his mind and began again. Black was planning a big job in the UK. He had men *in situ*, of which the dead guy had been one. Expendable, then – for someone with Black's background that wouldn't be a problem. And sure, if the gunman had given himself up he'd have been looking at a custodial sentence. Injuring a serving police officer, kidnap, threatening a member of the public with a firearm, breaking and entering. Possible membership of a terrorist group. Twenty years, probably – but he'd chosen a bullet instead. Had that been pre-agreed with Black? No prisoners, no risk to the job.

Moran scratched his head. Hell, how big *was* this job? And the answer came back, clear as day.

Very big indeed.

So, Caitlin Hannigan's abduction had, in all likelihood, originally been intended to be much more covert an operation than it had turned out to be. A cock-up, in truth. Black's operative had been spotted on CCTV, Charlie and team had had time to warn Caitlin – on the strength of O'Shea's intelligence, Moran conceded. The islander had been spot on.

Moran swirled his coffee dregs. The bar was quiet, just a few solitary drinkers in various locations; two at the bar, one at the small table in the opposite corner. All men, all middle-aged, unthreatening. He watched the barman move up and down his workspace, tidying, washing, polishing, smiling and exchanging mild banter with the men at the bar. An image of Jerry came into his mind, trussed and lifeless in the boot of the car. Moran's mouth set in a firm line. He'd get to the bottom of this for his old friend's sake, as well as for whatever Black was planning.

He rubbed his eyes, gritty and sore from lack of sleep, and tried to concentrate. Black had what he wanted, which was Aine. And so he'd allowed Caitlin to walk. Risk had been minimised with the gunman's suicide – preordained or otherwise. Thing was, he just couldn't figure out why Black needed Aine. And neither could she.

Or so she said.

His mobile buzzed. A text. Come to Geileis' cottage. Take a cab. O'S.

Geileis' cottage? Why Geileis?

Then he remembered the gun in the bureau drawer, the bullets.

He reread the message.

O'Shea seemed to be one step ahead. Which meant, Moran acknowledged, that he himself was at least one step behind.

'Come in, Brendan.'

Moran did as he was bid. O'Shea was sitting where Jerry had sat. He nodded a greeting. The evening was drawing in and Geileis had lit a few candles, kept the lights off. From the road the cottage had appeared unoccupied, lifeless. Moran hadn't known what to expect. A trap? An empty cottage, or O'Shea and Geileis waiting for him? Not knowing who to believe any more he'd taken a chance.

'A moment.' He went to the window, signalled to the cab driver; the guy raised a hand in acknowledgment and the car drew away.

'I have a little explaining to do, Brendan,' Geileis said, hooking her hair over one ear in a gesture he remembered from their evening together. 'Have a seat, now.'

'Well, I'd love someone to explain something.'

'Sure you weren't followed?' O'Shea prompted. He was wearing a rough polo-necked jumper and black jeans. His hands were muddy, oily perhaps, and his long hair was gathered as usual into a scruffy ponytail.

Dressed for business…

Geileis sighed. 'I didn't want to say much before, Brendan. I didn't want you caught up in it all.'

'I was caught up the moment I agreed to come.'

'Well, maybe,' Geileis agreed. 'But we were hoping that Joseph here–' she gestured to O'Shea, '–could sort things out. You know, before they escalated.'

Moran narrowed his eyes, looked over at O'Shea. 'You got word to this fella that I'd got myself locked up, right?'

'I knew I had to watch out for you, Brendan,' Geileis explained. 'When you said you'd been followed, I – well, I knew something was going to happen to you.'

Moran let his breath out slowly. He glanced at O'Shea. 'That's where the gun in the bureau came from. I did wonder.'

Geileis looked at her hands.

'Just in case,' O'Shea admitted. 'She's never had to use it.'

'There's more, I'm guessing?' He directed the question at Geileis.

'Me and Joseph have known each other for donkeys' years. Since the time he and Aine were – I mean, they had a thing, you know. Together.'

'What are you telling me?'

'Just that Joseph has a personal interest in Aine, particularly because of Caitlin.'

Moran glanced at O'Shea. The islander was nodding, agreeing.

Moran blinked. 'You're Caitlin's *father*?' he said slowly. 'Does Donal know?'

Geileis shook her head. 'No.'

Moran gave O'Shea a long look. 'She's safe and well,' he

said. 'My team are keeping her under observation.'

O'Shea nodded. 'Thanks for that.'

'I've been trying to help, Brendan. You see, I have–' Geileis paused and took a short breath '–*had* a friend, an admirer ... I met him at a local dance two months or so ago. He's in the gardai, but he's also one of Black's insiders. His name's Liam Buchanan.'

'We've met. I'm not a fan.'

'No. He's... well, he's proved useful. He came round yesterday and wanted to know where you were. I thought he'd figured out I was using him, but it was all right. *He* thinks he's using *me*.'

Moran shook his head in disbelief. 'I wouldn't have pegged you as a covert operative, Geileis.'

'I'm hardly that. But how can I sit by and watch all this happen without doing anything?'

O'Shea was on his feet. 'Time's marching on. I want to know what my brother wants with Aine, what she's got. It might give us a clue – *some* idea of what he's targeting.'

'We've all drawn a blank on that one,' Moran observed. 'Aine's clean.'

'You *know* she had links, Brendan.' Geileis was sitting forward on the sofa, her eyes alert and urgent.

'So what's her specialty? Communications? Money-laundering? Electronics? He should know, right?' Moran jerked his head towards O'Shea.

'It was a long time ago, the two of us,' O'Shea growled. 'If I knew, I'd tell you.'

Geileis shook her head. 'I can't believe Aine knows anything about that kind of stuff.'

'We can't be sure.'

'Sure, she hung out with Sean Black for quite a while, back in the day, yes. But she's hardly going to sound off about what she learned – what she was involved with – at that time, is she?'

Moran blew out his cheeks in frustration. 'Donal would have sussed her out, surely? If she'd been involved in illicit Republican activity her own husband would be the first to know.' He spread his hands. 'Don't you think?'

'He didn't know about me and Aine,' O'Shea muttered. 'We were careful.'

'Right. So careful you had a child together,' Moran countered. He tried to mask his disapproval, turned instead to Geileis. 'You were telling me about Buchanan. What did you get?'

'Only snippets. The UK job. Black has at least two men in London.'

'Timescales?'

'No. I tried. All he'd say was that it would be this year.'

Moran moved to sit next to Geileis. 'Think hard. Anything, Geileis, even some throwaway remark might be significant.'

Geileis shook her head, closed her eyes. A few seconds later she opened them again. 'It's probably nothing.'

'Go on,' Moran prompted.

'Buchanan was reading the paper, something about Prince William and Kate – oh, I know, it was the Middleton wedding.'

O'Shea frowned, muttered something under his breath.

'Pippa Middleton, right?'

Geileis nodded, remembering. 'He said something like, *"Oh, will you look at this? I tell you, Sean hates the Royals more than anything else on that island.*"

Chapter 24

The Royal Berkshire Hospital was blessed with an impressive frontage built from the same grade 2 listed Bath stone as Eldon Square, but since the Eighties the main entrance had been relocated to Craven Road on the east side of the hospital. Bola followed his nose a little further to the A&E department which was, predictably for this time of the evening, beginning to fill up. He checked briefly with Reception to make sure that Caitlin Hannigan had been registered. Yes, the receptionist told him with a patient but weary smile; Miss Hannigan was being seen immediately as a priority case.

So now it was all about waiting. Inconspicuously. Not one of Bola's favourite activities. He went outside where the usual early evening clientele was gathered in mutual support beneath an awning, dragging nervously at cigarettes or chatting morosely out of earshot of their injured family members. Calm enough now, Bola thought wryly, but come closing time plus half an hour the ambience would nosedive. Alcohol – the world would be better off without it.

Bola walked away from the smokers and down the concrete ambulance ramp to the pavement. The world *and*

DC George McConnell would be better off without it. Bola snorted under his breath. George was going to get it in the neck tomorrow, no doubt about that. Charlie enjoyed a drink like anyone else, but not on shift. Fine, so George was upset about Tess – they all were. But she was going to be OK, so, you know, deal with it, George. Hopefully he'd taken Bola's advice and gone home.

Bola paced for another few minutes. When the rain began he moved under the awning a second time, but the conversations going on around him were depressing and the smoke was getting up his nose. Literally. A thought occurred to him. Why not pop over to see how Tess was doing, just for ten minutes or so? Better than hanging around here waiting for A&E to do their thing with Caitlin Hannigan. She was perfectly safe in the hospital.

Better get an estimate, though. He went inside.

'I have no idea,' the receptionist told him, her earlier weariness giving way to irritation. 'Police, you say?'

Bola showed his warrant card.

'All right. A moment please.' She disappeared through one of the doors. Bola caught a glimpse of curtained cubicles, white-coated medical staff, heard a stifled cry of pain. Or was that just his imagination? He hated hospitals.

The receptionist reappeared and produced her best professional smile. 'She'll be another twenty minutes or so. They have to check everything thoroughly, as you can imagine.'

'Right. Thanks.'

Twenty minutes was plenty. Bola made his way out of A&E and followed signs. The hospital was a maze, though, a bewildering connection of corridors and wards, and before long he had to admit to himself that he was lost. He spotted an information desk and cut his losses. The elderly lady bobbed and smiled. 'Take the stairs or lift to level 2. Go through Main Entrance building into Centre Block, turn left at the Welcome desk and along the corridor, following signs to South Block. Then take the lift to level 3.'

'Right. Thanks.'

A few minutes and two wrong turns later he arrived.

'DC Martin? She's in HDU. High dependancy,' a nurse explained in response to Bola's blank reaction. 'But there's someone with DC Martin at the moment, I'm afraid,' she told him. 'You'll have to wait.'

Bola nodded. 'Sure. The doctor gets priority.'

'No, a visitor. A friend, he said.'

'A friend?' Bola showed his ID. 'May I?'

'Well…' the nurse hesitated. She was a pretty Indian girl in her early twenties.

'Just for a couple of minutes. I'll be as quiet as a mouse.' He flashed his best smile and watched the nurse trying to imagine the characteristics of a small rodent applied to the muscular black policeman standing in front of her.

She grinned. 'All right. If you're quick. Last bed on the right.'

Bola relaxed the smile as he made his way into the dimly lit ward. A friend? Not George, surely? They wouldn't let a drunk anywhere near the ICU. *HDU*, he corrected himself.

There was indeed a visitor – a young guy in jeans, T-shirt and a beanie, sitting at the head of the bed. Looked like he worked out a bit. Not exactly ripped, but close to it. Tess was conscious, and talking. That was good.

'Hello,' Bola spoke to Tess in a normal voice, then

remembered his promise. He adjusted the volume to more mouse-like proportions. 'How are you?'

Tess nodded. 'OK. Sore.'

Now Bola turned his attention to Beanie Guy. 'DC Bola Odunsi.' He extended his hand. The guy didn't take it.

'I'm just going,' he said, and turned back to Tess. 'If you remember anything else, DC Martin, you know where to get me.'

Tess gave a slight nod. The man got up and left.

Bola took his chair. 'Hey. What's up?'

'Not a lot. A girl's trying to have a rest, but all these blokes keep interrupting her beauty sleep.'

Bola grinned. 'Sorry. Just wanted to make sure you're OK. Look, Tess, I–'

'Stop.' Tess waved her hand in a small circle, the best she could manage while various drips and tubes impeded more expressive movement. 'Not your fault,' she said, and let her hand drop.

'Maybe, but I still feel bad about it. I should have been with you.'

'You *were*.' She sighed. 'It could have been the other way round, Bola. Easily.'

Bola chewed his lip, lost for words. She was right, but still…

'Did you *get* him, Bola?'

Bola was aware of the Indian nurse hovering in the background. She would swoop any time now. 'Tell you all about it later,' he said. 'Before I go, who was beanie man? Boyfriend?'

'Funny.' Tess made a face. 'I told you before – no time for boyfriends.'

'Then who?'

'He didn't say, exactly. But it's not hard to guess.'

Bola's eyes widened. 'A spook? You're kidding, right? What did he want?'

'Chapter and verse on the gunman. Description, anything else I could remember. Did I see his face, blah-de-blah …'

'DC Odunsi, that will do for now.' The nurse was behind him, tapping the chair back with her fingernail.

'Gotta go, Tess. Can I tell the boss?'

'Sure. Why not?'

'Did he give a name? Department? Anything?'

'Nope.'

The nurse prompted again, 'DC Odunsi?'

Bola stood. 'OK, OK. Catch you tomorrow, Tess. Get a good night's sleep.'

'In here? You're kidding. It's not going to happen.'

Bola shrugged, shot Tess a sympathetic grin, modified it a little for the nurse, and left.

'Just missed her.' the A&E receptionist announced with something close to a smirk.

Bola did a double take. 'But you said–'

'I can't be held responsible for how long the doctors take with each patient, can I?'

'Fine. She left on her own?'

'No. She was with a young man. Now if you'll excuse me, officer, I have one or two other patients to book in.' She indicated the heaving waiting room.

Bola exited via the smokers' entrance and ran down to the road, hoping to catch a glimpse. The apartments were within walking distance, but then Caitlin's companion might have brought a car …

Bola skidded to a halt on the pavement, looked right, left. The temporary pedestrian walkways skirting the water board's soon-to-be-completed (but never-apparently-worked-on) roadworks were empty and silent. Bola clanged along the metal ramp towards London Road. And there they were, under a street lamp.

Bola took a step towards them and checked himself. A heated discussion was in progress between Caitlin and the man, wiry, a little younger… Bola stood back, leaned nonchalantly against the low wall of the A&E perimeter, withdrew his mobile, began to fake a conversation.

'I told you to keep away from me,' Caitlin was saying in a low, angry whisper.

'I just wanted, you know… I heard what happened and–'

'You *heard?* This is all *your* doing. I know–'

'–I swear to God, I had no idea–'

Bola sidled closer. Irish accent. Quite strong.

Caitlin: 'Oh yeah, right. You had no idea. It was just coincidence, then, was it?'

'What d'ye mean?'

'That I get accosted by one of *his* guys two weeks after our, our … *discussion.*'

'Caitlin, let's go somewhere we can talk.'

The man grabbed her arm and Bola tensed, ready to intervene, but the Irishman glanced round, nervous now, checking if anyone was clocking what was going on.

Bola laughed into his handset. 'No way! He said what? Ha ha ha …!'

Caitlin shook the guy off. She was getting pretty agitated. 'I told you. It's no, no, *no.* What part of *no* do you not bloody

161

understand?'

'Please yourself.' He dropped her arm, took a step back. 'Just remember, you're not dealing with *me* anymore. I can't stop what's going to happen. If you don't play ball you know what he'll do.'

'*Go.* Leave me *alone.*'

Caitlin turned on her heel and walked towards Bola. He turned away, but she'd clocked him. As she passed, she shot him a knowing smile. The other guy stayed where he was for a bit, then set off in the other direction, hands in pockets, head down.

Bola waited thirty seconds or so, fought a brief battle with his conscience, pocketed his phone, and began to follow Caitlin Hannigan.

Finally. JC slipped from the shadows and started to follow the black copper. 'Charlie Two One, I have control on RED ROOSTER, leaving RBH and moving towards London Road. There's a friendly black in tow but shouldn't be an issue.'

'Confirmed Charlie Two One. You have control of RED ROOSTER.'

The radio was buzzing with the team's chatter as they organised themselves. Normally it would have boosted his confidence knowing he wasn't alone, but these days he felt more of a loner than ever. Charlie Two One today, tomorrow something else. Back at base, just his initials: *JC.* Like he'd lost the rest of his name somewhere along the line, even before he was recruited. Back in his army days.

A loner.

All the more since he'd woken up one morning with the

realisation that he'd never live a normal life; that he was so used to working and operating in what his shrink had called a 'hyper-vigilant state' that he could no longer differentiate between normal life and life on the grid. This had been brought home to him one Saturday afternoon in B&Q when he'd clocked a guy behaving suspiciously. He'd followed him, had been ready to take him out with a screwdriver if need be, but the guy had turned out not to be some crazy terrorist but just a small-time thief working with an accomplice to nick a TV in broad daylight, the cheeky sod. But he'd been ready to kill the guy, no problem. JC's wife and four-year-old daughter had seen it in his eyes, that look. Jane had smiled, said it was OK, but he knew it wasn't. He wasn't a normal husband and father; he was a dangerous weapon. He knew no other kind of existence. He looked after the British public, he hunted terrorists and foreign operatives, and he was damn good at it. And all was well, until the dreams had begun, the shakes, the sweats, and that time he'd tried to kill Jane at three in the morning because he'd thought that she was a suspect on his current op. His hands had been around her neck until he'd come to properly, realised he was strangling his wife. And his little girl, standing at the bedroom door. 'What's wrong, Daddy? Why are you hurting Mummy?'

PTSD, the shrink said. You should think seriously about a change of career.

But what else could he do? The family needed the security of a regular wage, even though, for what he did, the money was crap. There was no choice. He *had* to keep going.

And so he had, but with a few punts at the bookies thrown in to supplement the money. He'd won at first, but that hadn't lasted. A few months later he'd been worse off than ever. The team had started to notice his mood swings. There'd been a few close calls. And then, the Irish thing had come around. These people were organised – and to be *that* organised, they had to be well-funded. Which meant that money wasn't a problem for them. But *he* was about to become a problem for them, and a big one at that. He was about to bust their onshore operation right open. Unless they saw fit to make him an offer, of course.

And what do you know? They'd been highly amenable to his suggestion. A little taken aback at first, naturally, because they thought they'd been so damn smart that their every move couldn't possibly be tracked by British Intelligence. But he'd put them right on that score. *How much*, they'd asked. And they hadn't baulked at his figures. It was a nice little arrangement; they needed to be one step ahead, and now they were.

But for him, it had come at a price. And that price was fear and isolation. Not to mention shopping his mates; that was the worst part. What had happened to LK was down to him. The more he tried not to think about it, the worse it got. The dreams kept coming.

They'd found LK in a garage, in four pieces. LK was a nice guy. Nice family, wife, kids. The funeral had been the worst day of his life. Playing the supportive buddy, the family friend, when he was the one who'd delivered LK up to Niall Briggs and his torture team. At least Briggs was out of the picture now – but there'd be others. It wouldn't take them long to find a replacement. That guy with the scar, he looked like bad news. The idiot copper had got well lucky tonight. If he hadn't been there … what had happened made JC feel slightly better; he'd saved a good guy. But it was getting harder every day to live with the double game he was playing. That and the constant worry, of course; not about money, but when his luck was going to run out.

'Charlie Two One, update please.'

'Charlie Two One. I still have control. RED ROOSTER approaching King's Road apartment. Believe home to roost.'

'Base, Roger. Love the pun. Stay in position.'

'Roger, Base. Will do.'

Chapter 25

Geileis was preparing food.

O'Shea was out front, on duty.

Moran was thinking.

Or, more accurately, he was dealing with the irritation that he'd been outmanoeuvred by Black; Black had been waiting to pounce the moment he'd given Moran an address. He'd known the route Moran would take. A simple matter to lie in wait and make an early move, catch him off guard. And, Moran conceded, they had done exactly that.

He was angry with himself, worried for Aine, and unsure what to do next. But he was also nursing a hypothesis. Which went something like this: Black fails to entrap Aine, goes after Caitlin as leverage. He lets Caitlin walk after Aine is secured. Why? Maybe because now he's had the chance to brief Caitlin? *I have your mother. You'd better toe the line, do what I ask…*

But what could a young, high-flying civil servant possibly have to offer a man like Black? The answer had to be one of three things: influence, information, or expertise. Moran favoured influence. Information could be extracted relatively easily. But *influence*, having a key player at your beck and call – now that could be useful if Black was planning something

166

big.

But Caitlin was hardly a key player. Moran sipped his mineral water thoughtfully. Or was she? What if Black had gone for Aine purely and simply to get to Caitlin? And then, with Aine secured, Black contacts Caitlin, makes his threats, obtains Caitlin's co-operation. *Very neat,* Moran conceded. Black uses Caitlin to flush Aine out, and with Aine safely in the net he turns the tables, applying the pressure of Aine's kidnap against Caitlin. At which point the gunman finds himself surplus to requirements. He's done the job, albeit a little ham-fistedly – and surely more publicly than intended?

Maybe option three was the most likely, then: expertise. But what did Black want Caitlin to do? What *was* her expertise?

Did the basement finale hold the answer, perhaps? Sudden suicide, a bullet in the head? But why such a drastic ending? *If* the gunman had indeed shot himself – and there was a fifty percent probability that that was precisely what had happened. Only fifty percent, though, because there had been two people in that basement flat.

The gunman.

And Caitlin Hannigan.

His call went straight to Charlie's voicemail. Moran left a brief message: *Call me when you can. And check out any dignitary visits due in the county – royalty, celebrity, whatever. Could be something, could be nothing. Take care. Bye.* Charlie was flat out busy, so Moran wasn't unduly surprised he couldn't get through.

After they'd eaten, Geileis showed Moran into one of the spare rooms. He couldn't remember the last time he'd felt so exhausted. They embraced, and Geileis lingered at the door as he wearily removed his jacket. He sat on the edge of the bed and bent to untie his shoelaces. He didn't make it; sleep ambushed him before his hand had reached his shoe. He was dimly aware of someone swinging his legs onto the bed, the door closing softly. Then he was gone.

'The *where's* not a problem,' O'Shea was saying. 'It's the *how.*'

Moran joined Geileis and the islander at the table, neatly laid for breakfast in Geileis' inimitable style, tablecloth and all. *Crisis, what crisis?* seemed to be her watchword, and Moran admired her all the more for it.

'Well good morning, DCI Moran,' Geileis said as she poured him a generous measure of coffee. 'You're back with us, then? Nine and a half hours out for the count, I make it.' And then the smile, the subtle evocation of Janice gripping his heart. Flowers. He would take flowers to the grave when this was over.

O'Shea simply nodded a greeting. Moran wondered if the man had slept at all.

'Couple of hours,' the islander said as if reading his mind. 'All I need these days. Quiet night. I was half-expecting visitors.'

Moran thanked O'Shea for his vigilance. He himself had been in no state for guard duty last night. 'So why is the *where* not a problem?' Moran buttered toast and drank the coffee gratefully.

'That'll be because I know exactly where they've taken her,' O'Shea replied.

'I'm listening.'

'Cottage up on Slea Head. It's a partial derelict but one room's fit. Right on the clifftop, steps down to a small beach. He keeps a motorised dinghy there.'

'You're very well informed.'

O'Shea nodded. 'Thought that's why you wanted to work with me.'

'You followed them, after the ambush at the roundabout?'

Another nod. 'You were bound to cut and run. I had a few choices open to me for the ambush, but see, Inspector Moran,' he leaned forward, 'I *know* Sean. I know how he thinks.'

'Well, tell me how he's thinking now. About whatever's planned for the UK.'

Moran had considered whether to share his hypothesis with O'Shea but had decided against, primarily because his trust of the islander was cotton-thin. O'Shea was an ally for now, sure, but in Moran's head the guy was still working on his own. Moran was never comfortable with hidden agendas, particularly when they had the potential to blindside an investigation into potential acts of terror.

'Let's worry about Aine first of all,' O'Shea said, guardedly. 'I have every confidence in your home team, DCI Moran. We'll all play our part and things'll work out just fine.'

'D'you ever see Caitlin?' Moran asked.

The islander shook his head. 'What do you think? She's been brought up by Donal and Aine. She has her own life now.'

'She doesn't know, does she?'

'More coffee?' Geileis broke in.

Moran held out his cup, watched O'Shea's reaction.

'Better she doesn't.'

'But you've followed her career, I'll bet. She's doing well, her ma says.'

A trace of pride in his expression, the islander nodded. 'She's a bright girl.'

'So you know what she does for a living?' Moran eased the crack of the conversation open a fraction.

'Civil servant,' O'Shea said shortly. 'Ironic, in a way, you'll be thinking, with her old man how he is.'

'Kids go their own way,' Moran agreed. 'Different politics, different approach to life.'

O'Shea was watching him carefully. 'Where are you going with this, Moran?'

'I'm just wondering which way she'd turn, if push came to shove.'

'Meaning?'

'Nothing. Just wondering. I need to make a call. Excuse me.'

Outside, Moran breathed the unpolluted air. The contrast between his present location and Berkshire was polar. Perhaps he'd move back, one day. He thought of Geileis, the way she had waited at the bedroom door.

Perhaps, one day.

He dialled Charlie. *You've reached the voicemail of DI Charlie Pepper …* Moran muttered a curse under his breath, pocketed the mobile, went back inside. Enough talk, in any case.

It was time to get things moving.

Chapter 26

Charlie listened to Moran's message, tried to call back. No answer.

Royalty, celebrity? Surely not?

She rubbed her eyes. Better get onto it, but first…

Charlie popped her head out of her office. 'George? A word, please.'

'Boss.'

Charlie returned to her desk and sat behind it, drummed her fingers. She wasn't a fan of the type of conversation she was about to initiate, but some issues couldn't be ducked. George fell squarely into such a category.

George came in. He looked all right – a little tired, maybe, slightly red-faced. Wait. A bruise, on his head. Looked nasty.

Charlie came straight to the point. 'Feeling better?'

'Sorry, boss?'

'Bola said you went home with a migraine last night.'

'Oh, yeah. Right. I'm fine, thanks.'

'I can't have my team going awol with *migraines,*' Charlie made bunny fingers, 'when they're supposed to be working a case.'

'I know, it's just that – well, it was a really bad one, maybe the VDU issue again, like before when I needed to change my glasses, because–'

'Oh, *please*, cut the crap, George. What happened to your head?'

'Banged it on the cooker hood. Always doing it.'

'Bullshit.'

'No, really. It's got a sharp edge, badly installed. I should really get it seen to… ' George petered out into an awkward silence. He looked at his hands, placed one on top of the other.

'Shaking again? Don't suppose for *one minute* that I haven't noticed, George McConnell. I may be younger than you, but I wasn't born yesterday.'

George nodded miserably.

'You're upset about Tess. I understand. But this is *not* the answer.' Charlie sighed. 'Look, George, you're a good detective. A bit annoying sometimes, maybe, but we all have our little foibles. Foibles are fine. Getting pissed on the job isn't.'

George nodded again. It was unusual to see the little Scot lost for words.

Charlie pressed on. 'You're going to register with the AA.'

George looked up. 'I can't, boss.'

'Why not?'

'I can't sit there with all those … *saddoes*, and, and–'

'They're not *saddoes*, George. Just people like you who need help.'

George sniffed, took off his glasses, began polishing them on his shirtsleeve.

'You need help, George. If you register with the AA, keep off the booze, you get to stay on my team. If not–' she shrugged. 'I don't have a choice.'

George looked up, checked she really meant it, looked down again.

'It's been going on for a while, hasn't it?'

'I suppose.' George cleared his throat, swallowed hard.

'And you want to fix it, don't you? You want to keep your job? You want to live to collect your pension? Yes?'

'Yes.'

'Good. Go to the website. There's a national helpline – or just put your postcode in to find a local meeting that'll work for you.'

A nod.

'Right. That's that.' Charlie pushed a sheet of paper over the desk. 'Business. Two things. First, the guv thinks this Black guy is majorly anti-royal. Check on any visits due – countywide, OK? Second, mobile calls last night from the Eldon Square area. Contact the major providers, see what you can dig up.'

'On it, boss.' George folded the paper, got up and moved towards the door.

Charlie called him back. 'George?'

George turned in the doorway, eyebrow raised.

'Don't let me down.'

'So, you followed her back to the apartment? And she was alone?' Charlie motioned for Bola to sit. Her office blinds were open and she could see George at his desk, head down, busy with the job she'd assigned him.

'After the guy left her, yeah.' Bola scratched his chin thoughtfully. 'She went into her apartment. That was it. No more visitors, just our lot finishing off. They were done by midnight – I checked them all out. But there's weird stuff going on, boss. First the guy talking to Tess was a spook if ever I saw one. Second, the argument I overheard between the other guy and Caitlin Hannigan sounded more serious than some lover's tiff.'

'And he had an Irish accent?'

'Definitely.'

'Coincidence? She's from Ireland. An Irish boyfriend wouldn't be too much of a stretch.'

'They weren't discussing where to go on holiday, boss. It sounded heavy.'

Charlie nodded thoughtfully. 'OK, so maybe he's another link to Sean Black.'

'Maybe *Caitlin's* another link to Sean Black.'

Charlie pressed the heels of her hands into her eye sockets, tried to massage the tiredness away. She'd been up most of the night and the day wasn't getting any shorter. 'Maybe. Let's rewind a moment. According to the guv Sean Black is some A-lister Republican terrorist. He assembles his team for a new UK-based mission. But Black needs one particular person on his team, and she's not playing ball. Aine Hannigan – Caitlin's mother.'

'Right,' Bola nodded. 'So he arranges for her daughter to be taken hostage, to put pressure on, flush her out.'

'Yes. That's what the guv reckons.'

'Right.' Bola frowned. 'Then the hostage gunman tops himself, and Caitlin Hannigan walks free. Which means what?'

'Well, her being released makes sense, kind of, even though the method smells iffy. Because the guv and Aine Hannigan were jumped, and now Aine's nowhere to be found. They didn't need Caitlin anymore.'

Bola nodded. 'So, we assume Black's responsible. That means he must have got word to his gunman that the cat was in the bag and he could let Caitlin go, right?'

'But instead the operative turns the gun on himself. Why would he do that?'

Bola shrugged. 'Forensics report in yet? Might tell us something.'

'Any time now.' Charlie pushed her chair back and stretched. 'I'm due at Pathology shortly to find out what Dr Bagri can tell us about the gunman.' A thought occurred to her. 'Hang on, we didn't *find* a second mobile phone in the Eldon Square apartment, did we?'

'Apart from Caitlin Hannigan's, no. So did Black contact the gunman via *Caitlin's* phone?'

'Maybe. Unless Caitlin *removed* the gunman's phone. Either way–'

'We need to have another chat with Ms Hannigan.'

Charlie inclined her head. 'We do indeed.'

A tap on the door and George's head appeared. At Charlie's nod the little scot bustled in. 'Boss, we might have a problem.'

'Go on.'

'I checked the dignitaries calendar. We have something coming up.'

'Who and when?'

'Duchess of Cambridge, opening a new orthopaedic wing of the RBH. State-of-the-art operating theatres, all supporting electrics controlled by a special IT hub – completely customised operating system. They've been planning it for ye–'

Bola broke in. '*When*, George?'

'This afternoon. Three o'clock.'

Charlie was on her feet. 'Bola, get Caitlin Hannigan in *now*. George, with me.'

'Hang on boss, there's something else.' George almost tugged at her sleeve.

'Quickly, then.'

George produced his iPhone and Charlie clamped her lips together before she said anything disparaging about IT. 'George, will this take long?'

'No. Here, look.' He held the device up so Bola and Charlie could see. 'I recorded this earlier.'

Caitlin Hannigan's apartment CCTV. The foyer. As they watched, Caitlin came into view, went through a set of doors and disappeared.

'Back stairs,' George explained. He tapped a button on the app. Now they could see the underground car park. Caitlin appeared through the service door. She walked quickly to the garage doors and pressed a button. They slid open and she went out. Twenty seconds later she came back in, closed the doors, retraced her steps up to the foyer.

'What time was this?' Charlie shot Bola a look.

'Last night, around midnight,' George said. 'I'm betting she wasn't nipping out for a smoke.'

'No? Then what?' Bola folded his arms.

'I reckon she was getting rid of something,' George said.

Charlie pursed her lips. 'Right. And where would you dump something if you wanted rid?'

'Simples, Boss,' George said. 'In the canal.'

'Right. Get a diving team together, pronto. Whatever it is, I want it found, *yesterday*. Bola, why are you still here?'

*

George caught Bola in the car park. 'What? Can't it wait?' Bola had the car door open, was about to break a few speed limits.

'I only showed the boss half the story,' George said, producing his iPhone. 'Thought you might like to comment on the rest.'

Bola exhaled. He knew what was coming.

'This would be around, what? Three-ish? During your overnight 'observation' shift?' George offered the iPhone, which was playing a video with a familiar backdrop. The apartments. The corridor. Number five.

Bola watched himself on the screen, the discreet knock, the smile. The invitation. The door closing.

'What the hell were you thinking?' George felt his face colour. 'Are you completely off your head?'

'It was stupid, yeah, you got me. I know. But there was something about her.' Bola bristled, glanced around.

'So now you're going to arrest her? Awkward.'

Bola compressed his lips and nodded. 'I can trust you, George, right? Don't shop me, will you?'

'You're a bloody idiot.' George took the iPhone and pocketed it. 'If this goes to court, and I have a wee feeling that's exactly where we're going with Ms Hannigan, I'll have to produce any relevant recordings, won't I?'

'But this one, it won't be relevant, right?' Bola wasn't begging, but he was getting close to it.

George sighed, shook his head. 'Not clever, Bola. Don't ever do this to me again.' He thumbed the delete button.

'You got it, George. Thanks.'

'I'd get going if I were you,' George said. 'And give the

florist a miss.'

'Ha ha. Hey, by the way, what happened to your head?'

'Knocked it on the cooker hood.'

'Clumsy sod.'

George worked up a smile, shrugged. He watched Bola drive off with a squeal of rubber. His head didn't hurt that much. He gave it a short, experimental shake, probed the bump with his fingers. Probably looked worse than it was. He wasn't worried about the abrasion itself – more the fact that he couldn't remember how on earth it had happened.

Dr Moninder Bagri's autopsies were not mere medical procedures; they were *events*. Consequently there was always, inevitably, a gaggle of students assembled to watch the great man at work.

Bagri's routine was always meticulously followed, to the extent that fast results were seldom forthcoming, even when urgently required. Today, Charlie needed fast results. It was half past eleven. The clock was ticking and she still had no idea what, when – or where – the countdown would end. She chewed her lip as she waited behind the rectangular observation window, watching the little Indian begin his ritual.

'Good. So, we make the start.' Bagri beamed at the students. 'But, an unfortunate end, isn't it? As always, therefore, we shall pay our respects to human life, whatever kind of life it might have been. And so, let us be silent.'

Bagri bowed his head and the students self-consciously followed suit. One, a young man with John Lennon glasses, nudged a fellow student and was rewarded with a stifled titter. Bagri looked up and uttered one word.

'Who?'

The students looked blank. There was an uncomfortable shuffling of feet. Eventually, when it became clear that Bagri would not continue without a confession, the Lennon-lookalike raised his hand cautiously, tried hard to conceal a smirk, failed, and finished by shaking his head as he let out the burst of laughter he was unable to suppress.

'Something funny, young man, is it? About death? About this devastated face?' Bagri enquired in a soft voice.

'No, of course not.' Lennon had turned a shade paler under Bagri's scrutiny.

'Good. Because what you see here,' he indicated the ruined body, 'is what we all shall become. I would not wish for my remains to be the subject of mirth, would you, young man?'

Lennon shook his head sheepishly.

'Good. Then if you would be so kind as to compose yourself, this will be just like starting over.'

Charlie put her hand to her mouth. It was subtle, and there was no way the student would have got it, but Bagri had just namechecked the real John Lennon's posthumous chart-topping single. Beneath the *dignitas*, the little doctor concealed a wicked sense of humour; sometimes, it would leap out and surprise you, if you were ready for it.

Ceremony concluded, Bagri continued. He leaned in to inspect the gunman's face. 'Death caused, in all probability by the shotgun blast.'

Charlie was puzzled. In all probability? She was no pathology expert, but what else would have caused such damage?

'However,' Bagri looked up to Charlie's observation eyrie,

'one must not be quick to jump to fast conclusions, isn't it?' He turned to his students. 'We must never accept the face value. Always be looking for the deeper truth, especially in cases such as this, where a life is brought to an abrupt end. 'Poor fellow, we think, to take his own life like this. And in front of a helpless young lady. How desperate he was, how unhappy, how unable to face his future.'

Charlie was listening hard now. Something was coming up. Something she wasn't expecting.

'So, we look deeper, isn't it?'

Bagri's instrument probed the deep wound and Charlie's stomach groaned in protest. She'd seen worse, but this wasn't the kind of thing you ever got used to.

'Ah.' Bagri withdrew something from the tattered flesh and held it up for inspection. 'Observe. A shotgun death? I think not. This is a round from an automatic pistol. I am sure that DI Pepper's ballistics team will confirm.' Again Bagri's balding head turned up towards Charlie. 'But which came first, the shotgun or the pistol? To explore this question, I might ask, why shoot a pistol into this poor fellow's head, when the shotgun has already brought about the desired result? Mm?' Bagri looked at each student in turn.

Charlie was already on her mobile. Bola wasn't bringing in a harmless young woman for questioning. He was bringing in an armed and dangerous murderer.

Chapter 27

O'Shea slowed the car as a herd of sheep came into view. He eased around the animals with a wry shake of his head and a wave to the farmer. 'Only in Ireland,' he said. 'Main road, an' all.'

They were heading west on the R559, a well-maintained but narrow route which, in the height of the summer season, would carry endless carloads of tourists anxious to take in the sights of Europe's westernmost point. But the season was drawing to an end and apart from the farmer and his flock they encountered only one or two cars coming the other way and a lone pair of young hikers slogging along the verge.

'How's the head?' O'Shea asked.

'I've felt worse,' Moran replied, keeping his eyes fixed ahead for further obstructions. In truth, his head was pounding. He hoped that the blows he'd received outside Geileis' cottage – and as a result of Black's car ambush – wouldn't result in any further congestion of his own neural A-routes; traffic control in that department had been temporarily compromised by events at Charnford Abbey, the same events which had also left him partly lame. His recovery then had been in doubt, since at the time of the abbey explosion he'd also been recuperating from a near-fatal road accident. Black's roundabout intervention, by comparison, was small beer. Nevertheless, Moran fretted about his headache and promised himself a visit to Dr Purewal, his long-suffering GP, on his return to the UK.

'That'll be right, I reckon,' O'Shea said with a sideways glance. 'A man in your line of work'll see some violence over the years, sure he will.'

'But not today,' Moran said. 'No guns.'

O'Shea spun the wheel and the Land Rover cornered smoothly. 'Is that right, Brendan? Don't forget you're in my territory now.'

'It was mine too, once.'

'Sure it was. You can take the man out of Ireland, eh?'

'Something like that.'

O'Shea was silent for a moment, then: 'Look, at the end of the day, Brendan, he's my brother. Like I said, I want him stopped, but I don't want him hurt.'

'Let's hope Sean feels the same way, eh?' Moran said. 'I wouldn't put money on it after what's just gone down in Reading.'

O'Shea was about to reply but, Moran's mobile rang.

'Moran.'

Charlie's voice: 'Guv? At *last*.'

'Sorry, Charlie – the signal's a wee bit wayward out here,' Moran said. 'What's up?'

'We're bringing Caitlin Hannigan in.'

Moran listened, throwing occasional glances at O'Shea as he absorbed Charlie's update. 'Right. Thanks. Get the boyfriend in as well. Pronto.'

'We're on it, guv.'

'What about SECTU? What's their take on this?'

'They're covering the Duchess' visit, but only in lip service mode if you ask me. I've just got off the phone. It was a palm-off. Some snotty fast-tracker, by the sound of him. Quietly confident, can't foresee any problems, quote, unquote.'

'I'll bet – because they're not thinking Ireland. They're thinking ISIS, lunatics driving on the pavement, white vans and knives. They've dotted their Is and crossed their Ts in all the wrong places.'

'I'm starting on Caitlin soon as.'

Moran glanced at O'Shea again. 'While Black has her mother you'll have your work cut out.' He looked at his watch. 'Time is short. You'd better get cracking. Aine's your best angle. Caitlin and her ma are close. Play on that, you know, 'she wouldn't want you to do this' and so on. I'll call you as soon as our cat's back in the bag.'

Moran signed off. He wished he felt as confident as he'd tried to sound. He'd been right, but that didn't make him feel any better. Caitlin wasn't just leverage for Black to get his hands on Aine. She was a significant part of whatever he was planning. She'd got cold feet, but Black had upped the stakes, pulled her back on board.

O'Shea pulled over and killed the engine. 'He got to her, didn't he?'

There was a brief silence. Rain trickled down the windscreen, fogging the glass.

'Hang on to the brotherly love,' Moran said. 'Your daughter's not in any physical danger just now. She's in a lot of trouble, by the look of it, but at least she's safe, so let's concentrate on the job in hand: getting Aine clear. If we don't, Caitlin isn't likely to back down. Not with her ma's life at stake.'

O'Shea rested his head on the seat back, pressed both hands to his cheeks, scraped his fingers down to the point of his chin until they met in what could have been interpreted as a gesture of prayer. For a second he looked old and vulnerable.

'I can't believe she's doing this,' he said quietly. 'I thought, you know… I thought she was well out if it. Normal job, normal life, away from here, away from all the fear, the danger, the madness. A different life is what I wished for her, separate from the things I've done – just a chance to have a happy life, can you understand that, Brendan?'

'Yes,' Moran nodded. 'Yes, I can.'

'That's all I ever wanted for her. And now…' he trailed off. 'Ah well, enough sentiment. It's been a while since I've played this kind of gig, Brendan.' He fired up the land rover's engine. 'Still, old habits and all that. Let's get to work.'

Chapter 28

Charlie checked the camera position and hit record. '2nd October 2017, 11.25am. Interview with Caitlin Hannigan. Officers present: DI Charlie Pepper, DC Bola Odunsi. Ms Hannigan has requested a lawyer but has agreed to answer preliminary questions without a brief being present. Can you please confirm that for the tape, Ms Hannigan?'

'Yes, that's correct.' Caitlin's eyes were on Bola. Something there, different to before. Something hostile.

'You lied to us, Ms Hannigan. Your abductor was shot by a small calibre automatic weapon. The shotgun came afterwards. Would you care to explain?'

'No comment.' Caitlin pushed a lock of hair off her forehead with a steady hand.

'We have reason to believe that you are involved in a potential act of terror. We are also interviewing your accomplice, so you may as well tell us everything you know.'

Caitlin's composure was faultless. A little pale, maybe, but confident. 'Where's your evidence? I was abducted from my apartment. You know the rest.'

Very confident. Charlie leaned forward. 'We have reason to believe that you are part of an organisation intending to cause harm to a visiting member of the Royal Family.'

'You've been reading too many thrillers, DI Pepper.'

'I don't read thrillers. What happened in that apartment? Black called you, didn't he? He told you he had your mother, that he'd kill her if you didn't go through with it. Didn't he?'

'Go through with *what*, exactly?'

'So you know Black,' Bola said. 'Thanks for confirming.' He scribbled on a notepad.

'I never said I knew anyone of that name.'

'But you do, don't you?' Charlie pressed the point home. 'He called you. Told you what to do.'

'Not at all.' The hair push again. 'That guy might've killed me. I'm the victim here, not the other way round, for God's sake. Why would I be speaking on the phone to *anyone*? As a *hostage*?'

That's what you're going to tell us, Caitlin,' Bola said. 'We'll have the evidence within the hour.'

'I'm sure you're adept at sniffing things out, DC Bola.'

Bola's face gave nothing away under Charlie's sideways scrutiny. 'DC *Odunsi*,' he corrected her in a low voice. 'We have a diving team checking the canal outside your apartment building right now,' Bola said. 'If there's anything there, they'll find it.'

'Like what, exactly?'

'Like a gun, Caitlin,' Charlie said. 'And maybe a mobile phone.'

A shrug – and now, Charlie noticed, an avoidance of eye contact.

'We'll trace the calls, find out who made them.' Bola looked up from his notepad. 'And then we'll know, won't we?'

'Know what?'

'That you received instructions from a mobile phone network in Ireland while you were a 'hostage',' Charlie made the bunny quotes sign, 'in the Eldon Square basement flat.'

'Did you kill that man?' Bola's voice was steady, conversational. 'With a small handgun?'

'And then blow his head off with the shotgun? Make it look like suicide, a cornered rat's desperate last act?' Charlie followed through smoothly.

'Absolutely not,' Caitlin shook her head. 'I'm not answering any more questions without my brief.'

Bola glanced at his watch. 'Should be here anytime now. Suits me.' He looked at Charlie for confirmation.

'Yes, all right. Interview suspended at 11.37.' Charlie stood up. 'Don't worry, we'll be back soon.'

'Guilty as hell,' Bola observed as they made their way along the corridor to the incident room. 'And here's the man to prove it.'

George McConnell's unmistakeable figure had appeared at the far end of the corridor. He halted by the incident room door and his bristling body language told Charlie immediately that the little Scot had plenty to tell them.

'Boss.' A nod to Bola.

'Let's have it, George.'

The IR was bustling, electric with activity. Heads looked up as they entered. George's customary conversational speed, Charlie estimated, had accelerated by forty or so percent.

'The gun's with forensics now,' George was saying. 'And the mobile. There's no SIM, but they're doing what they can. The phone model uses NAND memory chips, so in theory there's always the option of extracting–'

'–OK, thanks George. As soon as we can prove anything conclusively about calls to and from Eldon Square, I want to know.' Charlie looked at the clock above her office door. Three and a bit hours. Not enough. What were they looking for? A sniper? A car bomb?

'George. How much do we know about the gunman? Who was he? Where was he based? What did he do for cash? Did he have a job? If so, where and what?'

'The team are working on it.' George indicated a knot of busy DCs in one corner of the IR.

'Help them out. I want to know *everything* about our late friend. And Bola, the boyfriend trace. Speed it up. You've seen him, you'll recognise him. I want him in here within the hour. Any problems, let me know and I'll squeeze Caitlin harder.'

Charlie went to her office, left them to it. This was the moment she had to share her fears with the Chief.

DCS Higginson was a good-looking man. Meticulous to a fault, his office exuded an air of calm, tasteful efficiency. Nothing phased him; disorder was not permitted either in his physical surroundings or in his thinking. He was a strong leader, approachable and supportive – traits which made him popular throughout the ranks. He was, however, a man who did everything by the book. And that was what Charlie was fretting about as she knocked on his office door.

'Ah, Charlie. Come in. Something urgent, you say?' The Chief looked up from his laptop. 'How can I help? Please, have a seat.'

'Thank you, sir.' Charlie took a brief moment to compose

herself; Higginson always made her feel like a schoolgirl sent to the headmaster for some minor classroom infringement. Did she fancy him? At times, maybe, if she was honest; she'd found herself on occasion concocting a dreamy fantasy or two, but recently she'd come to realise that the Chief was more father figure than potential conquest. And that was fine, because an authoritative steer was exactly what she needed right now.

Higginson arched an eyebrow. 'Any news on these warehouse break-ins?'

'Warehouse break-ins?' Charlie was momentarily fazed. It took her a couple of seconds to make the mental adjustment. The Portman Road raiders; they'd turned over two warehouses in the last month. She had DC Taylor and DC Butterfield on the case. Last thing she'd heard was inconsequential – Taylor and his sidekick were still on all-nighter stakeout duty.

She blushed, ran a hand through her hair to mask her embarrassment. 'Not yet, sir, I'm afraid. Soon as I have something, obviously–'

'Of course, of course. So, what's on your mind?'

Calm down, Charlie…

She cleared her throat and brought Higginson up to date with the latest developments, leaving out unhelpful details such as the guv's temporary working relationship with an ex-Republican paramilitary.

Higginson nodded. 'I see, I see. Well, my first inclination is to secure the evidence and pass all you have on to the SECTU team. They're covering the Duchess' visit, obviously. I'm quite sure they'll have taken every precaution.'

Charlie bit her lip. This was exactly what she had feared.

By the time they'd secured sufficient evidence *and* completed and passed on the paperwork, the Duchess' visit would already have happened.

'I suppose I'm thinking that our concerns may not be taken seriously enough, Sir. And we're almost out of time.'

'Let's run through where we are, shall we?' Higginson folded his large, dry hands and placed them on his spotless blotter. 'We have a young girl, apparent victim of a kidnap, or assault, whatever you will, a dead perpetrator and a slight anomaly as to cause of death. Have we proved that the bullet was fired from the handgun found in the canal?'

'We will, sir. Forensics are on it.'

'And what about proving that Ms…'

'Hannigan, Sir.'

'Thank you. Miss *Hannigan* actually pulled the trigger? She denies it, I believe?'

'Well, yes Sir, but—'

'So,' Higginson gestured by moving his thumbs slightly apart, 'in theory, the handgun *could* have belonged to the deceased gunman. He could have shot himself, agreed?'

'Well, he could have, Sir, but I don't think—'

'But it's possible, in terms of where we are at the moment?'

Defeated, Charlie let her breath out. 'Yes, Sir. I suppose so.'

'You see? We must be careful. We can't just pass speculative theories to the SECTU operation without hard evidence, and neither can we tread on their toes by conducting our own parochial anti-terror campaign.'

'Well, of course not, Sir. But DC Odunsi overheard a conversation which implied—'

'*Implied*. Implication is not hard evidence, Charlie.'

'There's an Irish connection, though, Sir.' Should she go on? Too late, it was all going to spill out. Well it would just have to. 'What I mean is that… well, DCI Moran is visiting a friend in Ireland at the moment, and he's made a connection which sheds some light on what's currently happening.'

'Has he, indeed.' Higginson sighed deeply. 'You really will have to make sure your guv'nor is confined to his home county, DI Pepper. I'm experiencing a strong sense of déjà vu.'

'Sir. But actually, DCI Moran *is* in his home county – I mean, he was raised in Ireland, near Dingle. And he's there to support a friend whose wife has been reported missing.'

'I fail to see–'

'It's Caitlin Hannigan's mother, Sir. That's what I mean by a connection.'

Higginson sat back in his chair and fell silent for a few moments, stroking his upper lip with a broad forefinger.

Charlie waited, the clock in her head ticking like a time bomb.

'I'll put you in touch with someone I know,' Higginson said. 'She's pretty high up in the SECTU pecking order, so tread carefully.'

'Of course, Sir. Thank you.'

'Run it past her, just to make her aware. If you feel you're not being taken seriously, then–' Higginson drummed his fingers, 'then I might not notice if you decide to take appropriate action – carefully and sensitively, mind.'

'Absolutely, Sir.'

The Chief made a satisfied noise in his throat. 'But listen, Charlie.' He leaned forward again and fixed her with his steady, fatherly gaze. 'This is the Royal County, after all. If our dignitaries aren't safe *here*?' Higginson spread his hands. 'The Irish issue was put to bed a long time ago. Personally, I think this is a storm in a teacup. Moran's jumping to all kinds of conclusions. Don't you go following his lead.' The forefinger was wagging now, kindly but firmly. 'I'm banning that man from taking any future vacations. You'd better warn him.'

'Yes, Sir. I will.' Charlie tried to smile but her face wasn't complying.

Higginson picked up a ballpoint and scribbled on a notepad. He tore off the leaf and presented it. 'There you are. Keep me posted, DI Pepper. And look after our Kate.'

'Sir.'

The DCS' attention returned to his laptop screen. The audience was over.

Detective Chief Superintendent Sally Gilmore sounded peeved. 'Irish? Are you serious? I can't imagine an Irish operation posing any kind of serious threat in 2017.'

'But Ma'am, the intelligence we have points–'

'Intelligence? We have specialist intelligence officers working around the clock here, DI Pepper. Do you not think that they might have alerted me to the possibility of a terrorist attack on the Duchess of Cambridge? It's so-called-Islamic-state terrorism we need to be on the lookout for, not some half-baked, retro-IRA plot.'

'Ma'am, if I may–'

'–We have the situation covered, DI Pepper. Now I suggest you attend to your crime-solving duties and leave bombs and terrorism to the experts.'

Charlie gripped the phone hard, bit her lip.

'If that's all, DI Pepper?'

'But at least check the route perimeters, Ma'am?' Charlie tried to keep her voice from adopting a pleading tone. 'The rooftops around the RBH, maybe – there are quite a few multiple-occupancy properties. I do feel that it would be … prudent.' *Prudent*? God … it sounded lame but Gilmore was a big cheese. She had to take care.

A slight hesitation. 'With your background I can understand why you might be a little jumpy, DI Pepper. I heard the Board were unexpectedly lenient? Well, jolly good, but you must learn to temper your reactions a little.'

'I *beg* your pardon?'

'Your disciplinary charge? Excessive force, as I recall?'

Charlie's eyes widened. The *nerve* of the woman. 'Yes, but I hardly think that that is rel–'

'–Well, thank you for letting us know, DI Pepper. You can leave this with us.'

'But I haven't given you any–'

The line went dead.

Charlie swallowed hard. Of all the arrogant, self-satisfied…

A young DC appeared at her shoulder. 'Boss?'

'Yes, Anne?'

'We've found the Irish guy. DC Odunsi's bringing him in.'

Chapter 29

'I don't see a cottage,' Moran said, as O'Shea pulled over and killed the Land Rover's engine.

'That's the point,' O'Shea replied. 'It's tucked into the lee of the coastline a few hundred metres along the track.' He jerked his thumb over his shoulder. The islander folded his arms and turned to Moran. 'Right. We're doing this your way, as I remember. So shall I take a stroll and knock on the door?'

'I'm thinking about it,' Moran said. 'How many, would you say?'

O'Shea made a noncommittal gesture. 'Two, three?'

'Will he be in residence?'

O'Shea laughed out loud. 'Sean? Not a chance. But he'll be somewhere close. Waiting it out.'

Moran got out, walked a few paces towards the cliff edge and surveyed the landscape. It was a clear day, a light breeze blowing in from the Atlantic. The restless movement of the waves mirrored Moran's anxiety; he had to get this right. The stakes had been high enough before; now, if he and Charlie were right, they were way off any measurable scale. Too late to stop the royal visit, too late for anything except to get Aine away from Black, pass the news to Charlie and pray. Security would be tight, he told himself. Especially given the current UK climate. But SECTU knew what they were about, didn't they? Surely nothing could slip through? If it did … but best not dwell upon that.

Moran turned away from the sea where the humps of the Blasket Islands floated, half submerged like a family of brooding plesiosaurs, and returned his attention to his immediate surroundings. Black had picked his spot well. You'd think you were in the middle of nowhere and you wouldn't be far wrong. The critical thing was the cottage, its topography, entrance and exits. O'Shea would know.

His lips were forming the first question when, at the edge of his peripheral vision, he caught sight of something large, half-hidden by a crumbling drystone wall and a few hastily placed branches. A car, or–

No, not a car.

A quad bike.

Damn.

He signalled to O'Shea. The islander quickly pocketed the Land Rover's keys and followed Moran's pointing finger. His eyes narrowed. 'Well, well. Pipped at the post.'

'Looks like you're not the only expert in covert observation around here,' Moran said. 'This isn't going to help.'

'Wait here. I'll bring the boy back.' O'Shea made as if to take the cottage path but Moran held up his hand.

'*I'll* do the recce. You watch the road.'

Before O'Shea could object Moran started walking. Keeping to the edge of the path where the untended bushes and stunted trees afforded at least some meagre cover, he advanced slowly until the path brought him to a curved drystone wall. On its far side, nestled in a slight dip, the cottage hugged the landscape like a rock formation – solid, impenetrable and impossible to approach without being seen.

Moran settled himself against the curve of the wall and peered around the corner. A single door, two covered windows and a rusty Ford Transit parked to the right at a slight angle, facing out to sea. Something familiar…

Moran felt a cold jab in the back of his neck, immediately followed by a terse whisper. 'Back out. *Easy*, now. Hands where I can see 'em.'

He did as he was told.

'Slowly turn, so's I can get a look at you.' The whisper was unsteady, the breath carrying it laced with alcohol.

Moran turned.

'Ah, God. *Brendan*.' Donal Hannigan lowered his shotgun.

Moran was equally surprised. 'What on earth … I thought Padraig–'

'Aye,' Donal said, 'he's in there all right. I don't know what the hell he's up to, but he's keeping poor company.' Donal's eyes were bloodshot, his hands shaking as he cradled the shotgun.

Moran placed a steadying hand on Donal's shoulder. 'You're right. Listen, Donal, I have someone here, helping. You'd best come back to the road, leave this to us.'

'He's my *boy*.'

'It's going to be all right, Donal. Just come back with me, OK?' Moran threw a glance over his shoulder. The cottage was still, wrapped in silence.

Donal's face took on a bewildered expression. 'Where've you been, Brendan? And what's this to do with Aine?'

There was no easy way. 'Listen, Donal. Aine's in there too, but—'

'*What?* Why—?'

'I'll explain once I've got you out of here.'

Donal brushed Moran's hand away. 'I'm going *nowhere*. My *wife*, my *son*…'

'Donal, please—'

Donal pulled back and lurched into the open, fully exposed to whoever might be keeping a watch on the cottage's approaches. Moran watched helplessly as his friend weaved unsteadily towards the front door.

A tread behind him. O'Shea appeared at his shoulder. 'What the hell's going on?' The islander caught sight of Donal. 'Oh *great*.'

Moran hesitated. If he broke cover both he and Donal were very likely to be shot before they reached the cottage. If he waited … no; he'd never forgive himself for not trying.

'Stay here. Cover me.'

'Are you crazy—?' O'Shea made a grab for his sleeve but Moran was already out of reach.

He was half-way across the open space when a window cover flickered, like a blink of an eyelid. At the same moment Donal let the front door have both barrels. The noise was shockingly loud in the confined area, a thunderous report that echoed against the cottage walls and bounced out to sea, carried aloft by the strong breeze. Donal's boot followed through, the door caved in and Donal pitched in after it.

Above the racket Moran discerned a higher frequency, the tinkling of shattered glass. Something thin and black protruded through the window, following his progress, tracking his steps. Moran threw himself flat and felt the bullet pass above his head like an angry mosquito, a zipping thump of compressed air. He rolled, rolled again, grimacing as his leg spasmed in protest.

Another shot, this time inside. O'Shea passed him, ducking, weaving. His ribs and leg telegraphing their objection, Moran scrambled to his feet, hobbled to the door, hugged the wall opposite O'Shea.

'No further.' A voice Moran recognised. 'I'll put a bullet in his head, sure I will.'

Padraig's voice raised in confused protest: 'You said no one would get hurt. I'm with *you*. Why are you–' A muffled thump, the sound of metal against flesh. Padraig fell silent.

A woman's voice now, a howl of protest. 'Leave him be, you *bastard*.'

Moran made a sign to O'Shea, held up one finger, questioning.

O'Shea nodded.

'Let them go, O'Mahoney,' Moran shouted through the wrecked door. 'I'm coming in.'

The female voice again: 'He has a gun. Someone's hurt–'
Someone?

'I mean it, Moran,' O'Mahoney shouted. 'You want blood on your hands? Come right in and you'll have it. In spades.'

'I'm unarmed. Just let me in and we'll talk.'

O'Shea had moved slightly to the left, adjacent to the broken window. A knife appeared in his hand, a conjuror's deft movement.

'One more step and I pull the trigger,' O'Mahoney said. 'The next one's all yours.'

From the corner of his eye Moran could see O'Shea sizing up the odds. The broken pane was perhaps fourteen to twenty inches across. The islander would have to risk O'Mahoney taking a shot at him as he lined up with the gap – and before he moved into position there was no way of knowing what sort of target O'Mahoney would present, with Padraig or Aine potentially shielding the bent garda's body.

O'Shea made another sign. Two fingers. A count. Moran understood, braced himself. One finger…

Go.

Moran stepped inside. His eyes, accustomed to the brightness of the early afternoon, struggled to adjust to the gloomy interior. A quarter second, maybe, had elapsed.

Donal, groaning on the floor. A woman, sitting on a stool against the far wall, hands behind her – tied, probably. O'Mahoney's closed fist, just clear of Padraig's shoulder, gripping the handgun, the other arm pulling the boy in closer, tighter. The automatic's barrel, a tiny, snub-nosed aperture, growing in importance, suddenly the only significant object in Moran's world. He wondered if he would catch the slight jerk of the recoil as the bullet began its short journey towards him, or if the pain would come first, the numbing shock of impact as the round tore through flesh and bone …

Half a second gone.

A whistle of air as something came whickering through the broken window. O'Mahoney gave a surprised grunt. The automatic wavered, clattered to the floor as the garda's hand instinctively went to the most significant object in *his* world: a six-inch throwing knife embedded in the muscle wall of his shoulder. Padraig took his opportunity, driving his elbow deep into O'Mahoney's solar plexus. He doubled up, and Moran waded in with a finely-aimed kick to the side of

O'Mahoney's head.

Two seconds.

O'Shea appeared at the threshold, took in the scene, looked straight at the woman and voiced Moran's concurrent thought: 'And you are?'

'Mary. Mary O'Riorden.'

Same height, same hairstyle as Aine.

Decoy.

Moran bent to attend to Donal. The bullet had penetrated his thigh; there was a lot of blood, but he'd been lucky, it was an in-and-out wound. Moran hoped the alcohol had taken the edge off the pain for his friend's sake.

'Padraig, give me a hand here. Hold this against his leg, that's it. Tightly now.' As Padraig obeyed his command Moran could see how frightened the boy was. His hands shook as he held a handkerchief to the wound. Moran quickly fashioned a makeshift tourniquet from the tail of Donal's shirt and propped Donal against the wall.

'Where are they?' O'Shea was bending over the fallen *garda*, had a hold of his lapels. 'Don't make me work the handle.' The islander raised his hand towards the knife, which protruded from O'Mahoney's chest just below the collar bone. It had been a well-judged throw, Moran noted; any lower and the blade would have pierced the garda's heart. Any higher, a miss.

'Take a hike, O'Shea.' O'Mahoney grimaced.

'Don't say I didn't warn you,' O'Shea said.

O'Mahoney's scream set Moran's teeth on edge. He grabbed the islander's shoulder. 'All right, O'Shea, that's enough.'

'Black's taken the woman,' O'Mahoney spat. 'You can see

she's not here, for God's sake.'

'Padraig, take the girl outside,' Moran said. 'And bring the Land Rover. Quick as you can, now. Your da needs medical attention. And so does this fella. O'Shea? Keys.'

O'Shea dropped O'Mahoney, patted his pockets, pulled out the keys, but before handing them over he fixed the boy with a level gaze. 'Sure which side you're on now, son?'

Padraig moistened his lips, nodded.

'Right you are. Careful now, it's a fine vehicle.' He dumped the keys in Padraig's shaking hand.

The lad gestured to Mary O'Riorden who allowed herself to be led away without a word. Her eyes said it all: *What just happened to me?*

The muscles in O'Mahoney's jaw worked as O'Shea turned his attention back to the wounded garda. 'OK. Who is she?'

'No one. Works in a bar.' O'Mahoney replied in a pained hiss. 'Get me to a hospital, O'Shea.'

'And Black?'

'Gone to pay you a visit,' O'Mahoney said, this time with a trace of satisfaction. 'Leastways, that's what I reckon.'

'He's taken Aine to Blasket? Why?'

'Distance. Security. And he knows you're agin' him now, sure he does. I believe he's a mind to evict you from your cosy wee house.'

'We'll see about that.' O'Shea aimed a kick at the garda's ankle and found the spot. O'Mahoney howled. 'That'll learn youse to scare an innocent young woman half to death. And what about the boy? What lies did you spin him, eh? Another kick, another yelp.

'I need a doctor, *please.*'

'Then *talk*.'

The Land Rover coasted to a halt outside, Padraig's face the colour of cheese through the windscreen.

'Leave it, O'Shea,' Moran said. 'Give me a hand, would you? All right, Donal, take it steady…'

Donal was trying to make light of his injury. 'I'm all right enough, Brendan. It's Aine you should be attending to.'

'And I will, I promise … O'*Shea*, for God's sake, man…' Moran tried to pull the islander away, but O'Shea was getting into his stride; his next kick caught O'Mahoney square in the ribs.

'All right, all *right*!' O'Mahoney tried to make himself smaller, curled up, shuffled backwards. 'Black told the boy about his ma, and, and … and *you*, you fornicating bastard–' That earned another kick. O'Mahoney, was panting now. 'The kid wanted to get back at her. Black told him he could be part of something really big, something for Ireland.'

O'Shea drew back for another blow but this time Moran succeeded in restraining him. O'Shea struggled, but Moran's grip was secure. 'Listen, O'Shea,' Moran hissed in his ear, 'I need help with this man. And we're short of time, remember?' He twisted O'Shea around, keeping the pressure on. For a second they were eye-to-eye, nose to nose, close enough for Moran to see the pores in the islander's skin. A second passed.

Another.

O'Shea's mouth broke into an appreciative grin. 'Not a bad move for an auld fella, Brendan, right enough.'

Moran let him go. 'Padraig,' he called, 'come and help your da.'

Between the three of them they got Donal into the Land

Rover. Donal had sobered up and was losing more blood than Moran was comfortable with, slipping in and out of consciousness. 'Hospital, Padraig. *Go*.'

'My ma—'

Moran raised his hand. 'Just *go*. Leave Aine to me.'

They watched the Land Rover bump down the path.

'Trust him?' O'Shea spat on his hands, rubbed them together.

'Lesson learned, I think.'

O'Shea nodded. O'Mahoney's yells and curses were escalating in volume. 'What about him?'

'I want to know what his buddy's up to,' Moran said.

O'Shea rubbed his hands together again. 'I'll ask.'

'*I'll* ask.' Moran pushed past O'Shea into the cottage.

O'Mahoney watched nervously as Moran approached. 'I'm bleeding to death here. You're a policeman for God's sake, Moran—'

'And so are you,' Moran said evenly. 'So don't tell me what I should or shouldn't be doing.' He bent and inspected the wound. 'You're not bleeding to death. It's in the muscle, nothing vital. When the blade comes out, you'll be stitched up as good as new. Now, where's Buchanan?'

Silence.

'I have to leave shortly, O'Mahoney. If I were you, I'd be wanting that to happen when my friend here is feeling more kindly disposed towards you, if you get my drift.'

O'Mahoney threw a glance at O'Shea, hovering in the doorway, rubbing his hands and massaging his fingers.

'All right. He's gone to sort the woman.'

'Woman?' Moran's heart jumped.

'The spy. Geileis.'

'Get up.'

'I want a doctor.'

Moran hauled O'Mahoney to his feet. 'You'll go with O'Shea, *now*. And you'll call your buddy and tell him to back off.'

'Can't. He's off the grid.'

'You'll be permanently off the grid if anything happens to her,' O'Shea snarled.

'Take the quad bike,' Moran told the islander. 'Do what you have to.'

'And you?'

Moran looked at his watch. Ten past one. Under two hours left. 'I'm going after Black.'

O'Shea made a gesture of mock astonishment. 'It's walkin' on the waves now, Brendan, is it?'

'I'll get the ferry.'

'End of season. Next one's in April.'

'What do you suggest?'

'I'll drop you near Dunquin. I've a dinghy stashed there, near the ferry. Good motor.'

'What about me?' O'Mahoney whimpered.

'I'll call a medic later,' O'Shea told him. 'If I remember.'

'You can't leave me here…'

Moran shut the door behind him.

Chapter 30

'I'm saying nothing – I've done *nothing*.'

'Keep your voice down, please, sir, if you would.' Bola guided his man along the station's familiar corridor, past the interview room where Caitlin was being questioned and into an adjacent, identical, room. It had been relatively easy to pick the guy up. CCTV outside the hospital, a quick sniff around the local Irish pubs and bingo – second pub, Oxford Road. End to end, an hour and a bit. Bola was pleased with himself.

ID had been straightforward enough, too. No prints on file, no previous – at least in the UK – but standard database queries revealed Bola's collar to be one Brian Keelan, age twenty-seven, native of County Kerry, resident in the UK since 2015. Currently unemployed, single, and, judging from the noise the guy was making, possessed of a serious problem in the anger management department. Now they just needed the forensic report from the canal.

Bola ran through the formalities, set the camera recording. The clock on the wall above the small window pointed to twenty-five to two.

'OK, Brian. Let's start with an easy one. Do you know a

woman named Caitlin Hannigan?'

'Maybe.'

'Relationship?'

'Just a friend.'

'Right. How do you know her?'

'Friends.'

'When did you last see her?'

A shrug.

'Try again.'

'Couple of days, maybe.' Keelan scratched his cheek with a grubby finger.

Bola raised his eyebrows.

'Yesterday, then. I dunno.'

'Been here long?'

'What?'

'In Reading.'

'A while.'

'Where are you from?'

'Ireland.'

'No, really? Specifically.'

'County Kerry.'

'Thank you. Know a guy called Sean Black?'

Keelan's eyes darted this way and that, as if looking for an escape route. He licked his lips. 'Nah.'

'Sure?'

'Yeah.'

Bola leaned forward. 'I don't believe you.'

'Your problem.'

A knock on the door. Bola paused the tape. 'A moment, Mr Keelan.' He left the room. 'Yes, PC Bradley?'

'Message from DC McConnell to phone him. Says it's

urgent.'

Bola found a quiet corner, dialled George up, listened. 'Great stuff, George. We took Keelan's prints a half-hour ago.'

He went back into the interview room.

Keelan looked up, cocky still, over-confident. 'You can't hold me for long – unless you're arresting me, which you're not.'

'Really?' Bola sat down, folded his arms. 'Under the Terrorism Act 2006 the pre-charge detention period was extended to twenty-eight days. Depends on your definition of 'long', I suppose.'

'You can't do that!' Keelan jumped up, banged the desk. Bola wasn't alarmed. He was a big guy, a lot bigger than Keelan.

'Sit down, Mr Keelan. I want to tell you a little story.'

Glowering, Keelan did as he was told.

'We found a gun in the canal.'

'So?'

'We have good reason to believe that the gun belongs to you.'

'Yeah? Even if you could prove it was mine, it's still not a crime to own a gun.'

'Agreed. But if said gun was used to blow someone's head off, that would constitute a crime, right?'

Keelan sniffed, looked away.

'Anyway,' Bola went on, 'it was nice and clean, all fingerprints carefully erased.'

A trace of a smile now on Keelan's face.

'But you didn't clean the ammunition,' Bola went on. 'Did you know that fingerprints can be revealed on bullet casings even if they're wiped clean?'

Silence.

'Well, there you go. You learn something new every day. And this isn't the first time forensic advances have come to the rescue for us hard-working coppers. Amazing what those guys can do nowadays, isn't it, Mr Keelan? Yep, even if there's very little of the casing to work with, all that's needed is a tiny bit of corrosion left by the sweat. They use powder and apply an electrical charge, you see. That makes the dust stick to the corroded areas, and hey presto! We have a fingerprint.'

Keelan licked his lips.

'It's not foolproof. A lot of people don't secrete enough salt in their sweat to corrode the metal, so…' Bola shrugged, 'no print.'

Keelan sniffed again, relaxed a fraction.

'But *you*, Mr Keelan. Well, you're a sweaty one, for sure. You left enough salt on one of the bullets to mine a whole lab's worth of prints.' Bola leaned in, 'Did you give this handgun to Caitlin Hannigan, Mr Keelan?'

'No.'

'Did you *force* her to take it? Did you load the bullets for her? '

'No!'

'What *were* you doing, then? Giving them a polish? This is sounding like accessory to murder, isn't it, Mr Keelan? Did you threaten Caitlin Hannigan? Were you *blackmailing* her to do something she didn't want to do?'

Sweat was forming on Keelan's forehead. 'No! Are you crazy? I want a lawyer.'

Bola sat back. 'Thought you'd never ask.'

*

'We found the gun, Caitlin,' Charlie said. 'Or rather, DC McConnell here found it.'

'Remind me, which gun was that?' Caitlin Hannigan replied smoothly. Her brief, a short guy with round glasses, ruffled his papers and took out an expensive-looking pen.

'The one you dropped in the canal.' George McConnell slid a plastic folder across the table. 'Showing Ms Hannigan Exhibit 1A.'

Caitlin gave the photo a cursory glance. 'Can you prove I touched it?'

'Your friend did,' Charlie said. 'His prints are all over the bullets.'

'Well, that's not me, is it?'

'What did Sean Black tell you to do?'

'Sean *who?*'

'You're an electronics graduate, right?' Charlie continued. 'You're doing well in your career, I understand. Government engineering or somesuch?'

'I work hard.'

'I'm sure. No time for boyfriends? Attractive young woman like yourself?'

Caitlin gave her brief a look. 'Not much.'

'Brian Keelan an exception?' George chipped in. 'Taste of home, maybe?'

'Meaning?'

George shrugged. 'Nice Irish lad. Not bad looking, so DI Pepper tells me.' George glanced at Charlie for confirmation, who shrugged.

'He's just an acquaintance.'

'Ever discuss politics, Caitlin?' Charlie tried not to look at the clock. This had to be by the book, nice and steady. PACE compliant.

'I don't really follow politics.'

'No? Unlike your mother, then. You haven't asked about her, Caitlin. Why is that? She's missing, remember?'

'I presumed you'd let me know if there was any news.'

'You're a cool one and no mistake,' George said. 'Unless, maybe, you already know your ma's going to be all right.'

'Because you're keeping your side of the agreement,' Charlie said.

'What agreement?'

'The agreement Black forced you into. The agreement which means you're going to carry out your side of the bargain.'

'I have no idea what you're talking about.'

Caitlin's brief nodded approvingly. His pudgy hands moved the pen across his sheet of foolscap.

Charlie interlocked her fingers and rested her hands on the table. 'I'll tell you what I think, Caitlin. You're a bright girl. You're aware of the political thread running through the centre of your family, going back a long way. Maybe you subscribed to those ideals when you were old enough to understand. But you moved away, life happened, time passed and you found you weren't as completely sold on the ideals as you used to be. But then the past came calling in the shape of a guy called Sean Black. Your mother probably mentioned him from time-to-time. Bad news. Very intense, very focused. A lot of hate. He needed a favour. Your background was right, an easy connection. But better still, you're an electronics expert.'

'I like gadgets,' George added. 'But I don't reckon I'm in

your league, Caitlin.'

For the first time Caitlin's composure wavered. She looked away, swept her hair back. Folded her arms. A defensive posture. The truth was getting closer. The brief had stopped writing, his small eyes alert behind the thick lenses, hanging on for the next question.

'Is that what Black wanted?' Charlie said. 'What did he ask you to do, Caitlin? Something clever? Something technical?'

'If you don't have any evidence, you can't keep me here, can you?'

'We can keep you for long enough,' George said. 'Anyway, what's the rush? Got to be somewhere?'

'Somewhere important, maybe, Caitlin?' Charlie added. She sat back, folded her arms, appraised Caitlin from top to bottom, woman to woman. 'You didn't really want to do this at all, did you? You still don't. But Black's got your mother. You have no choice. Am I right?'

Silence.

'If I can guarantee your mother's safety, will you call it off?'

Caitlin looked away, looked back. Did the hair thing.

'*Will* you?'

'Call *what* off?'

George abruptly got up. 'Right. Have it your way. I'll have a chat with Mr Keelan. Maybe he'll tell us more about what you've been up to.'

'Whatever.'

'I'm due an update on the mobile phone, Caitlin,' Charlie said. 'I wonder what that will tell us? Won't keep you long.'

George went through the 'pause interview' formalities. Caitlin's brief put his pen down, spoke quietly in Caitlin's ear. She smiled, nodded.

In the corridor Charlie took a breath. It was nearly two o'clock. An overwhelming sense of dread washed over her. She wanted to call high-flying-Gilmore and yell at her until she saw sense. *Fly with that, babe…*

'You OK, boss?'

'I'm fine, George.' Charlie set her mouth in a determined line. Yelling would make her feel better, sure, but there was no point trying to reason with Gilmore. It was down to her. And maybe the guv. She punched Moran's number. 'George, get Bola out here. *Now*. And find out how they're getting on with the canal mobile.'

'Will do.'

Charlie put the phone to her ear. Four rings. Five. No answer.

She gave up, put the phone away. Whatever Moran was up to, he'd find a way to let her know.

Just make it soon …

Bola appeared looking slightly – what? Guilty? Worried? She frowned, still slightly annoyed that the big DC had tried to cover for George. She understood why, but still. She'd need to have a chat with him later. 'How's it going with Keelan?'

'Brief's due any minute. I think he'll cave in.'

'I'll talk to him. I want you to chase up forensics and pathology on the gunman's identity. I *need* that info *now*, Bola. And where's George got to? Ah, talk of the ginger devil—'

George, red-faced and clearly excited, materialised from the direction of the IR. 'Got it. Asda network. Calls made to and from Ireland to Eldon Square area at time of shooting. They're working on tracing the exact location, but because the SIM's missing it means they'll definitely have to analyse the–'

'Prints?' Charlie interrupted. It was a speculative question. There wouldn't be, she knew. Keelan was the weak link here, not Caitlin.

'Nope. Clean as a whistle.' George shook his head. 'Sorry.'

'And the gunman?'

'Yep, good progress, I believe. Five minutes, OK? James and Phil are working on it.'

'Tell James and Phil five minutes is too long.'

'Right. Will do.' He turned and scuttled away. Half-way along the corridor he stopped, turned. 'Almost forgot. Tess is OK. They're discharging her this afternoon.'

Charlie threw him a grin. 'Thanks, George, that's great news. That girl is not going anywhere *near* anything remotely dangerous until I say so. Bola?'

'Boss?'

'Keep an eye on Caitlin while I'm with Keelan, would you? Just an eye, no questions.'

Bola spread his hands. 'I thought you wanted me to–'

'Just *do* it, Bola.'

Tess Martin swung her legs out of bed and gingerly placed both feet on the floor. Her bandaged midriff made her feel like the Michelin Man, ungainly and awkward.

She was sore but feeling a great deal better than she'd felt during the night when she'd had to call for a nurse and a sick bowl. That was just post-anaesthesia nausea, though. *Just*? Being sick was the worst. Still, she'd felt so much better afterwards and had even managed to sleep a little which, in this busy ward, was nothing short of miraculous.

She pushed forward so that her weight was on her legs. Nothing bad happened. Everything appeared to work. She began to shuffle along the row of beds towards the toilet. She was a bit light-headed but that was also to be expected. She nodded at the nurses' station on her way past and received a tight smile from the ward sister in return.

So far so good. She was burning with curiosity about what had happened last night. Hopefully her mobile was still in her handbag. Number one priority, toilet. Number two: nip out and make a call.

Tess pushed the toilet cubicle door open and sat down. As she did so she noticed that her hands had begun to shake. She pressed her palms onto her knees. It took a full five minutes to steady them enough to tear off a small piece of toilet tissue.

She got up presently, a little unsteadily this time, and went to the mirror.

The grey-blue eyes which looked back at her swam in and out of focus; it took Tess a good few seconds to realise that the woman in the mirror was crying.

Chapter 31

Geileis moved slowly around the cottage, clearing up and tidying, even though there was hardly anything left to wash, dust or put away. It had been good to have company, for a while at least. The feeling of emptiness had returned with Moran and O'Shea's departure, and to this she could now add the nagging worry – all right, *fear* – that she might not see either of them again.

What they were doing was crazy, off limits. Anything could go wrong, and probably would. Black was an animal, a lone wolf who'd stop at nothing to get what he wanted. But there was nothing further she could do. She'd done her best, helped O'Shea as much as she had been able. She bent to retrieve her empty glass and flinched as she felt the familiar, sharp ache in her stomach. They'd told her it might get worse. The good couple of months she'd enjoyed following her last round of treatment had lulled her into a false sense of security. It had been easy to pretend that all was well – and when Brendan had arrived, even despite the less than ideal circumstances, she had found herself playing a dangerous game of make-believe. He liked her, that much was obvious. She wasn't Janice, never could be, but surely something good could be salvaged from such a tragic past? Surely they could learn to love each other? In time…

But time was a commodity she wasn't sure she could lay claim to.

She looked up at the sound of car tyres crunching on the gravel. A door slammed. Heavy footfalls outside.

Oh no, surely not?…

The knocker rapped three times in quick succession.

She opened the door. 'Liam.' She tried a smile. It felt as though it would crack her face but he didn't seem to notice.

'Can a man get a drink around here?' Buchanan strode proprietorially into the lounge.

Geileis told herself to be calm, but she could sense the garda's agitation. 'I'm not feeling well, Liam. A headache–'

'Is that right, now?' He was beside her, reaching for her. Geileis backed away.

He grabbed her arm. 'You were keen enough last week,' he said softly. 'Are you going to reject me, is that it?'

Geileis began to feel the first stirrings of fear. Her first thought, *call the gardai*, bounced back at her with plain absurdity. Buchanan *was* the gardai. No panic button these days, not like her office in London. She was in the middle of nowhere with a man she hardly knew. 'Let go of me, Liam.'

He drew her closer until she could smell the sourness of his breath. She flinched and cried out as his grip tightened.

'I'm not messin' about, Geileis. I know Moran was here. And I know that he knows more than he should. Has he been back? Have you been helping him? All your questions, eh? You'll be knowing where he is, I'm sure.'

Geileis gasped in pain. 'I don't. I haven't seen him since Tuesday.'

'You know what happened to Jerry?'

The grip tightened. '*Yes*. I told you; Donal told me. Don't hurt me, please…'

Buchanan released her and she staggered back, rubbing her arm. She felt faint.

Buchanan looked her up and down. 'God, look at you. I don't know what I ever saw in you. You're just an old, desperate woman.'

Geileis backed away until she bumped against the bookcase. Her hands went behind her, looking for a weapon. The gun was locked in the bureau, on the other side – now the wrong side – of the room. And the keys were in the kitchen, on the hook … her fingers closed instead over a brass candlestick.

Buchanan advanced on her, wagging his finger. 'You're lying, you old witch, aren't you? Moran's been here. I can *smell* him. What is it, eh? You'd rather have him than me, would you? Well, I'm going to end this little episode. The way I should've ended it before.'

Geileis waited, biding her time. She moved back further, and further still until she was at the kitchen door. Something moved across the lounge window – just a flicker, but Buchanan had his eyes fixed on Geileis. Her heart beat wildly in her chest. Maybe there were others, keeping watch outside the cottage.

Buchanan lunged. She brought the candlestick around in a wide arc, caught him a glancing blow on the side of his head, ducked under his grabbing hands.

'Oho, you bitch.' He felt his head and his hand came away red. 'Now you're dead.'

He caught her by the throat, lifted her off her feet. The

room darkened, stars blipped and fizzed across her vision. She could feel her feet kicking, trying to find purchase.

Think, think, think…

But her strength was ebbing. She stopped kicking, summoned her resources for one last effort and brought her knee up into Buchanan's groin. The pressure on her throat lifted instantly as Buchanan doubled over, his mouth a wide O of agony.

Geileis staggered, almost fell, found her feet, and kicked out again, this time connecting with Buchanan's knee which gave a satisfying *crunch* on impact. Buchanan howled. She hefted the candlestick and lashed out, striking the top of Buchanan's head, then followed with another blow to the side of his face. Buchanan keeled over, twitched and lay still.

Geileis dropped the candlestick and held onto the sink for support. Her legs were unsteady and there was blood on her hands and forearms. It was only when she looked around for something to clean herself that she noticed O'Shea's familiar frame filling the doorway.

'Looks like I rushed for nothin'', he said softy. 'Come here, my lovely. It's all right now.' His arms opened and she fell into them gratefully, sobbing like a small child.

Moran fired up the dinghy's engine which started – gratifyingly and rather surprisingly – on the first turn. He gave O'Shea a mental nod of appreciation and fixed a course toward the dark shape of Great Blasket. The weather, thank God, was calm and looked likely to remain so – at least for as long as he hoped it'd take to get to the island.

Two hundred metres from the mainland he tried to recall O'Shea's hasty instructions. 'All three initial fixes are set on the alignment of 015° T – or 195° T southbound – of the site of the old tower on Sybil Point and Clogher Rock, off Clogher Head, Brendan. This'll lead you through Blasket Sound – the An Tra Ban initial fix gives a good point to break off for the anchorage off the beach. Have you got that? You've sailed a bit before, I'm hopin'?' The answer to that question was a cautious 'yes', but his sailing experiences were a long time ago. He took heart that the beach, if he got that far, would at least be recognisable.

He glanced anxiously at the compass. Despite the favourable conditions, the small craft was still being buffeted about more than he'd expected; he'd forgotten how exposed the open sea could make you feel when all you had between you and a watery end was a thin layer of plastic, aluminium and rubber. He tried not to think of the Armada, who'd found themselves literally all at sea among the Blaskets' rocky hazards. Two had miraculously got through; others hadn't fared so well, running aground on the hidden rocks known locally as Stromboli and Scollage.

To the north, An Fear Marbh, the Sleeping Giant, northernmost island of the Blaskets, was a low shadow on the grey water. Moran glanced at the waterproof map, checked the compass again. His bearing was good. Visibility was good – a blessing given the notorious sea mists which often made the Blaskets invisible from the mainland. Once in the sound the sea would be less choppy and it would be a relatively easy steer into An Tra Ban and a beach landing.

But what would be waiting when he got there? What was Black planning?

He'd know that Moran would follow. He'd be ready. Moran felt a bigger wash on the port side of the dinghy. For a moment he thought he'd imagined it, but there it was again; a grey shape just beneath the surface. His heart leapt. A shark? Surely not in these latitudes?

He looked again and grinned with relief. A dolphin had joined him on the crossing. It skipped along in front, maintaining a distance, then sank out of sight before reappearing on the starboard side. It repeated this trick twice before turning on its back and waggling its flippers. A good omen.

Thanks, my friend, I needed that…

The dolphin seemed to know where he was headed, diving and plunging along, zig-zagging towards the long mound of Great Blasket. Moran kept his hand firmly on the tiller and followed his new guide until the waves quietened and the dinghy settled into the calmer water of the sound.

Chapter 32

Charlie nodded to Keelan's brief, a businesslike black girl with designer spectacles and expensive taste in suits. The nod back gave nothing away. She'd be good, this one.

Just my luck.

Preliminaries and formalities attended to, Charlie went for the jugular.

'Mr Keelan. We have a gun. We have your prints on the bullets. The weapon was used to kill a white male, aged thirty to thirty-eight-ish, in a town basement flat yesterday evening. Who was that man?'

'I dunno.'

'Come on, Mr Keelan. We'll get an ID very soon anyway. It'll go a lot better for you if you co-operate. You know how this works.'

'Can I smoke?'

'No.'

A short consultation with the brief – low voices, exchanged whispers.

Keelan moistened his lips. 'It's my gun, right enough, but I lent it to Caitlin.'

'And why would you do that?'

'She was worried about her safety. In her new apartment.'

'And why would she be worried?'

Keelan made a non-committal gesture. 'Women, you know. They worry.'

'Do they? What about?'

'Stuff. Being on their own.'

'I don't keep a handgun in my house.'

'Maybe you should,' Keelan sneered. 'Maybe you'd better watch your back.'

'Are you threatening me, Mr Keelan? I suggest you retract that last statement.'

A stern look from the brief led to another whispered consultation.

Keelan sat back in his chair, reluctantly repentant. 'I retract that last statement.'

'Good. In which case, I'll overlook it. Whatever happens, Mr Keelan, you're very likely to go to prison. I've unearthed a little previous to help that on its way.' She hadn't. There would be previous, no doubt, but none had been easily discoverable in this timeframe. 'So, my strong advice to you would be to cooperate. I'm sure your brief, Miss–?'

'Ilo.' The voice was soft, cultured.

'–Miss Ilo, will be in complete agreement with me on this.'

Another low exchange.

Charlie waited, tapped her biro on the formica. Too slow. Push, push, push…

'Miss Hannigan is going to be released soon, Mr Keelan. She doesn't seem to mind what happens to you.'

A fierce stare of denial. 'That's bullshit.'

'I don't think so. Her prints don't show up anywhere. It's her word against ours as to what happened in the basement flat last night.'

'She's lying. She shot him. She told me.'

'Really?' Charlie affected nonchalance. 'That's not what she told us.' She let her words hang provocatively in the empty air between them.

'I haven't done *nothin'*. It's all her. She's done the lot.'

'What *has* she done, Brian? Let's get it sorted, shall we?' Charlie spoke softly, sensing an opportunity. She sat back and watched Keelan wrestle with his fear, facial muscles twitching. She held herself in check.

Keelan grimaced. 'Sure, I was only to make sure she was up for it, you know. Push her a bit. Her family, they've got the history. But she came over here. And he didn't know where her head was these days. Y'know, if she cared anymore – about home, about Ireland. But he wanted her to be a part of something. When the time was right.'

'Sean Black? Is that who you mean?'

A reluctant nod.

'Good. Now, what was the deal, Brian? What did Caitlin have to do?'

'Electronics, it is.' Keelan took a swig of water from his polystyrene cup, wiped his mouth. 'She's a bloody whiz kid. And he knew that.'

'What did she do, Brian?'

Keelan looked Charlie directly in the eye. 'You'll get me off? You'll make it easy?'

'I promise I'll do my very best. Now…' Charlie tilted her head to one side, widened her eyes a little.

'It's a bomb.'

Charlie went cold. 'Where?'

'She didn't tell me, did she? Black told her to keep it tight.

Need to know basis an' all that.'

An image of a sleek, black limo, purring its way along the M4, filled Charlie's head. Destination, Royal Berkshire Hospital.

'She must have confided in someone, Brian. She wouldn't have planted an explosive device on her own, would she? Was there an accomplice? If not you, then who? The gunman?'

'I don't know. About him. She never told me his name.'

'Oh, come on.'

'She *never* said.'

'Brian. I'm giving you a chance to make life easier for yourself.'

Keelan's mouth twitched. His fingers gripped the cup tightly.

'You and Caitlin – you're an item, right?'

A dismissive snort. 'Supposedly. She'd never stitch me up, anyhow.'

'Don't be so sure.'

A knock. George's head appeared round the door. 'Boss?'

Charlie paused the recording. 'I'll give you a minute to think things through.'

George was in the corridor, gnawing impatiently at his finger. 'I can't get hold of the guv.'

'Still?'

'Going to voicemail.'

'Gunman ID?'

'Still checking. We have a possible.'

'I want *definites*, not possibles.' She read George's expression. 'What else, George?'

'The Duchess. She's ahead of schedule.'

Charlie's world froze. 'By how long?'

'Twenty minutes or so. She's due to hit Reading in around–' George examined his phone, '–thirty minutes.'

'It's a low-profile visit,' Detective Chief Superintendent Sally Gilmore spoke quietly, reasonably. 'We have everything covered. All is well, DI Pepper. Please be assured.'

'The route,' Charlie pressed. 'Which way is she coming in?'

'Well, there's only one way from London – via the M4, Cemetery Junction, left into Craven Road.'

'She's not using the multi-storey, surely?'

'No,' Gilmore replied with exaggerated patience. 'She'll enter the hospital via the main entrance. Her car has been allocated a reserved space right outside. The public have been diverted to the old London Road frontage for the day. I have resources covering Craven Road at both ends even as we speak.'

'But the roadworks? Surely they're smack in the way?'

'Thames Water have cleared the site. They're done.'

'Since when? They've been there for *weeks*.'

'Since I told them to. Actually the work was completed a few weeks ago. They've been short-staffed. It was simply a question of removing the walkway, traffic control, cones and so on. They finished everything off last night. By midnight, as I mandated.'

Mandated. Talk about smug. 'You're one hundred percent on this?'

'I'll ignore that, DI Pepper. I understand your concern. But do, please, remember who you're talking to.'

'Oh, I will. You can be sure of that, Ma'am.'

A pause. Then, 'Let me be *quite* clear, DI Pepper. Leave this to us. Understood?' Gilmore spaced the words out for extra emphasis.

'Ma'am.' Charlie stabbed the red button to kill the call.

The clock on her wall read twenty-five to three. Charlie sat on the edge of her desk, ruffled her hair with an impatient gesture. In her mind's eye she saw the limo pause at the police filter at Craven Road. The duty officer would smile, perhaps nod to the Duchess, wave them through. A few hundred metres, indicate right. Pull up by the main entrance. Waiting there, the reception: hospital management, senior medical staff, shuffling feet nervously in anticipation. A little banter, perhaps, a few in-jokes. 'She's charming.' Or 'Nothing to worry about. She's lovely, you'll see.'

I have resources covering Craven Road at both ends ...

But none along the road itself. Charlie would have deployed a team at intervals, probably in some of the medical units on the left-hand side, one or two outside the entrance. But who knew what or *whom* Gilmore had seen fit to deploy? Charlie bit her lip fiercely. Time for one last crack at Keelan? Why not. But Charlie believed the guy; he only knew what he had to know. Caitlin was the one with the answers, and she wasn't budging. Only Moran could provide the key to unlock Caitlin's silence.

Charlie made a fist and banged the desk hard.

Guv, where are you when I need you?

Chapter 33

'Boss. Update.'

'Make it good, whatever it is, George.'

'Gunman's name was Niall Briggs. Lot of history – dodgy, most of it – in the extended family. Irish. Been working over here for a couple of years. Last employer, Thames Water.'

Thames Water.

Charlie swallowed hard. 'George. The *roadworks*.'

George's face blanked, and then, as realisation set in, reddened in horror. 'Outside the RBH? I'm on it–' He made as if to leave but Charlie stopped him with a look.

'No time, George.'

'The uniforms–'

'At each end of Craven Road. Sealed off, Gilmore said.'

'But she must have people nearby? I mean, trained guys who–'

'Who'll do what? Look for something to shoot at? There isn't going to be anything to shoot at, George.' Charlie's fingers were dancing over her iPhone. No choice, as usual. None. But she'd promised herself ... no, not possible. Too much at stake.

Bola was at the door. 'Eyeball on the London Road traffic

cam, boss. She's just been waved through. It's not a limo either, it's a Beamer. Inconspicuous I suppose–'

'Just an ordinary girl. Only she's not.' *Pick up, Tess, pick up.* George was hovering, dithering. 'Get in there with Caitlin, Bola. Tell her anything. She can't let this happen.'

'She might not be able to stop it, Boss.'

'I don't *care*. Just *try*.'

Bola followed George out casting a backward, rather hostile, glance at Charlie as he went. What was all that about? Never mind. Later. *Pick up, Tess…*

'Tess Martin.'

'Tess? Oh, thank *God*. Listen. Where are you?'

'Just outside the hospital, why? It's all happening here, I can tell you. The Duchess of Cambridge? She's opening the new orthopaedic wing–'

'–Tess, listen to me–'

'There's a right old reception committee – hang on, I can see the car–'

'Tess, *listen*, I *have* to ask you to do this. I'm so sorry.'

George McConnell was standing in the empty interview room. 'How?' he hissed to no one in particular. '*How*–?' he repeated, as if repetition could reverse the situation. Where the *hell* was Bola?

Don't jump to conclusions, George…

Next stop: duty sergeant. Maybe it wasn't too late; maybe she hadn't left the building. Maybe she'd gone to the toilet.

Denis Robinson was on duty, as always. An affable man close to retirement, Denis' organisational and administrative skills had attained legendary status throughout Thames Valley. Never known to pass up the opportunity for a chat,

Denis was well-liked but usually avoided at times of crisis when his meticulous record-keeping and penchant for labouring a point could become counter-productive. As he raced down the stairs George planned his approach. Simple, direct questions worked best.

Luck was with him. Denis was stirring a mug of tea at his desk and one of the juniors was working reception.

'Denis. Young girl, late twenties. Shoulder-length reddish-blonde hair. Caitlin Hannigan. Any sign?'

Denis looked up from his task. 'Ah. Young George. Tea?'

'Bit of an urgent one, Denis.'

The spoon was replaced carefully in its saucer. 'Hannigan, Hannigan.' Denis went to his log book and his broad forefinger travelled down the page. George watched its snail-like progress with a sinking heart.

'You must remember her, Denis? Striking girl. Brought in earlier for questioning regarding the Eldon Square incident.'

Denis' finger paused on its journey. The sergeant tilted his head to one side, frowned. 'I believe I do, George, now you mention it.'

'And?'

'We have a lot of people come through. It's been like Piccadilly Circus today. Give us a moment.' The finger resumed its line-by-line examination.

'I mean, has she been signed out?' George bit his knuckle, waited.

'Patience.'

George held his tongue. The reception area was half-full. A grey-haired lady in a floral dress was giving the PC at the window a hard time. As far as George could tell it was something to do with motorbikes and late nights, suburban teenage angst and her husband's escalating blood pressure. George undid his top button; it was uncomfortably warm in Denis' orderly domain. By the gods, he could murder a drink. One wouldn't do any harm, would it?

'Here we are.'

George peered over Denis' shoulder at the rows of beautifully-crafted copybook handwriting, an art form which would disappear forever from the record books come the sergeant's retirement.

'Hannigan, C.' Denis tapped his entry and glanced at his watch. 'Fifteen minutes ago.'

'I don't understand,' George said. 'She just came down and asked to leave?'

'Don't be daft,' Denis said. 'She was with your buddy, the big fella. It all looked pukka. Just popping out to her car, your fella said. Hang on, that's odd; they said they were coming straight back.' Denis' finger resumed its line-by-line inspection. 'Nope, they've not booked in again as far as I can see … wait a sec – where are you off to?'

'Run it,' Charlie said. George pressed *play* and the DVD player obligingly showed the interior of Caitlin Hannigan's recently vacated interview room. In the heat of the current activity, they'd forgotten to switch the machine off during interview breaks. Good news for them, bad news for DC Bola Odunsi.

'Just need a private word,' Caitlin-on-screen said to her brief.

'Understood.'

Exit brief.

'I need to make a call, DC Odunsi. I left my phone in the

car.'

'Sorry, no can do.'

Caitlin opened her handbag, produced a sheaf of glossy prints, spread them on the table. 'Shall I run these past DI Pepper?'

Bola looked at each in turn, shook his head slowly. Not much left to the imagination. 'You wouldn't.'

'If I have to. Now, can we pop to the car park, please? You can accompany me, of course.'

They watched as Bola wavered. It was uncomfortable to watch.

Caitlin-on-screen arched an eyebrow. 'Shall we?'

Caitlin and Bola stood up together, left the room without a glance at the camera.

George clicked the *off* button. 'I could say something rude at this point.'

'Save it, George. Get the car. Back door, under a minute – quicker if you can.'

Bola was being careful to adhere to the speed limit, not for any legal or dutiful reasons, but because there was a pistol pointing at his head. Oldest trick in the book, and he'd fallen for it. 'Glove compartment's stuck, Bola, would you mind?'

Caitlin had stepped back, given him space to reach into the car, but as he had done so she'd grabbed the pistol from the front seat storage box and jammed it into his temple. 'Get in. Drive.'

She'd sounded serious, so Bola had thought it best to comply. Out onto the IDR, past the Oracle shopping centre on the flyover, and towards the RBH.

'Nice and steady, DC Odunsi, please,' Caitlin Hannigan

said. 'Take the next right, then left into Eldon Square. There's usually a space.'

Bola risked a sideways glance. Caitlin was fiddling with what looked like a cheap mobile – not a smart phone, a burner maybe. She had the back off and was making some deft single-handed adjustments to the phone's internal components, the gun steady in her left hand.

'Eyes front, Bola.'

'You're the one, right? You're the trigger.'

'Keep driving.'

'You're not serious. You can't blow up a duchess. *The Duchess…* It's just–' Bola shook his head, searching for the right word, couldn't find it, gave up and fell back on cliché. 'It's *mad*. Crazy. They'll lock you up for *years*.'

'I think not.' She snapped the phone together, switched it on and gave a murmur of satisfaction as the LED lit up.

'Left here?'

Caitlin checked right, checked left, looked ahead to where they could see the police cordon at the junction of Erleigh and Craven Roads, glanced at her watch. She took something from her bag, placed it in her ear, went quiet, frowned as if she were listening hard for something.

Bola felt sweat trickle down his forehead. Should he jump her, drive the car into a wall? But that might detonate the bomb. He glanced at his abductor again, remembering the fate of the gunman in the basement flat. 'So what am I doing? Left or *what*? We're about to miss the turn.'

'Roger that,' Caitlin said. 'This is DUSTER, repeat, DUSTER, almost in position. Give me an update on QUEEN OF HEARTS, please. Twenty seconds? Roger that. Ah, I see her.'

'What the *hell*…?' Bola glanced sideways again, his eyes widening in surprise.

'Eyes on the *road*.'

Bola returned his gaze to the junction, saw a black BMW glide up to the cordon, slip though soundlessly, waved on by a smile and a nod from the attending police officers.

'Change of plan,' Caitlin said. 'Drive straight on, towards the cordon, please.'

'Lights are red.'

'Drive. Fast as you can, please.'

'Oh *shiiiiit–*' Bola floored the accelerator and shot over the junction. Tyres squealed as cars tried to get out of his way. He clipped one, sent another spinning. The two uniforms at the cordon stepped forward in alarm. The tail lights of the BMW were half-way up the road, heading for the reception committee.

Half-way across.

Bola prayed, bracing for impact.

A guy on a racing bike banged the roof in passing, shook his fist, carried on riding.

They made it. Bola brought the car to a halt half-on, half-off the pavement by the cordon.

The uniforms were at the window, motioning for him to open up. Caitlin had the mobile in her hand, was punching numbers.

Now or never.

Bola lunged for the mobile, Caitlin shouted, pulled away. Her left hand came up.

She fired the pistol.

The uniforms fell back, white-faced, shocked.

Bola's ears were ringing, but the shot had missed, torn

through the roof, not him.

Caitlin's attention was back on the phone, fingers moving rapidly across the keypad.

Bola lunged for it.

'Let *go*, you idiot … you don't *understand*…'

She bent forward and bit his hand. The pain was sudden, shocking and intense. He let go. Caitlin opened the door, got out. Bola followed, using his momentum to attempt a clumsy rugby-tackle which Caitlin nimbly sidestepped. Bola hit the tarmac hard, looked up … Caitlin's eyes were focused on the BMW, concentrating, calculating… Her fingers resumed their dance on the keypad…

Bola had been a fair basketball player in his teens. This target was smaller, if a little closer than usual. A big ask though, under the circumstances. Nevertheless … Bola slipped off his shoe, took aim, threw.

Bola's size eleven struck Caitlin's wrist, heel first. The phone flew from her hand, went spinning. Bola watched it hit the tarmac, bounce once, break open…

Tess felt a little light-headed. Everything had taken on a surreal quality; the air was buzzing with the excited chatter of the reception committee. She pushed through. 'Excuse me, please… thanks…'. Now she was outside, the glass doors behind her. Down the steps to the pavement, slowly, purposefully, keeping her movements steady, unthreatening. Three senior hospital staff on the pavement, the vanguard. A middle-aged lady, a grey-haired man in a charcoal city suit, and a younger guy, nervous, shuffling his feet, fiddling with his cufflinks. Hospital admin. He glanced at her as she took the last step and joined them by the road.

Tess looked to the right. Clear. Not a uniform in sight. Wait, there, right at the top. By the junction, arms folded as if nothing special was happening. One uniform. Were there others? Charlie had said not. SECTU had ranked this a low-profile visit. Tess looked the other way, towards the London Road. A car, a BMW, half-way along the road and closing. Tess estimated the speed at not more than fifteen to twenty.

She tracked up from the moving vehicle. Eight to nine metres away the fresh tarmac of the recently completed road works was a raised rampart, maybe four metres across and just a couple of inches proud of the original road surface. You wouldn't know it was there. Probably wouldn't even feel the bump in a car like that.

Tess moistened her lips and began to walk along the pavement. She winced as the dressing beneath her blouse shifted slightly, catching on the wound. She still felt light-headed. The medication, perhaps; they'd warned her she might feel a little drowsy. She could see the driver now, a good-looking bloke in a tweed jacket. Someone in the back seat. A woman. Long hair, elegant. The car would cross the roadworks in about twenty seconds.

Tess walked a little faster. It would be all right. Step in front of the car. Hold your hand up. Show your warrant card. She fumbled in her handbag but her hand was shaking so much she gave up. The priority was to stop the car. They could worry about ID later.

Would she make it? Yes, just, if she hurried. She broke into a trot. She would pass the roadworks before the BMW reached them. Easily. The road repairs looked like…well, nothing. Just tarmac. Impossible to think of it as dangerous in any way. Just a few metres to go. Come on, Tess. Be professional. God, her stomach hurt. Ignore it, girl. Everything would be all right, of course it would.

Her breath was harsh in her throat, her heart pounding. No one else around. No pedestrians. All clear. Here we go, Tess. Slow down a little, don't alarm them. *Your ID*, come *on*. *Think*. Dip into the bag again. Hands a bit better now. *Got it.* OK – step out in front, nice and easy…

Chapter 34

From the ground floor bay window of a Victorian semi-detached house directly opposite the maternity unit entrance, JC slipped an automatic from his inside pocket. Precautionary, Gilmore had told him at the hurried briefing. *Just turn up. Hang around. Be available and unobtrusive.* No problem, that's what he did; that's what he was trained for. Just a low priority gig. Watch the lady arrive, make sure she gets inside safely. Pop in after a few minutes, keep a discreet distance. See she gets back to the car, off to wherever privileged young women go after official visits. Bucklebury, no doubt, to see the parents. Just a few miles west of Reading; near the Blue Pool, he recalled, where that MP had topped himself after some call-girl scandal last February. The name escaped him, but it was a rich, middle-class area, anyway, packed with cosy country pubs where stockbrokers and lawyers rubbed shoulders at the bar and put the world to rights over Sunday G&Ts or pints of real ale.

It was a world he resented. The privileged set – public school, captains of rugby, cricket, football. Head of House. Oxford or Cambridge. What the hell did *they* know about what he did, about the crap he had to go through to protect the likes of them? The endless hours of surveillance, the fear, the sheer discomfort of undercover ops.

Anyway, such were his orders. Keep the lady safe. But unofficially, of course, he was here for entirely the opposite reason. At briefing he'd pushed himself forward for prime position and there'd been no objections. Which meant he'd been able to call the shots – no pun intended – for which team member went where today, and in particular where he was going to position himself, which was in just the right place to make sure nothing stopped the car driving over the prepared ground. Come to think of it, he couldn't think of a time when the team had been quite so willing, so compliant. Funny they'd all fallen into line so easily. Was that something he should worry about? Probably not. It had been a busy few weeks. Nobody fancied being stressed out today, that was the prevailing vibe, so the job was all his. Perfect. His hand went to his pocket, felt the contours of the mobile phone. One code, one call. *Boom.* And then at the debrief, sharing the disappointment, the outrage. Pointing the finger – well away from himself, naturally. 'We missed it; how did we not *know?*'…

He'd been able to keep the primary snippet of intelligence well hidden, the location and nature of the threat, which was pleasing. It was all about distraction, misinformation. And he was damn good at that, though he said so himself. It hadn't been easy; his team hadn't been recruited for their gullibility or lack of incisive thinking. They were all bright sparks, which made his counter-operation success even more satisfying. The Irish should be paying him a lot more. Maybe he'd ask for a rise at their next meeting. Shame about the Duchess; she seemed a decent sort, but that wasn't his problem. Tomorrow's newspapers would be ablaze, just like her car.

JC glanced at his watch. Right on cue, his headset sprang into life.

'Charlie One Eleven, update please.'

'Charlie One Eleven. In position. All quiet.'

'Base, roger. Stay in position. Keep us updated. ETA two minutes.'

At that precise moment JC caught sight of a woman walking unsteadily along the pavement on the opposite side of the road. Probably nothing, but there was something about her which brought him to full alert. She seemed purposeful, not just some random outpatient walking to the bus stop.

He glanced to his right where he had an unobstructed view down to London Road. *There we go.* A black BMW was smoothing its way up towards the hospital. There was nothing connecting the woman to the vehicle except his intuition. Not sixth sense, *hyper-vigilance.* It was probably nothing, but he slipped the safety off anyway and watched.

The woman and the car were equidistant from the slick tarmac stain of the recently completed roadworks. He watched the woman carefully. She was looking in her bag for something. She withdrew her hand and he saw the tremors even from this distance. A nut job? Harmless, probably. Not bad looking… Wait a minute, though… she looked familiar.

The woman broke into a run. He was at the door in seconds. She hadn't spotted him yet. He paused by the low wall of the semi's drive, crouched low. The BMW continued its effortless glide along the road. Now it was barely a couple of metres from the woman. He gripped the handgun and prepared to call a warning. That was when she changed tack and ran into the road, straight in front of the Beamer.

Damn. It's the copper. DC Martin.

DC Martin's hand went into her handbag a second time. She was going to stop the bloody car.

Stop. Put your bag down. Now!

She turned in surprise, saw him, but her hand stayed in the bag. The BMW had slowed, just a metre away, engine purring. From the corner of his eye, a flash of red hair in a parked car – this side of the police cordon, twenty metres distant, maybe twenty-five. His old friend, RED ROOSTER, the electronics whiz, nicely in position, backing him up like she'd said.

Wait, there was some disturbance, some kerfuffle by the cordon…But he had to get Martin out of the way, she mustn't stop the car. He curled his finger around the trigger, lined up the shot, kept his eye on the copper. *Stupid cow.*

She saw him. '*No!* It's all right,' she shouted back, wild-eyed. 'I'm a *poli–*'

Something in the corner of his eye, something not right. Someone else, watching. Not his team mate. Recognition failure. Too late, anyhow; he was committed. He squeezed and felt the gun buck as the bullet discharged. Martin went down. Was the car close enough? The Beamer was still moving, the driver maybe trying to process what he'd just seen, or *thought* he'd seen.

Was it close enough?

It would have to do.

He took out the mobile, punched the number. Stepped back …

The road erupted, parted like an earthquake. The tarmac

tore open as if some subterranean monster was clawing its way up to the surface. A blinding flash gave way to a warm funnel of air which lifted him off his feet and threw him across the pavement into the front garden of the house he'd just left.

He lay on his back, dazed, for ten, twenty seconds before his training kicked in. He scrambled onto his belly, peered over the wall. A pall of smoke hung over the road. The Beamer was slewed to one side, seemed intact, maybe a broken windscreen, front tyres melted, rear door opening, uninjured passenger by the look of it but the all-clear not yet given…

Running feet, a blur of uniforms, high-vis jackets coming from all directions. Smoke drifted and curled around a single body lying at the roadside by the lip of the yawning crater formed by the explosion. The blast had been directed vertically, as RED ROOSTER had predicted. Max force into the car cab, that was the idea … except that the car hadn't reached the spot. His gun was lying a few metres away. He couldn't remember dropping it. Sloppy.

He retrieved the weapon, pocketed it, moved towards the Beamer in a running crouch. At the junction with London Road the parked car he had seen had its doors open. RED ROOSTER was over the bonnet, held down by a black guy – ah, the copper, Odunsi. Others, too – the DI, Pepper, and two uniforms … anyway, that was RED ROOSTER's problem. He'd played his part. JC joined the paramedics gathered around the fallen woman's body and saw that she was holding a lanyard on which hung a photo ID – *Detective Constable Tess Martin.*

A gaggle of uniforms had surrounded the BMW. A tall

woman in her thirties, instantly recognisable, was being helped out. She seemed unhurt, just dazed. She wanted to go to the copper's assistance but an aide was saying *no*, holding her back. The BMW driver was standing on the pavement, shaking his head, bleeding from facial cuts, arguing with the paramedics, insisting they look to his passenger, leave him be. Shock: it did funny things to the mind. The guy was just doing his job.

Just like he was.

But now it was time to leave.

Worry about the fallout later. As he walked away he threw a backward glance at the medics working on Tess Martin's prone body. If she kicked it, he'd be OK – no witnesses. He glanced around, nervous now. That other guy he'd caught in his peripheral … no sign of him. Maybe the old hyper-vigilance thing was playing him up – had *made* it up. The shrink said that was always possible, but it usually happened after the job, not during it. Like what happened with Jane, during the night. His daughter, in the doorway. *'Why are you hurting Mummy?'*

Another glance back, through the drifting smoke. Crowds were gathering. The defib machine had appeared, was being applied. Tess Martin's body jerked once, twice. He kept going, thumbed his radio button.

'Charlie One Eleven, aborting. Heavy police presence onsite. Asset safe.' He felt a stab of frustration hearing himself say the words. 'Charlie One Eleven, I repeat, asset safe.'

He was halfway along London Road, hood up, trying to ignore the sirens, the constant flow of emergency vehicles, when the black car pulled up alongside. He made a rapid assessment. Not the Irish, too obtrusive. Not the team – they'd use a van, leastways that's what they'd always used before for quick pickups and in any case, Control hadn't been in touch to say they were picking him up.

He kept walking, past the Chinese students' building, keeping to the inside of the pavement, ready to cut away if need be. But there was a guy waiting, just ahead by Kendrick Road. JC glanced behind. Another guy, walking towards him in a leisurely fashion. OK – other side, by the garage. He made a further, quick mental reconnaissance. Three cars, one filling up, one driving away. One waiting in one of three parking slots away from the pumps. Red hair, shoulder length. Watching him. Watching the pick up. RED ROOSTER. *What the hell?*

He tried his radio. 'Charlie One Eleven. I have a slight problem. Please acknowledge.'

No response.

'Charlie One Eleven. Require assistance urgently. Please respond.'

Nothing. Not even static.

The electric rear window of the black car slid down soundlessly, and a cultured, well-mannered voice spoke. 'Hop in JC, old chap. No fuss, there's a good fellow. We'd like to have a word.'

JC moistened his lips. This time, he knew there was nowhere else to go.

Chapter 35

Moran hauled the dinghy up the beach and secured it alongside a group of jagged, seaweed-encrusted rocks. It would be partially hidden from any casual observer, something which might be desirable in the not-too-distant future. Thankfully, the weather had remained fair and the sea calm; he doubted whether his half-remembered seamanship skills would have risen to the challenge of poor visibility, or even worse, high winds and rain.

Not for the first time he wondered how Charlie was faring, how close they were to exposing Black's plot. He fished out his mobile. Dead. His home team were on their own. Best just to concentrate on what he could achieve in the here and now. He checked the dinghy's moorings with a firm tug and, satisfied, set off inland.

The silent, sorrowful derelicts of Blasket observed his progress with hollow-windowed indifference. Moran headed the way his instinct told him to go – that and O'Mahoney's vitriolic aside to O'Shea, *I believe he's a mind to evict you from your cosy wee house…*

O'Shea's house it was, then. And Black probably had a great deal more than eviction on his mind; Moran couldn't recall precisely how many of the long, shallow boxes he had counted on his last visit, but it was more than a few – more than enough to guarantee a warm reception. Moran tramped on, noting familiar landmarks as he went. He paused to mop his brow, glanced at his watch. Two o'clock. Later than he'd thought.

Moran picked up the pace and his leg shot him a reminder. He shrugged it off and concentrated on putting one foot after the other and thoughts of failure aside. There was nothing he could do about Geileis; he had to trust to O'Shea's expertise. Donal would recover. Padraig's issues would be mental, not physical. Which left two women: one a commoner, one as high-profile as you could get, but both relying on the half-baked plans of an inappropriately dressed and ill-prepared middle-aged policeman. The odds, he acknowledged, weren't great. But they never were. It was how you played your hand that counted, not the hand itself.

There was something bright on the path ahead, catching the rays of the afternoon sun. Moran reached the spot and picked up a silver charm bracelet. It was Aine's; he recalled commenting on the various objects dangling from its circlet. A cluster of stars, an angel, a crucifix, a lucky pixie – or leprechaun more likely – and a half-moon. A smorgasbord of superstition and religion. Moran called it hedging your bets, had commented as much while they'd been holed up in O'Shea's house. 'You have to believe in *something*, Brendan,' Aine had replied. And he, insensitive as always, had responded: 'Something, maybe, but not *everything*.' Moran pocketed the bracelet and continued along the path. Here, in the shadow of An Cro Mor, Great Blasket's brooding mountain, he could understand why human beings, particularly in isolated communities such as had existed here, clung to such superstition, their stories and traditions handed down generation by generation until one day there was no one left to receive them.

Moran tramped on, battling a growing sense of despondency at the futility of his mission. Even if he succeeded in freeing Aine from Black's clutches, how could he communicate his success to Charlie? His mobile was dead, and even if some spark of charge could be coaxed from the battery, the likelihood of obtaining a signal was remote. He would be too late; Caitlin Hannigan would carry out Black's plan and there was nothing he could do about it.

Too late.

The voice in his head whispered again. *As usual. You were too late to save Janice; now you'll be too late to save Aine.*

And too late, maybe, to save a future queen.

Moran set his teeth to the wind and concentrated on placing one foot after the other. He half-expected to see O'Shea's distant figure leading him on as before, the occasional turn of the head to check on his slower progress. Was it his imagination, or was there indeed a figure up ahead? He shielded his eyes from the glare of the sinking sun. Yes, just where the path meandered around an anvil-shaped bluff which jutted over the rocks, a stooped figure appeared to be making slow but steady progress, pausing occasionally as if waiting, as O'Shea had done, for him to catch up.

Moran wasn't superstitious by nature, but he was well-versed in the folklore of the region, having spent many a dark evening during his teens scaring the pants off Janice, Geileis and Donal with tales of, among others, the *Hag of*

Beara, the goddess of winter – a deity said to grow younger and stronger as the seasons gave way to spring. By winter, however, she had metamorphosed into a hideous old crone, holding the fate of the people in her hands during Ireland's harshest season. Legend had it that the hag was eventually turned to stone.

Moran shaded his eyes again. The figure had disappeared, in its place a mound of rocks. He rubbed his eyes.

It's not the goddess who'll decide the outcome here, Brendan, just yourself…

A few minutes more and he would reach the bluff. From this vantage point, he remembered, he would catch his first glimpse of O'Shea's eco-house. The ground was rising and the going getting tougher but Moran set his mind and feet to the task and tried not to think about his leg. *Take it easy*, Dr Purewal had advised. *Your hiking days are over.*

He made the bluff, rested up for a minute or so. As he'd recalled, the eco-house was visible, lying in the lee of the hill facing the sea. He could see someone on the decking, although he was still too far away to make out any detail. Not a wasted journey, then. No point trying to be covert; he was in the open now, easily visible from the house. He set off at a steady pace towards O'Shea's DIY creation.

He'd only taken ten or so paces when he heard it: a high, piercing, whistle similar to the noise of a low-flying jet, only faster, louder … there was a tremendous *whoosh* as something passed overhead. Moran hit the ground. The explosion came from some way behind, but he still felt the force of the blast. A storm of tiny particles pattered to earth around him and lay, fizzing and smoking on the mossy grass. It was a new experience for Moran but he knew exactly what was happening.

Mortar.

He racked his brains for survival rules. *Lie flat, don't move when the first one hits. Better to let the shrapnel rain down than have it pass straight through you … find the lowest point. Look for water. Water lies low.*

He lifted his head. The smoke was clearing; the danger from the first round was over. But what about the next?

Moran glanced around. He'd been saved by the rock formation; his goddess had come good. The shell had fallen directly behind the rocks, where he'd been standing just a minute before. Damn good ranging. Which meant the next one would be more accurate still…

Think, Moran, think…

Had he read somewhere that you shouldn't run *away* from a mortar attack, you should run *towards* it. Because it's more difficult for the enemy to get the trajectory right…

But run? He could hardly *walk*, let alone run.

Moran got to his feet and began an awkward, bent-over trot towards the distant eco-house. He was out of cover now. He just had to trust that Black's marksmanship would be off. Maybe he'd used the only available shell. Maybe…

This time he heard a soft *whump* as the shell left the mortar tube. As the whistle escalated in volume he scanned the ground ahead. There was a dip to his right – not much of a dip, true, but it was the lowest on offer, so he altered course slightly and went for it, pitched himself forward in an awkward dive, hit the ground hard, felt his ribs protest on impact. He covered his head, pressed his nose into the grass.

The noise was huge this time, a sky-rending crack of doom. Clods of earth and soil crashed down around him and his lungs filled with acrid, foul-smelling smoke.

The shot was long. Moran counted to three, got to his feet. Dazed and shocked, he staggered forward. The eco-house swam in and out of focus. His sanctuary, his nemesis.

His legs weren't working properly. Had he been hit? No, no blood. All limbs intact. Running was beyond him for now so he did what he could, stumbled on…

The whistle was louder this time; Black had gone for a lower trajectory. Moran pitched himself forward, spreadeagled his body onto the springy turf. This time he prayed.

And waited.

He heard the wind catch in the shell's fins as it succumbed to gravity, spiralled lazily down towards him. The ground trembled as if someone had struck it with a mallet.

Closest yet…

Moran covered his head with his hands and waited for the explosion, or oblivion.

Nothing.

He risked a quick glance. The mortar's tail fin was embedded in the grass three metres ahead.

Dud.

Moran got to his feet, fear lending him, if not wings, then at least sufficient motor ability to keep going. He gulped air, saw that he was closing the distance between him and the artilleryman. His leg shot him bolts of pain as he pounded across the canted expanse of grass.

Better lame than in bits, Brendan…

He kept going, his lungs on fire and his breath coming in short gasps. Now he could see the figure on the decking more clearly. Black, had to be, bent over a cylindrical tube, working the mechanism, preparing one last attempt to blow him to pieces.

He was too close now, surely? Yes, the guy had straightened up. Hands on hips, watching him approach. Moran slowed to a standstill, bent at the waist, hands on knees, gasping for breath. When he looked up again Black had disappeared inside the house.

Another minute passed as Moran took stock, felt himself all over, checked for shrapnel damage. His heart was pounding and his ears ringing from the blasts. He'd been lucky.

Damn lucky.

The house was silent now. No movement.

He was completely exposed, but so what? He felt strangely elated, self-aware. Two minutes ago he'd thought he was going to die, but here he was, miraculously intact. Another omen from the goddess. Moran sank to his haunches at the perimeter. He could taste the dry, acidic tang of explosive and his tongue was sticking to the roof of his mouth. He found his water bottle, drank deeply, and noted with surprise that his hands were steady. At least he now knew for sure what kind of man he was dealing with, if there had ever been any doubt; Black had lived up to his reputation in spectacular fashion. Sure, Moran might have expected the guy to take a few pot shots at him, but not on this scale. The guy had tried to take him out, plain and simple. Survival rates weren't the best when it came to mortar strikes, that was a given. Yet here he was.

Lucky, Brendan … lucky, lucky…

The contrast between the last few adrenaline-fuelled minutes and the absolute silence now surrounding the house was eerie, almost unreal. Moran was struck again by the same sense of isolation he'd felt on his first visit. O'Shea's home was, to all intents and purposes, Europe's last outpost, a lone sentinel perched here on the island with only the gulls and waves for company. Under the circumstances, Black could hardly have chosen a more appropriate location.

At that moment, as if on cue, the door opened and the same tall, well-built guy appeared on the decking. There was a passing resemblance to O'Shea, but the eyes were narrower, darker, the body language and facial expression hard and uncompromising. Moran was familiar enough with the look to recognise the stamp of fanaticism when he saw it.

'Bit late in the day, DCI Moran. Enjoy the fireworks?'

No doubt now. It was the brogue he had last heard on the mobile phone – the unmistakeable mocking tone of a man confident that he had the situation under complete control.

Moran nodded. 'First rule of battle: check your weaponry. Bit sloppy, I thought.'

'Ah well, I'll be blamin' my wee bro for the dud. But it does give me the opportunity to meet you properly.'

'I trust you won't be disappointed.'

Black laughed. 'Well I have to say you're lookin' fair dishevelled, Brendan, but good on youse – you made it, despite my best efforts – not that I was *really* trying to hit you, you understand. Just a bit of fun. But tell me, did you enjoy meetin' my little bar girl? Dead ringer, I thought.'

'I'd rather it'd been Aine, to be honest.'

'Honest! There you go. An honest man is hard to find these days.'

'I'd like to contact Caitlin. Let her know her mother is safe. I assume she *is* safe?'

Black scratched his cheek. 'Come away in, Brendan. I can't be offering hospitality out here.'

'Let me see Aine first.'

Black came down the wooden steps, two at a time. His movements were languid but surprisingly quick for a big man. Although the mortar tube was on its side, smoking gently, harmless now, Moran took an involuntary step back.

'Jumpy, Brendan?' Black came to a halt just outside the boundary of Moran's personal space. 'Can't blame you for that, I suppose. But you've lost, my friend; better get used to the idea. The game's over. Too late, the hero.'

Moran saw the pistol nestling in Black's easy grip. The Irishman could kill him where he stood, throw him over the cliff. It would be days, weeks maybe before his remains washed up on a beach somewhere.

'You can't know for certain.' Moran kept his voice low and conversational to match Black's. 'You'll be lucky to get any kind of signal out here.'

'Sure, but if I hadn't thought of that you'd be callin' me a stupid Irishman, am I right?'

'You have a radio?'

'Satellite phone, Brendan. Heard of them? You being from the bakelite era an' all?'

'Of course.' That was one less thing to worry about. He could get hold of Charlie.

'So, what's the story?' Black looked at his watch. 'Around eight and a half minutes till zero hour, I make it. All you have to do is knock me over the head, make the call, and hope your home team can persuade Caitlin not to hit the button. Does that about cover it, Brendan? Or am I missing somethin'?'

252

'You might be, as it happens.'

'I'm listening.'

Moran would have liked to tell Black exactly what he was missing, but that would have meant putting Aine in a potentially life-threatening situation. He tried to keep his eyes focused on Black instead of Aine's measured, creeping progress from the eco-house's front door to the top of the wooden steps. A resourceful woman as ever, the lock hadn't presented much of a problem. Aine's face was pale, her expression murderous. In her right hand she held what looked to Moran like a short length of lead piping.

He kept eye contact with Black, moved his arms, tried to channel the Irishman's focus. 'Caitlin won't do it, Sean.'

'Oh, she'll do it all right.' He jerked his head towards the eco-house. 'Her and her ma – they're like two peas in a pod. Inseparable.'

'You'd kill Aine? With your history?'

Black's face expressed mild surprise. 'Ah, you know, then. I suppose that's fair play, you bein' the big detective man. A one-sided attraction, Brendan. Useful back in the day, but you know how these things are, affairs of the heart? Well, the one you're talkin' about is well past its expiry date.'

Aine's mouth curled into a snarl as she edged closer, bare feet soundless on the decking; another two steps and she'd be within range.

'As are contra-UK paramilitary campaigns.'

The Irishman's expression changed in an instant. 'No, no, no.' Black shook his head. 'You're so wrong, Brendan. I'm not done with England yet.'

'But most, if not all, your contemporaries *are*. 1998? Good Friday? Mean anything to you?'

'Nothing. It means *nothing*.'

'You're decommissioned, Sean.'

'*Never*.'

At that moment Aine swung the piping but Black seemed to sense something, moved forward a fraction, turned...

The blow caught Black on his shoulder blade. He staggered, almost lost his footing, righted himself as Aine came in for a second strike. Black recovered fast; he ducked under Aine's swing, spun around and caught her by the throat. The piping clattered to the decking. It was over in a split second.

Breathing hard, Black hoisted Aine off her feet. Her hands scrabbled and scratched at his muscular arms but Black's grip was firm. Moran made as if to assist but Black's eyes shot him a warning. Aine's cheeks were turning blue, eyes bulging, legs kicking. Black relaxed his grip a fraction, set her feet back onto the decking. She took a whoop of air, coughed, spat, cursed, struggled.

'Fiery little girl, you are, eh?' Black said in Aine's ear. 'I should've remembered. But memory's a funny thing; not always to be trusted, eh, Brendan?'

He dragged Aine towards the door, all the while keeping his arm wrapped firmly around her neck, the pistol pressing into her flesh. Aine's heels trailed helplessly along the boards. 'Come on in, Brendan, why don't you? We'll drink a toast and you can be on your way, back to your English lords, eh?'

Moran accepted the invitation. No point staying out here; whatever chance he had would have to be taken at close quarters. He kept his eyes fixed on Black as he took a cautious step forward.

'What good'll it do you, Sean? D'you think high-profile

murder'll get you more support?'

Black hauled Aine over the threshold, breathless with the effort of keeping a conversation up while dealing with a kicking and twisting woman. 'They'll pay a damn sight more attention, that much I know. But this is just the *beginning*, Brendan. They'll soon know who they're dealing with. Now, you'd better come away in, my friend, where I can keep an eye on you.'

Chapter 36

The interior of O'Shea's house was unchanged since Moran's last visit. A recently kindled fire burned in the islander's improvised grate. As his eyes grew accustomed to the flickering light he saw that the packing cases were still in situ. No, he was mistaken. One was missing. Moran glanced through the skirt of glass which formed the rear of the eco-house. The missing box was just outside, lid half-on, half-off, as if O'Shea – or perhaps Black – had been interrupted during an inspection of its contents.

'Let her go, Sean.'

Black jammed the pistol harder into Aine's neck. 'She'd have brained me without a second thought and you want me to let her go? I don't think so, Brendan. We'll just sit the next few minutes out, if it's all the same to you. Help yourself to a drink.'

Moran cocked an eyebrow. 'It's your brother's hospitality you'll be offering, Sean, but I'm sure Joseph won't object.'

'Him? The faint-hearted sibling? Keep *still*, will you?' Black tightened his grip, and although Aine dug her nails into his flesh, drew her closer. Aine's eyes were signalling Moran; she was trying to tell him something …

'Don't think I've come alone, Sean. The gardai aren't far behind.'

'Right, and the whole army along with them.'

'I'm serious. Take a look if you don't believe me. You've seen Joseph's observation tower?' Moran indicated the rear door beyond which O'Shea's Heath Robinson contraption was sited on a raised platform like some cast-off attraction from a downbeat travelling fair.

'Maybe you can take a look for me, Brendan. On you go.' Black motioned with his gun hand, easing the pressure on Aine's neck.

Aine reacted instantly, grabbing Black's wrist and jerking the automatic towards his head; her slim finger curled through the trigger guard, clamped over Black's finger and pulled.

The gun went off, the bullet striking the roof somewhere above Moran's head. He ducked instinctively but Aine wasn't finished; in control of the automatic's trigger, if not the direction of its bullets, she fought against Black's stronger arm, the gun waving this way and that until, inevitably, Black gained the upper hand and heaved the pistol's muzzle to Aine's chest.

Moran hadn't been idle during this frantic exchange; the shotgun was now firmly in his grip. All he needed was a clear target.

'Go on, Brendan. Blow us to kingdom come, why don't you?' Black was breathing heavily, sweat clinging to his brow like drops of rain on a cracked windscreen.

The gun was over Aine's heart. Moran had no clear shot; with an automatic, possibly, but with a shotgun? The spread would annihilate both of them. He lowered O'Shea's weapon of choice.

'Break it.'

Moran broke the shotgun. Two new cartridges were in place. He hadn't been sure. At least he knew now, for all the good it was likely to do him.

'Put it down. Carefully. On the table.'

Moran put the gun down.

'Brendan, I'm sorry.' Aine's voice was a husky whisper.

'Don't be – just keep calm. I–'

'No, you need to listen.'

Aine's finger was still jammed against Black's, against the automatic's trigger. Something about her tone made Moran's heart begin to pound in a slow, unsteady rhythm.

'A story, is it, Brendan?' Black was breathing heavily. 'Well, let's listen to the lady. Nothing else to do, eh?'

'I want you to know that I'm truly, truly sorry.' Aine's eyes never left Moran's. She spoke as if Black's presence had become immaterial, as if he had been relegated to some ghostly location where he could do them no harm. Black seemed to feel this too, and it showed in the subtle change of his expression.

The Irishman sniffed. 'Get on with it, woman.'

'I was young,' Aine continued. 'Not to make an excuse, but we were all idealists in those days, weren't we, Brendan? I followed a call, just as you did. But mine was wicked, and wrong. This man was my guide, my leader, and I want you to know that I regret my discipleship deeply.'

Moran could only listen. He felt a creeping dread at what might be coming.

'That day, when you met her for lunch. It was such a fine day, wasn't it? Until the clouds came, and the rain began –

slowly at first, I remember, just a fine mist, then heavier and heavier till it was a downpour. But by then I was running, as fast as I could. I heard it, you see; I heard the explosion even as I ran. As I've heard it every day since.'

Moran shook his head. This wasn't right, couldn't be right. 'No, *no!*' he shouted. 'It was Rory Dalton. It was done under *his* orders—' he broke off, opened his hands beseechingly, willing her to deny it '—but *you?* What are you saying? My *God*, Aine, what—'

Aine's hand was steady, her finger steely, curled and ready. 'It wasn't Dalton, Brendan. Although he might have taken credit for it to rile you – sure that's the sort of thing he'd have done. Now listen to me; I can't atone for what I did. I won't try. But maybe this, at least, will help. Stop this terrible thing from happening. Speak to my daughter. Tell her I died for something worthwhile, at least. And tell Donal and Padraig that I love them.'

Moran held up his hands. 'Aine. Please, you don't have to do this, you—'

In that instant Black understood Aine's body language, tried to twist away, but Aine held him close. 'I'm so sorry, Brendan,' she whispered, and squeezed down hard.

The shot threw the entwined couple against the wall. Aine slumped forward. Black staggered into a half-crouched position, his shirt bright red with Aine's – or his own – blood; Moran couldn't be sure. Black straightened, was trying to extricate his grip from the gun, but Aine's lifeless finger had his right hand trapped. The shotgun was lying on the table, broken, where Moran had placed it.

Up for grabs.

Moran got there first, grabbed the stock and turned, but

Black, using Aine's body for cover, had raised the automatic again. Moran fell back, made contact with the rear door, fumbled the shotgun, dropped it as Black's round clipped past his head. The shotgun crashed to the floor, still broken, lost a cartridge. The round rolled diagonally across the floor and came to rest against one of the table legs.

Black had managed to extricate his finger; he discarded Aine's body like a sack of unwanted clothing, began to close the distance between them, savouring the moment.

'Just me and you, Brendan. And that's how it should be.'

'You had a woman do your dirty work.' Moran edged towards the open hearth where he could at least be sure of partial cover. 'Too much of a coward to do it yourself, Sean. Eh? Is that what you're like? Does it give you a feeling of power, having women under your control?'

'I didn't know she was going to be drivin' your car that day, Brendan.' Black shrugged, as if apologising for some minor offence. 'I liked both the Hannigan girls, sure enough. What can I say? You got away with it. I never got a second chance to take you out. But now...' Black crept forward another pace. 'Now we're full circle; it's all come around again. Like I hoped it would.'

Moran stepped briskly to the fire and seized the cool end of a burning shard of timber. It wasn't much but it was something. Splinters scored his flesh.

'You'd hit me with your wee piece of wood, would you now, Brendan? Well I don't *think* so...'

Black jinked to the left, snapped off a shot.

Moran felt it zip past his right ear, strike somewhere on the eco-house's set of aircraft windows, blow out a pane. He retreated to the back door, pushed against it, felt the decking beneath his feet, a brisk wind blowing in from the Atlantic. How many bullets did Black have left? One at least. Two, maybe…

The decking afforded little cover, just the steel gate of O'Shea's scissor lift. Steel was good. Moran backed away from the door, right hand outstretched, waving the burning log as if warding off some lumbering Hollywood monster.

The monster appeared in the doorway. The gun rose to Black's eye level, steadied. This one was going to count.

This one might have your name on it, Brendan…

Moran continued his retreat, feeling behind him with his left hand, never taking his eyes off Black's automatic. His hand found metal and he felt a slight give; the gate was unlocked.

'Game over, Brendan.'

Moran judged his throw. He'd always been rubbish at football; rugby was more his thing. He remembered the fly-half's job; stoop low, scoop up the ball, a lobbing spin out to centre, the feeling of elation as the centre picked it up, dodged, made his own pass.

Job done.

He had one shot at this, and it was a hard target. Not fair, but then life never was.

Moran took aim and let the brand fly; it was more a lob than a throw. The burning wood arced across the short distance and for a moment Moran's stomach lurched; he'd missed completely. He'd pitched long. But his goddess was still on point; the brand struck the eco-house's wall of many windows and bounced off at an angle.

The angle was good.

The glowing timber disappeared into the half-open

ammunition box before Black had the time or wit to mock Moran's effort.

Moran reckoned he had a precious few seconds. Not long enough, but he gave it a go. He fell back again, this time onto – and into – the scissor-lift platform, felt the steel shutter spin shut on its spring. His hand reached out to the two buttons. One was blue, the other red. Blue for go.

Blue. *Please God.*

Moran's stomach protested as the lift shot up at the speed he recalled from O'Shea's demonstration.

The explosion came a fraction of a second later, a crackling crump of exploding ammonal which sent a shockwave outwards and upwards. Moran felt the lift judder and rock, and for a moment thought the whole contraption was doomed. How high was he?

High enough…

The lift held. Once the initial blast had dissipated the violent swaying eased, settled into a gentle, horizontal, side-to-side bumping.

Moran lay on the platform and waited until the movement had eased to a point where he thought he might be able to stand and take stock. His hands grasped the platform's flimsy walls, just steel netting stretched over thin, supporting rods. He pulled himself up and peered over the side.

The devastation below took him by surprise. The decking was matchwood, the lift's survival presumably due to the strength of the steel base which supported it. The eco-house too was half-demolished; the glass wall lay in glittering shards among shredded woodwork and O'Shea's personal belongings. Far off to the right he caught sight of Black's shirt, ripped, reddened and blackened. The half-destroyed roof revealed Aine's prone body, still lying where she had fallen.

Moran prayed and pressed the red button. If the electrics had been damaged he'd have no recourse except a risky descent; he'd have to shin down the lift's scissor-frame, hope his strength would hold out and avoid any exposed high voltage cables on the way down.

The lift, however, obediently began a slow, if shaky, descent. Moran clung to the rail and tried to calm himself. His head was pounding and his hands shaking.

As he stepped off the platform his legs threatened to give way, but somehow they carried him automatically across the debris-strewn landscape and into the remains of O'Shea's house.

A search of the room revealed Black's satellite phone, secreted in an empty drawer along with a passport and some papers Moran didn't bother looking at. There was something lying on the floor, next to Aine's lifeless body. He bent and picked it up. Her photographs, fallen from her jeans pocket. He flicked through them; they were all of Caitlin. Here was the one she had showed him in the safe house. And another.

Wait. The background looked familiar. He studied the print. Thames House, surely? The photo had been taken on Lambeth Bridge, the unmistakeable bulk of MI5's headquarters looming behind.

The penny dropped with an almost palpable *clunk*.

Moran shook his head in disbelief. How had he missed it? The answer came quickly.

Because she was damn good, Moran, you thick Irish clod. She had you fooled, and Black too.

But not her mother. Not her closest buddy...

Moran looked from the photograph to Aine's pale face, back and forth, back and forth.

You knew, didn't you? You ran because you didn't want to compromise your daughter's operation. Not because you thought Caitlin would be forced to commit an act of terror if her mother's head was in Black's noose...

Moran fiddled with the satellite phone. He figured out how to turn it on after a minute or so; it took a while to get through. But time was of no consequence now. What had happened, had happened.

'Charlie? Yes, I'm all right. Listen, I'm sorry to have to tell you this...'

When he'd finished he threw the phone aside, went to the tattered sofa, sat down. Charlie had confirmed his theory: MI5 had caught a mole – an operational one at that, the most dangerous kind. So some good had come out of this after all.

Now there was no wall to hide it, he could see the sea directly ahead, the horizon a clear pencil line separating white-topped waves from grey-white sky.

And the lady was safe. The one who mattered. Moran repeated it over and over, taking the information in, rationalising everything, as he always did when ... well, when things were over.

The ones who mattered.

But who mattered, really, in the end?

He got up, creaked over the boards, knelt down by Aine's body. Took her hand. There was a lot of blood. But at least it would have been quick, no suffering.

She had tried to make amends the only way she could, and in doing so she had undoubtedly saved his life. Now he knew what had happened, all those years ago. He knew who was responsible. She'd made her last confession.

He found himself stroking her hand, trying to warm the cooling flesh. 'It's all right,' he told her. 'I forgive you.'

Tears stung his eyes, blurring his vision.

'God help me,' he said. 'God help me, but I do. I really do forgive you.'

Chapter 37

'How was I supposed to *know?* Just tell me that.'

'You couldn't have known, Bola,' Charlie said. 'None of us could.'

'I thought she had the trigger, that she was going to blow it—'

'I'd have done the same, Bola. I wouldn't have known either.'

'If she'd just *told me* that she was trying to jam the signal—'

'—then you wouldn't have believed her. There was no time, Bola, no time.'

'Tess was *there*. I mean, she was right *there*. If she hadn't been there, then—'

Charlie nodded. 'Yep, I know.'

Smoke was still rising from the crater outside the Craven Road entrance and a partial evacuation of the hospital was underway. The road was newly cordoned off by five squad cars, parked bumper-to-bumper across the junctions at each end. Eldon Road and London Road had been closed and hospital admissions transferred to the west entrance in Redlands Road.

A car was being waved through the cordon, a blue Lexus

saloon.

The Lexus parked on the opposite pavement and a slim woman in a smart, charcoal business suit stepped out. Her hair was short, brunette, no make up. She looked up and down the road, beeped the car locked and walked towards them.

'DI Pepper?'

'Yes. Who wants to know?'

'Detective Chief Superintendent Gilmore. Pleased to meet you at last.' She extended a slim hand.

Charlie looked at it. Looked at Gilmore.

Gilmore dropped her hand.

'You're upset. I understand that.'

'Upset? *Upset* doesn't cover it.'

Gilmore touched her arm. 'Can we go somewhere? Somewhere private?'

'DC Odunsi comes with me.' Charlie glanced at Bola. 'If you want to, that is, DC Odunsi.'

'You can brief me later, boss,' Bola said, looking Gilmore up and down. 'I'll be with Tess.'

'Of course.' Gilmore nodded. 'The gardens, then, perhaps, DI Pepper?'

Charlie nodded.

They crossed the strangely empty London Road and went into the memorial gardens. The square seemed sombre; borage weed was rampant and there were few perennials to lighten the impression of neglect. Gilmore perched herself on a bench and invited Charlie to join her on the peeling woodwork.

'I'll stand, thanks,' Charlie said.

'Very well.' Gilmore joined her hands together. 'The first

thing is, you must realise that I wasn't at liberty to impart any information which would be likely to compromise the operation.'

'You could have said *something*. I didn't need details. Just that there was something big going down. That's all.'

'I did make it very clear that we had everything covered, DI Pepper.'

Charlie said nothing. That was true, up to a point.

'And you thought I was being obstructive, uncooperative. Isn't that right?' Gilmore's tone was reasonable and measured.

'If I'd known—'

'—If you'd known, that would mean that I'd told you, which in turn would mean that sensitive information had been shared concerning a top secret operation, yes?'

Charlie fumed silently. She tore at a low-hanging branch, pulled a few leaves off.

'You must see that it wasn't within my remit to divulge such sensitive information.'

'To *hell* with your bloody remit.' Charlie waved her arm towards the hospital. 'I have one of my *best* officers in there. She might *die* because of your sodding *remit*.'

'I'll thank you to keep your voice down, DI Pepper.' Gilmore leaned forward. The senior officer's eyes were clear, as was the translucent skin at her temples. Creaseless; no laughter lines. A career woman, as Charlie had guessed, married to the job. 'The important things here are—' Gilmore spread the fingers of her left hand and rapped her pinky with her right forefinger. 'Number one. The Duchess is unharmed. Number two, we have caught a very dangerous mole, an on-the-ground operator who'd chucked in his chances with a terrorist organisation. He'd been on the highly suspect list for quite a while, and MI5 have gone to great lengths to expose him.'

'Via Caitlin Hannigan.' Charlie folded her arms.

'Yes.'

'Who was he? *Is* he?' The question took Charlie by surprise. But it mattered, she realised; she wanted to know. She owed the team that much. She owed it to Tess.

'A senior operative, sadly. One of our best. Money problems – he took a bribe.' Gilmore reached into her pocket, produced a passport-size photograph, handed it to Charlie. 'Keep it.'

Charlie examined the photograph. Young guy, mid-thirties. Good looking, in a rough sort of way. Nondescript, really. The type of bloke you passed every day in the shopping mall, down the pub, at the gym.

'Caitlin put her neck on the line to catch him. We owe her a great deal.'

'I arrested her, for God's sake. I was going to charge her with *murder*.'

'We had the situation under control. And we had faith in Ms Hannigan's abilities. It's not *any* Tom Dick or Harry who gets selected for her kind of deep cover work, I can tell you.'

'What a mess. What a bloody awful *mess*.' Charlie threw the crushed leaves down, swept a hand over her hair.

'Not from our perspective, as I'm trying to make clear. Our mole has been outed, our asset is safe. And furthermore, we have the names of most – if not all – of the top UK-based contacts associated with Sean Black.'

'DI Pepper?' A uniform appeared at the gate.

Charlie raised her arm. What now?

'I have DCI Moran patched through on my radio. He wants a word.'

'Coming.'

'I expect we'll want a word with DCI Moran too,' Gilmore said. 'When he sees fit to return.'

'Not now, George.' Charlie didn't need to look up. She recognised the knock.

The door opened anyway.

'I need to know. Sorry, I just–' George McConnell made futile gestures with his hands.

Charlie took a deep breath, pressed her hands wearily to her eyes. 'She'll live. That's all I can say. That's all they could tell me. She lost a lot of blood. Her heart stopped. They got her back while she was still on the road. She's burned, but not badly – the bomb was designed to explode vertically, which probably saved her life. She was in theatre within five minutes. She was in the right place, in that sense.'

George nodded. 'The right place.'

'Look, George, I know what you're thinking. I had no choice, you understand that, don't you?'

George stood in front of her desk, tight-lipped, nodded again.

'If I hadn't sent Tess in, the car might have been a few metres closer to the bomb. The Duchess–'

'Right, right. The Duchess.'

Charlie swallowed hard, moistened her lips. She could see that George was trembling, keeping himself under control with some considerable effort. She opened a drawer, took out the photograph Gilmore had given her. 'This is the guy MI5 were after. The mole.'

George took the photograph and gave it a cursory glance. 'So we can all sleep safe in our beds tonight. One less baddie to worry about.' He handed it back.

Charlie wasn't fooled. 'You recognise him. How come?'

George shook his head vehemently. '*Recognise* him? No way. Never seen him before in my life.'

'Are you sure?'

'Of course I'm sure.'

Charlie narrowed her eyes. Should she probe further? Was it significant?

Let it go, Charlie – now's not the time…

'Like I said,' George ploughed on. 'He's just another bad guy off the street, right?'

Charlie nodded. 'Right. And who knows how many lives saved? It's a good result, George, despite the fact that we nearly screwed the whole thing up.'

George opened his mouth to reply, thought better of it, contented himself with a muttered expletive.

'It's over, George. There's nothing else we can do.'

'Aye, it's too late, so too bad.'

Charlie had no answer to that, so she just gave her officer a tight smile. 'Thanks for your efforts, George. Go home. Tomorrow's another day.'

She watched George McConnell's retreating figure, anger and hurt radiating from his body like a force field, until she lost sight of him at the far end of the IR. Charlie looked at her desktop with its piles of files and papers. The file directly in front of her, in its buff vanilla folder, was labelled

Theresa Jane Martin. DC. TVP. DOB 10/12/1981.

Should she go back to the hospital? Or wait for news? She wanted to be there when Tess came round. It was only right.

Because, at the end of the day, Charlie, it was down to you. It was your call.

Charlie went to the internal window and shut the blinds.

What would Moran say on his return? How would he judge her? He'd left her in charge…

Charlie sat back down at her desk, thumbing Tess Martin's file, bending the corner up and down, up and down until the label blurred and swam out of focus.

I'm sorry, Tess. I'm so sorry.

George McConnell waited across the road from the unremarkable-looking semi-detached house, loitering in the lamp light like an assignee on some undercover stakeout. Which would have been a strong preference; it had taken a huge effort of will to get *this* far, especially with two pubs en route. To say that he could murder a drink would be a wild understatement. But truth be told, the photo had shaken him badly. It had all come back in a rush. The pub, the fight; the guy who'd tried to bottle him.

The mole.

He'd had a close encounter with the mole, the centrepiece of the whole operation, and frankly, *anything* could have happened. Everything had been a blank the following day; a blinding headache, total amnesia. But one glance at the photo had lit the whole scene up as if under a spotlight: the guy had pushed him outside, made a spectacle of him – and in doing so had probably saved his life. George remembered his reaction, what he'd said to Charlie.

Just another bad guy off the street…

But what was bad? What was good?

George stamped his feet. He *really* needed a drink.

Come on George, this isn't for you. A pint and a whisky chaser instead. What harm? Just the one, then head home, grab a takeaway, watch a film…

But he knew it wouldn't be just the one. It never was. By the time he got home he wouldn't be able to *find* the TV let alone watch a film. It was time to sort this out, once and for all.

A middle-aged woman was walking her dog on the opposite pavement. She shot him a suspicious look while the animal gave the lamp post a thorough watering. Neighbourhood Watch, I'll bet, George thought. She'll be reporting me as a dodgy character as soon as she gets in.

The nearest pub was just round the corner – the Bull. George knew it well. And they knew George equally well. Quieter than the Falcon, the station's favourite watering hole, and a better selection of Scotch to boot. A no-brainer.

George took the invitation from his trouser pocket, glanced through the last few paragraphs.

Attendees will usually be asked to keep an open mind, to attend meetings at which recovered alcoholics describe their personal experiences in achieving sobriety, and to read AA literature describing and interpreting the AA program.

AA members will usually emphasise to newcomers that only problem drinkers themselves, individually, can determine whether or not they are in fact alcoholics.

At the same time, it will be pointed out that all available medical testimony indicates that alcoholism is a progressive illness, that it cannot be cured in the ordinary sense of the term, but that it can be arrested through total abstinence from alcohol in any form.

George sighed, folded the invitation, put it back in his pocket. He thought of Tess, lying unconscious in the hospital ward. What would she say? What would she want him to do?

It was a short walk to the front door, but a walk, nevertheless, which had taken him many years to begin. The porch light was on and, through the curtained lounge window George could hear voices raised in friendly conversation. He took a deep breath, reached out and rang the doorbell.

Chapter 38

If Moran never saw the inside of a hospital again he'd be a happy man, but fate seemed to have other ideas. He found his way to Donal's ward easily enough, but hesitated on the threshold. What could he say? How could he explain what had happened? A white-coated doctor brushed past him, buzzed the door open. Moran followed, his nostrils flaring at the conflicting smells of antiseptic, institutional food and that indefinable smell of illness which was, in his mind, the worst of the three.

A ward nurse directed him to the left, and then to the right. He caught sight of Geileis first and then Padraig, the former sitting attentively at Donal's bedside in what seemed to be the only supplied chair, the latter standing awkwardly on the other side, passing his smartphone self-consciously from one hand to the other and clearly wishing he was somewhere else.

'Brendan.' Geileis' smile was wide and welcoming. 'How are you? Donal's been anxious to see you.'

I'll bet. Moran conjured some facsimile of a smile as he approached.

Donal raised his head from the pillow and grunted a

greeting. He looked pale and washed out. 'Ah, it's yourself, Brendan.'

He doesn't know. Geileis' loaded look conveyed Donal's ignorance loud and clear.

Donal raised his hand weakly. 'Will you have some fruit, or—'

Moran waved Donal's offer away. 'Listen, Donal, I'm glad to see you're on the mend, but I have something to tell you.'

Donal rested his head on the pillow and listened without comment as Moran brought him up to date with the events which had taken place on Great Blasket. When he finished there was a silence in which the background noises of the ward seemed magnified; the chink of syringe trays, the rustling of privacy curtains being drawn, the quiet chatter from the nurses' station, a phone ringing, long and unanswered.

Geileis reached out and took Donal's hand, careful to avoid the cannula site on her brother's wrist with its slight discolouration and bruising.

'I had no idea. No idea,' Donal said quietly. 'Oh my God. I had no idea.' He shook his head repeatedly from side to side, as if his disbelief alone would counter the truth of Moran's words.

'Did she *suffer*?' Padraig's smartphone had fallen onto the bed, forgotten, and his voice was a barely controlled blurt.

Moran shook his head, put his hand on the boy's shoulder. 'No, son. She died instantly. I'm so sorry. There was nothing I could do.'

'I don't blame youse,' Padraig said. 'It's my fault. I should never have listened to him.' He covered his eyes.

'No,' Geileis said. 'It's not your fault Padraig. Sean Black was a manipulator. An expert manipulator. You're not to feel responsible, isn't that right, Brendan?'

'Listen to your aunt, son. She's spot on.'

'Oh god,' Donal was saying under his breath. 'I never knew. How did I not know?' He looked up at each of them in turn, desperate for an answer. 'I should've known, isn't that right? It was my *business* to know.' His eyes misted over and his head sank back into the pillow.

A nurse came by, fiddled with his cannula, checked the drip, tapped the plastic bottle with the back of her index finger, made a satisfied noise in her throat, smiled and withdrew. Donal hardly noticed the intrusion. His mouth worked soundlessly as he wrestled with impossible questions.

'I'd better be on my way,' Moran said. He bent and kissed Geileis' cheek, turned to Padraig. 'Look after your da, son. He needs you now.'

O'Shea was waiting, as he had said he would, by the roadside at Dunquin. Moran left the car on the verge and got out. A seagull circled overhead, cawing insistently as it scanned earth and water for sustenance. The islander was standing with his arms loosely at his sides, looking out to sea where the Blasket Islands squatted, dark and mysterious, in the grey waters of the sound. Autumn was closing in, the clouds were gathering, and Moran wondered what O'Shea was planning for the winter. It was a harsh life on Great Blasket, even with O'Shea's highly-honed survival skills. Moran felt a pang of conscience at the damage he'd caused to the islander's home, but what could he have done to prevent it?

'So.' O'Shea looked him up and down. 'Time for you to

be off, is it? Leaving me with the mess to clear up?'

'I'm sorry about your house.'

'But not my brother?'

'Honestly? Not so much, no.'

The islander nodded. 'We had a deal, remember?'

'He was pointing a gun at my head – and that was *after* the mortar. What would you have done? I had no choice; it was him or me.'

O'Shea sniffed, weighing Moran's words. 'Drink?'

Moran accepted the hip flask. The wind was chilly and he was only wearing a light jacket and chinos; he'd had to bin his heavier winter coat, burned and torn as it was.

'Thanks.' He handed O'Shea the flask. 'Aine told me – what she did, all those years ago,' he said. 'You knew didn't you?'

O'Shea stroked his beard contemplatively. His cheeks were red and weather-beaten, but the big man radiated fitness and vitality. His hand shifted from beard to ponytail, toyed with the rope-like coil. 'I knew, yes.'

'But you didn't see fit to tell me.'

'Now I didn't think it would improve your motivation to track Aine down, Inspector Moran, if I'd been stupid enough to let out something like that.'

'I might never have found out.'

'Ah, I think you're underestimating her, sure I do. That kind of guilt is hard to live with. She'd have found a way to tell you, eventually.'

'Eventually.' Moran faced the sea, felt the salt breeze on his own cheeks. He reached into his pocket, took out the photo album. 'Here.' He held it out. 'Aine would have wanted you to have this.'

O'Shea took it, nodded. 'Thanks.'

'You can be proud of your daughter. Her mother certainly was.'

'I don't need to hear that from the likes of you. I'll feel what I feel, and be proud of whom I'm proud of without your say so.'

'I did what I could, O'Shea. Aine saved my life. It could have worked out very differently.'

'I've lost a brother, Moran. And a very old friend. I could work things out differently for *you*, if I were that way inclined.'

'But you won't. And you're not.' Moran looked into O'Shea's deep-set eyes. 'You know what your brother was. A man out of time. A man who couldn't let go. It was always going to end badly for him. You *know* that.'

'You got lucky,' O'Shea replied. 'Sean killed better men than you in his lifetime, so he did.'

Moran nodded. 'I'm no better man than the next, O'Shea. And I've always said you make your own luck.'

'Maybe we'd better leave it there, Inspector.' O'Shea extended his hand. 'We won't meet again.'

Moran shook the islander's hand. 'I'm genuinely sorry about your house.'

'Houses can be rebuilt,' O'Shea said. 'Some things can never be repaired.'

The islander made his way down the stone steps to the low cleft in the rocks where he stored his dinghy. A few minutes later the sound of an outboard engine floated up from the beach. The dinghy soon came into view, cutting a white wake in the water as it forged across the strait towards the waiting islands.

Moran sat on the wall and watched the dinghy's progress until the sound of its engine had faded and the only sound was the susurration of the waves against the rocks and the background cries of the gulls.

The sun was low in the sky by the time Moran opened the little churchyard gate for Geileis and stepped aside to allow her through. Wordlessly, they followed the winding path through the gravestones towards the familiar spot. Moran was thinking of Aine's guilt, how she had carried it for so many years, living with the knowledge that one day, perhaps, it would all be revealed. And yet she could hardly have predicted how that was to work itself out, how she had become a pawn, a hostage in her daughter's web of spies, murder and terrorism.

Now I know. But it makes no difference. Nothing will ever make a difference.

Geileis slipped her hand into his and Moran felt a small shock at this demonstration of her warmth towards him. Full circle, he supposed, of a kind. Perhaps this was it; the possibility of some alternative existence to the life he had endured for so many years. An end to all the deaths, the deceit, his sheer ongoing dismay at the hopelessness of the human condition.

'It's peaceful here, isn't it?' Geileis murmured. 'She'd like it.'

'She would that,' Moran agreed. 'She was a country girl at heart, like yourself.' He gave her hand a squeeze. They separated naturally as they approached the grave, took up positions facing each other on either side, heads bowed. The silence was profound.

Geileis was the first to break it. 'You see,' she said, 'she'll always be between us. No matter how hard we try to make it otherwise.'

Moran had a lump in his throat. He could only nod.

'You can visit as often as you like, Brendan.' Geileis smiled at him across the gulf. 'In any case, you're not ready for the quiet life. Not at all.' She shook her head. 'What was it you said to me that first evening? About the fear of slowing down, being stuck inside all the time?'

'The thought of being trapped inside all day filling me with horror, you mean?'

'Yes, that. You'd be lost without your job.'

'I could change.'

Geileis looked down again, at the inscription on the headstone. 'Maybe you could,' she said. 'I have my doubts, but just maybe you could.' She drew her coat tightly around her as a strong gust of wind blew in from the sea, ruffling the grass and disarraying her hair. She swept the red locks behind her ears, drew her collar up. 'The thing is, Brendan, although we might be able to change the future, we can't change the past. That's the way it is.'

Moran nodded. 'Yes. You're right, of course.'

'You think so?'

'I do. But at least we have the present. The here and now. No one can take that away,' he said, the lump in his throat reducing his voice to a husky whisper.

She smiled, the skin taut and thin over her cheekbones. 'Yes, of course,' Geileis said. 'We have now.'

They stood together for a long time, and then eventually, as if at some unbidden, unheard signal, retraced their steps along the path, away from the spot where the deep shadows hugged the earth, beneath the high wall which faced west, out to the wind and the open sea.

Epilogue

Thames House is instantly recognisable as the home of British Intelligence, if not by courtesy of many a scene-setting movie shot, then certainly by the heavily-armed police presence and the security bollards studding the pavement. Moran had received his invitation – or summons, as he preferred to interpret it – via DCS Higginson, the day after his return from Ireland.

Side door, Brendan, I think.

Tradesman's entrance. Well, not quite, but close.

Moran moved away from the imposing row of main doors beneath the front arch and walked along the side of the building, where he soon came to a smaller, self-evidently bomb-proof alternative, which in turn led into a tiny security room, lined ceiling to floor with thick ballistic glass.

A security team scrutinised him suspiciously from the other side of the barrier. One beckoned him to the intercom. Moran cleared his throat and introduced himself.

Ten minutes later, after a rigorous set of security checks, he was shown into a nondescript room with two chairs and a table and told to wait. Presently a severe-looking middle-aged woman in a dark purple jacket and trousers put her head around the door and told him to follow.

They walked along corridor after corridor, past closed doors marked with bewildering combinations of letters and numbers. Moran wondered what was happening behind them. Probably best not to know. Eventually his guide paused before one, marked simply 22Ac, and knocked. A muffled 'Come in'; his guide opened the door and indicated that he should enter. The door closed behind him and Moran found himself standing before a leather-topped bureau, behind which an avuncular looking man in his early fifties was busy cleaning out an elegant meerschaum pipe. Two chairs of the sturdy, functional type had been placed before the desk.

'Ah.' He looked up at Moran and gestured to his pipe. 'Can't smoke the damn things in here, but at least I'm able to conduct a little maintenance work, eh? Have a seat.'

Moran chose a seat, sat down and crossed one leg over the other. It cramped almost immediately and he was obliged to uncross and stretch the offending limb.

'Leg still a problem? Bad business, that Charnford case. Irish again, if I remember correctly?'

'Yes, it is – and yes. But not in a paramilitary sense on that occasion,' Moran replied. He wasn't surprised that this elegant stranger knew of his near-fatal episode at Charnford Abbey. He was inside the place of information, after all – the house of secrets.

The man looked across the desk at him – not analytically, but with, Moran felt, some small degree of scrutiny. 'Quite so,' his host said at last, tapping the bowl of his pipe gently against a pewter ash tray. A few remaining shards of tobacco fluttered into the ash tray and the man grunted with satisfaction. 'That'll do for the time being, I think.' He rested the pipe carefully against the ash tray. 'Now then, good journey?'

'Fine, thanks.'

'My name's not important,' the man went on, 'but we wanted to be sure of a few things before we allow you to return to active duty, Inspector.'

Not *before you return*, Moran noted, but *before we allow you...* And there was the plural, too. 'We?'

'Indeed.' The man pressed a button on his desk. 'Send Caitlin in, would you please.'

Caitlin Hannigan was, in many ways, a taller, younger version of Aine. The hair was shoulder-length, the same shade of auburn and red, the mouth full and eased up at the corners. Sure, her mother's traits were clearly discernible. But the brightness of her eyes, the easy, confident movements, the way she carried herself – they were pure O'Shea.

Caitlin sat down, turning her chair in towards Moran. A guest of the man behind the desk, but a co-inquisitor nevertheless...

'You're sure Black's dead?'

No messing around, just like her ma.

'As sure as I'm sitting here.'

'What happened? I want to know everything.'

Moran told them.

The man behind the desk nodded occasionally, toyed with his pipe. Caitlin listened, stopping him if she wanted more detail, waving him on impatiently when he was giving too much. Although he took care to tone down the details of Aine's confession and suicide, Moran could see that his narrative was taking its toll; the colour had begun to drain slowly from Caitlin's face and her hands were involuntarily clasping and unclasping as she struggled to keep herself under control. Moran's words dried up. 'I'm sorry. This must be hard for you to hear.'

She waved him on again. 'I'm all right.' She bit down hard on her bottom lip, stuck her chin out. A single, rebellious, tear slid down her cheek, which she flicked away with an angry gesture. Moran offered his handkerchief, which was declined. Pipe-man affected not to notice any of this, the maintenance of his smoking machinery apparently the primary focus of his universe. Moran started up again. By the time he'd described the arrival of the rescue helicopter Caitlin's eyes had regained their icy clarity, her voice its steady confidence. 'So,' she said. 'O'Shea wasn't involved?'

Moran shrugged. 'As I said, only in the sense that he was helping me. He wanted his brother stopped.'

Caitlin and the man exchanged glances.

'What about the explosives and weapons?' she asked.

'Yes. Well, I can't say whether or not O'Shea was planning to do anything with them. I was under the impression they might have been, how shall I put this? Old stock.'

'And the mortar?'

Moran paused, remembering the sound the shells had made as they dropped from the sky. He'd had one or two nightmares since his unlikely survival. Hardly surprising. If they reoccurred, he supposed he ought to see somebody; that was what people did nowadays, wasn't it? PTS wasn't something that would go away on its own, not without trying to bring the trauma to some kind of philosophical full stop. But he'd managed all right in the past, after Charnford … so what was different? Maybe it was an age thing?

He realised that Caitlin and the man were looking at him, waiting. He cleared his throat. 'The mortar, yes. My guess is he was saving that for official visits – you know, the eviction order kind. I wouldn't put it past him to fire a few warning shots. As for the other boxes,' Moran went on, 'for all I know he was using the explosives for quarrying. He's a resourceful guy. He told me he just wants to be left alone. I believe him. I'd be more concerned about Buchanan and O'Mahoney.'

Caitlin waved her arm dismissively. 'That's already sorted. They won't cause any further problems.'

Moran had a few questions of his own. 'Why didn't you tell DI Pepper that you were working deep cover? You could have saved yourself a lot of trouble.'

'Simple. I didn't know who could be trusted. The golden rule, DCI Moran, is *never* to voluntarily blow your cover. With anyone, even investigating police officers.'

'Let me get this straight,' Moran said. 'You contrived a set of political views guaranteed to make Black believe that you would agree to help; he took the bait, if you like.'

'That's right. With my mother's background in mind, he kept an eye on me as I was growing up. He was like that. Always on the lookout.'

'But he wasn't looking carefully enough to notice that you'd joined MI5.'

'It's not something we tend to advertise.' The man smiled benignly. 'It's all done very discreetly.'

'Black just believed you to be a communications and wireless expert, trained through the usual channels?'

'Exactly,' Caitlin said.

Moran's mental list scrolled on. 'So why did you pretend

you'd got cold feet? That's why Black went for Aine, wasn't it? To get you back on board?'

'For strategic reasons.'

'What kind of strategic? You must have known it was a gamble.'

Caitlin's composure faltered once again, but only momentarily this time. She paused, took a breath. 'It's all a gamble, Chief Inspector. I pretended to withdraw to encourage our mole to step up to the plate and take responsibility for the bomb. JC hates royalty, the upper classes. Toffs, he calls them.' Caitlin wrinkled her nose and Moran saw Aine in the gesture, clear as day.

'And I mean really hates them,' Caitlin went on, 'just like Black. We needed JC to nail his colours to the mast, find a way of catching him out. And lo and behold, he took the bait; he stepped up. Which left me free to return to the fold in suitably penitent mode, but in a supporting role.' She leaned forward. 'My decision, Chief Inspector. I knew the risks. But you're right, of course, I didn't expect Black to do anything quite so overt as to threaten my mother. Nor did I expect Niall Briggs to lose it in such spectacular fashion.'

'The basement gunman?'

'Yes.'

Moran sat forward in his chair. '*You* shot him, didn't you? And my guess is you did it on Black's orders. My doctor friend in pathology described the bullet and Ballistics confirmed our suspicions. Unusual. Government issue, I believe? Not something a paramilitary group would be likely to obtain. Ergo, it was your gun.' He sat back, flushed, realising that he'd raised his voice, was close to losing his cool altogether.

'Briggs was out of control,' Caitlin said. 'Black gave him orders to encourage me to keep on with the job in hand, not come after me with a shotgun. He was going to wreck the whole operation. He had to be taken out. He was always trouble. That's just how it was.'

'Probably not a helpful line of enquiry, in any case, DCI Moran,' the man interrupted smoothly. 'You must understand that certain, um, unpleasant actions are sometimes necessary. We won't be troubling the CPS on this particular account.'

'No. I suppose not.' Moran shifted in his chair. This was a different world, and not an altogether comfortable one. Nevertheless, his curiosity spurred him on. 'It was a risky strategy, surely? Relying on a wireless jamming device to stop the bomb being detonated? What if it had failed?'

'We test our devices thoroughly,' the man said. 'If your enthusiastic DI had backed off as we'd suggested and DC Odunsi had not been present, all would have gone to plan.'

'And had DC Tess Martin not been in situ, it might have been a very different story,' Moran countered.

'Ifs, buts and maybes, DCI Moran,' said the man. 'No point dwelling on those. How is DC Martin, incidentally?'

'She'll recover. She's a damn good officer.'

'Good, good. Delighted to hear that.' The man tamped at the meerschaum bowl's phantom contents.

'What will you do with JC?' Moran had to ask.

'You don't really want to know,' the man said.

And actually, he realised, he didn't. So Moran let it go. His imagination, if he allowed it, would fill in the blanks.

Caitlin had stood up. 'Will that be all, Sir?'

'Indeed so. Thank you, Ms Hannigan.'

Moran stood too. The audience was clearly at an end, but Caitlin had paused at the door.

'How *is* my father?'

'He'll mend. He's at home now. Padraig will be looking after him. I have no worries on that score.'

'I didn't mean Donal.'

'Ah.'

There was a moment's awkward silence. The man was busy with a fresh pipe-cleaner. Caitlin helped Moran out. 'I work for British Intelligence, Chief Inspector,' she said. 'It's my job to know the facts.'

'Of course. Well, I probably wouldn't be here now if it weren't for him,' Moran said. 'Whatever he's done in the past, I wouldn't hold it against him. To answer your question, he's fit and well. As I said before, all he wants is to be left alone.'

Caitlin considered this for a moment, then gave a small nod of acquiescence. 'Thank you, DCI Moran.'

'Nice to meet you, Chief Inspector,' Meerschaum Man said. He didn't offer to shake hands, so Moran didn't either. 'If you wouldn't mind stepping outside, I've a few calls to make. Someone'll be along to collect you shortly.'

Half-way across Lambeth Bridge Moran stopped, leaned on the balustrade by one of the latticed lamp stands, took a deep breath and exhaled slowly. It would have been just about at this spot that Caitlin had had her photograph taken. Perhaps Aine had taken it herself, on some weekend break to visit her daughter.

Her daughter, the spook.

Light years away from her mother's background, a

juxtaposition of loyalties if ever there was one.

Moran blew out his cheeks, took in the view. To his left the spires of Westminster; to his right the slowly revolving London Eye. Beneath him, passing to and fro on the murky waters of the Thames, a constant procession of pleasure boats, barges and tugs. He watched them awhile, enjoying the movement of the water, the wash breaking over rusty prows, the smells, sounds and general hubbub of London's river. Compared to the stifling atmosphere of Thames House it made him feel free and unencumbered. Moran felt the wind on his face, filled his lungs, and continued walking, towards the familiar sounds of a city in homeward mode; offices disgorging weary white-collars, construction workers filing from building site turnstiles, pub pavements teeming with early drinkers, impatient taxi drivers honking at weaving cyclists and despatch riders. He reached the Tube entrance at Lambeth North and paused briefly, reluctant to let the feeling go. It was only after rain began to spatter his coat, just a few droplets at first, and then more persistently, that he turned on his heel and vanished into the depths.

Glossary

SECTU

South East Counter Terrorism Unit

ONH

ONH is one of three republican dissident terror groups still active in Northern Ireland alongside the New IRA and Continuity IRA factions

RBH

Royal Berkshire Hospital

IR

Incident Room

PACE

Police and Criminal Evidence Act (1984). An Act of Parliament which instituted a legislative framework for the powers of police officers in England and Wales to combat crime, and provided codes of practice for the exercise of those powers

The DCI Brendan Moran Crime Series

Black December

Creatures of Dust

Death Walks Behind You

The Irish Detective (Omnibus)

A Crime for all Seasons (Short Stories)

Silent as the Dead

Standalone novels

The Trespass

The Serpent & the Slave

The Ley Lines of Lushbury

Sign up to Scott Hunter's newsletter to be notified of special discounts, offers and news, and to receive a FREE eBook

www.scott-hunter.net/signup